CHANDLER

LAURELIN
PAIGE

*everafter*ROMANCE

EverAfter Romance
A Division of Diversion Publishing Corp.
443 Park Avenue South, Suite 1008
New York, New York 10016
www.DiversionBooks.com

This is a work of fiction. Names, characters, places and incidents either
are the product of the author's imagination or are used fictitiously.
Any resemblance to actual persons, living or dead, events or locales is
entirely coincidental.

First edition September 2016.
ISBN: 9781942835042

The following story contains mature themes, strong language, and
sexual situations. It is intended for adult readers.

CHANDLER

CHAPTER ONE

"Can you manage to keep your dick in your pants for one night?"

Hudson's question is meant to grab my attention, and it does. To be fair, I heard most of what he'd said up to this point. The parts that were of interest, anyway.

Okay, maybe that wasn't much.

"Probably not. I don't sleep in my pants, for one, and I do plan on sleeping." I pull next to the valet podium at the Whitney Museum of Art, and add, "eventually," because I know it will rile my brother up.

His sigh is heavy with exasperation. "Can you keep your dick in your pants *at the gala?*"

I grab my phone from its dock, automatically switching it out of Bluetooth mode, and bring it up to my ear. I pretend to consider as I step out of the car and button my tux jacket. "Hmm."

"Nice wheels," the valet says, unconcerned that I'm on the phone.

I pull out my wallet and flash a fifty-dollar bill. "Take care of her and this is yours."

"Yes sir, Mr. Pierce."

If Hudson were here, he'd wince at the recognition. It's possible the valet knows me from the latest list of "Richest Men Under Thirty"—it's the first year I've hit since I only got my trust fund when I turned twenty-four a few months back. But one look at the tattooed, pony-tailed Italian says he isn't the type to read *Forbes*, which means he recognizes me from the gossip sites instead. Honestly, I don't mind that I have a rep. It's the elder Pierce who seems to care.

Speaking of the elder Pierce…

"Can I keep it in my pants until after the gala?" I repeat his earlier question as I stride toward the entrance of the museum. "I don't know. How long is this thing supposed to last?" I'm messing with Hudson. It's too easy not to. And really, what does he expect me to say? It's not like I'm planning to try to get a girl to blow me on the event premises.

Though, if one were to offer…

"And don't hit on anyone while you're there, either."

Now he's going too far. "Is that a baby crying?" I don't really hear a baby crying, but the likelihood that there is one somewhere near him isn't too slim. The recent birth of his twins is the whole reason I'm stuck going to this stupid shindig in the first place.

"I mean it, Chandler."

As if on cue, a baby actually *does* start crying in the background. "Shouldn't you go put a pacifier in it or something?"

Hudson ignores me. "This is an important event," he

chides. "Accelecom is looking to strike a deal with Werner Media, and it's crucial we make a good impression."

"Yeah, yeah, yeah." It's not like I don't know this. He's told me seventeen times just today, plus several hundred times earlier this week. In fact, every conversation we've had in the past few days has been about Accelecom's charity gala tonight, which is more than a little strange, even for my work-obsessed older brother. Mainly because Werner Media isn't a company we own. Sure, it belongs to family friends, but the Pierces haven't been that close to the Werners since, well, around the time I graduated from high school. So why the fuck does he care so much about the impression I leave?

It suddenly occurs to me to ask. "What exactly is it you hope to gain from my presence here tonight? The Werner-Accelecom merger has nothing to do with Pierce Industries, does it?"

A beat goes by. "It's a good opportunity for you," he says finally. "There will be a lot of press there this evening, and if you play nice, you could get a good write-up, one that doesn't involve the mayor's daughter."

His answer is irritating. Though he's easing me into the family business, I'm technically an owner of Pierce Industries, just like he is, and I hate it when he treats me like an average employee. We're completely different people, from our attitudes about our careers to our physical looks— my eyes blue where his are brown, my hair blond where his is dark. But, despite our differences, I want our company to succeed as much as he does. I want our efforts to bear fruit, just like he does. He slaves away at the job, but I work hard, too.

Well, hard enough.

But I'm not in the mood to argue.

I'm in the mood to deflect. "Man, that kid of yours is really howling. I didn't know you subscribed to the cry-it-out method. I knew you were old, but 1990's parenting? Come on."

"Chandler." Hudson's tone is clipped and stern. He means it to be intimidating.

Spoiler: Hudson doesn't scare me.

"I'm hanging up now," I say, pushing through the doors of the museum.

"Do you understand what I'm saying?"

"Yes. I understand. *Dad*."

I expect him to growl about my latest poke, but he's distracted. "I'll take him," I hear him say, his words muffled as though he has his hand over the mouthpiece. Then, more clearly, "Chandler, I have to help Alayna with the babies."

"Finally. Wouldn't want to have to accuse you of child neglect." Without saying goodbye, I click *END* and, after putting it on silent, slip my phone into my inside jacket pocket. Hudson's children can only preoccupy him for so long. Sooner or later, he'll be back to riding my ass, and even though I'm here at this event in his place, as far as I'm concerned, I'm off the clock.

• • •

The thing is, Hudson's concerns are somewhat legit. Not because I *can't* keep my cock in my pants, but because most of the time I don't *want* to.

What can I say? I'm a guy who loves women.

Lucky for me, women usually love me too. And why

wouldn't they? I'm charming, young, good-looking, smart. Decent at my job, despite what Hudson tells anyone. Oh, and let's not forget, filthy rich. I'm shower masturbation material come to life.

Most impressive, though, is my bedroom portfolio—it's not a secret that I'm a giver. Swear on the Pierce family name, I do not let a woman leave my sheets before she's received at least two orgasms. The goal is always three, but I'm willing to concede that there are sometimes other factors besides me contributing to that outcome. Maybe she's tired. Maybe her head's too into it. Maybe she's not good at relaxing. Whatever, I get it. But she's getting two O's regardless.

Before I start sounding too noble, let me clarify— the orgasms are for *me*. There's nothing like the feel of a pussy clenching around your cock, milking you to your own climax—that's got to be the best definition of heaven around.

But the biggest reason I deliver is because of the cost-benefit ratio. I'm a firm believer in *what goes around, comes around*. The happier she is, the happier she'll want to make me. I'm talking Happy with a capital "H." And while I'm a one-night-only kind of guy—a fact I always make clear from the beginning—I've done really well with referrals. Call it a successful "business" model.

Sometimes *too* successful, considering the way some of the ladies are eyeing me as I glance around the museum.

It only takes one sweep of my gaze to know tonight is not going to create any problems for my brother. The room is filled with the kinds of women I'm one hundred percent not attracted to. Trophy wives looking for a distraction. Cougars who sit on the boards—and the faces—of whatever-and-whoever-is-*in*-this-week. Rich dames with so much Botox and spandex their bodies don't even jiggle when they're supposed to—and if she's lying underneath me, it's supposed to.

That just leaves the women I've already been with, and I don't do repeats.

Well then, let's make this trip an easy in and out, just like I like it. This time when I glance around, I look for the quickest opportunities to achieve the "make a good impression" edict that Hudson has given me. I make a plan. Mingle with the execs from my father's country club, say hello to Warren Werner who I've just spotted by the fondue station, and then put in a bid at the auction in the adjoining room to make sure the Pierce presence is duly noticed.

But first, I need a drink.

A waitress passes by with a tray of caviar. "Excuse me. Is there a bar somewhere?"

She tilts her lip into a flirtatious grin as she checks me out. Now this woman might be an option…

But she's working, and I'll have to stick around until she gets off before I'll have any chance of getting off myself, and I can already tell this thing is going to be a snooze-fest.

Especially when she answers. "There's champagne floating around. And some punch that should be spiked if it hasn't been already."

"Well, shit. I should have brought my flask." Though, if I had, it would have been filled with a single-malt scotch and not something I'd ever mix, let alone with fruit punch. I wink. "But thanks for the heads-up."

I can tell she wouldn't mind more cozy conversation, but I slip away before she gets any ideas, and after a quick chat with some men I've done business with in the past, I run smack into Warren.

"Chandler! I didn't expect to see you here tonight. Where's Hudson?" The man is practically a father to me, or rather, he was around while I was growing up about as much as my own dad was, which is to say, not much. In other words, I have to talk to him, but it's going to be boring as hell.

I put on my friendliest grin. "Alayna had her babies early. He's taking some time 'off.'" I use air quotes around the word *off* because Warren and I both know my brother works in his sleep.

"Oh, yes. I recall hearing that." He goes on to deliver heartfelt congratulations and the like before moving to the obligatory inquiries about the rest of my family, which I give, dutifully.

This kind of small talk is the worst. I'm dying inside with every polite word. I only manage to tolerate it by dreaming about the real drink I'll get later at The Sky Launch or another one of the nightclubs where hooking up is practically an item on the drink menu.

Eventually, after Warren's told me all about his upcoming plans to retire, I courteously ask about his daughter, Celia—Hudson's childhood peer/possible lover/almost-baby-mama/part-of-a-complicated-friendship-that-I've-never-understood.

Though Warren's expression remains warm, his eyes harden, and I sense he'd prefer not to talk about her with me. While I was too young to be privy to the rift that happened between our once-close families, I have a feeling most of the bad blood has to do with Hudson not marrying Warren's daughter.

"Celia's good," he says curtly. "She's in town at the moment. In fact, she was supposed to be here tonight but ended up canceling because of a headache." *Or because she was afraid she'd run into Hudson.* "You know she's married now, and her husband—"

His sentence is cut off by a younger gentleman tapping on his shoulder. "Sorry to interrupt, but Mr. Fasbender is looking for you."

Fasbender. I recognize that name. He's the owner of Accelecom and probably one of the people that Hudson would most prefer I be seen with tonight.

Which is why I decide not to bother. I've done a fair bit of schmoozing already. If Hudson wanted more from me, he could have been more specific when he asked. Besides, he needs to learn to deal with disappointment, and who better to teach him but me.

Grabbing a glass of champagne from a passing waiter, I head to the area where the silent auction has been situated. I peruse the items up for bid, quickly bypassing the most popular draws—a houseboat, a vineyard in France, a private island off of Malta—and settle on the gaudiest piece of art I've ever set my eyes on. Complete with a five-inch thick ostentatious gold frame, the six-foot square canvas is covered with abstract red-hued phallic brush strokes. It's bold and brusque. It makes me angry just to look at it.

It's perfect.

I pull a Montblanc fountain pen from my breast pocket and find the next blank line on the auction sheet. Tripling the last amount offered, I fill in my own bid. Then, with a gleeful smirk, I sign Hudson's name and his office phone number before tucking the pen back in my jacket.

There. I'll pose for a picture at the door on my way out for good measure, but otherwise my work here is done. And without causing any trouble. *Consider it a baby gift, Hudson.*

Downing the too-sweet champagne, I turn to search for a place to set my empty glass before making my trek back across the museum floor.

That's when I see her.

My breath is knocked from my chest the second my gaze slams into her. I swear there's a spotlight on her. Cliché, isn't it? But I pull my eyes up toward the ceiling to see if there's a fixture directed at her and am surprised when I find none. Because she literally *shines.*

Frozen to my spot, I ignore the people pressing past me coming to and from the auction tables, drinking in every detail I can of the beauty across the room. Her long shapely legs, her lusciously curved hips, her pouty mouth drawn into a tight line. She's wearing a lace shift dress—my sister owns a boutique, I know these terms—simple in shape, but the pattern is elegant, making her look classier than many of the older women here in their skin-tight bling-bling gowns. She's on the tall side, but not too tall. With her modest heels, she's just the right height to kiss. Just the right height to devour without having to bend. Just the right height to be able to look in her eyes as my hand presses gently at her throat.

Jesus, did I just fantasize about choking a woman? What the fuck is wrong with me? I'm the first to admit I'm a pig, but I've never had those kinds of kinky thoughts. I've never not been a gentleman. Never wanted to not be *nice* like I want to not be nice looking at her. She's just so…captivating.

I'm not the only one who notices. She's surrounded by a flock of men who are not very good at hiding their eagerness to see what's beneath her dress, and I can't say that I blame them. She's *that* alluring. That *hypnotizing*.

She's not even the kind of girl I'm attracted to. Too thin, too brunette. Too young—she can't be more than twenty-five. But there's *something* about her. Something that separates her from the crowd. Something in her gestures as she patiently tolerates her would-be suitors. Something about her posture, which is polished, but aloof. Something about her entire being that keeps my eyes pinned to her like a lion's pinned to his prey.

I should leave. I know this. It's not my M.O. to stalk. I prefer to be the one reeled in—again, part of the model I've successfully honed. But I'm stuck, glued to the spot, staring at this intriguing creature with graceful movements and delicate features.

And then there's a clearing in her swarm of admirers, and I'm suddenly not stuck, but moving toward her, drawn as if on the descent of a zip-line. She hasn't noticed me, and I take advantage of that, circling around her so that I can approach her from behind. It gives me a chance to check her hand, when I'm near enough, for signs of a ring. A ring is a deal-breaker for me. I don't do infidelity, never have. Once, I came close. Or rather, the situation *felt* close to cheating, and it was terrible. I won't do that again.

But that was five long years ago now and not only has that lesson been learned, it also seems to be unnecessary tonight. The slinky brunette that has lured me across the room is ring-less. I'm assuming she's also date-less, or if not, she should be, because no way in hell would any decent man leave his girlfriend alone around the predators here. Predators like me.

It briefly occurs to me that I've never once thought of myself as a predator, and that maybe these ideas in my head are a sign that I need to get the fuck out of Dodge.

But I can't. For reasons I can't explain. Reasons that are primal and base and as out of my control as breathing.

As well as being ring-less, she's also drink-less, and so, as a waiter passes, I drop off my empty flute, and retrieve two fresh glasses.

When my prey turns casually in my direction, I'm ready.

I hold out a glass in her direction. "Champagne?"

Her grey eyes spark when they catch mine, sending a jolt straight to my dick. I'd know that look anywhere—she likes what she sees, and thank god, because now that I've seen her close up, I'm absolutely certain that I have to have her. Have to possess her. Have to do unspeakably dirty things to every inch of her body.

Tighten those reins, boy. Get ahold of yourself.

I almost do, but then she narrows her stare and twists her lip. It's the lip that does me in.

"How do I know you didn't put anything in it?" she asks, and JesusfuckingChrist, she's got an English accent. I'm instantly hard.

Okay, semi-hard. I'm not twelve. I have some control.

"Well," I consider, "I have two drinks. You choose which one, and I'll drink the other."

She hesitates, suspicion vibrating from her body. Which is crazy—I'm a puppy.

Except I'm not a puppy. Not right now, not around her, and her distrust increases my interest in her tenfold.

"How about you drink from both of them? And then I'll choose one."

Whichever she chooses, she'll have her lips on the glass after mine. That's so hot.

Maybe I am only twelve.

With her eyes still caught in mine, I take a swallow from one flute and then from the other. "Now choose."

"I'll have this one," she says, claiming the glass I drank more from. "Thank you." Her skepticism relaxes slightly, but she's still wary. As she should be.

I'm surprised how much it arouses me.

Tipping it forward, I clink my flute to hers. "You've been surrounded all night."

"And?" She's polite enough not to sigh, but I can hear the weariness behind the single word.

I should leave her alone.

I can't. "I didn't like it."

She tilts her head, her expression both appalled and intrigued. "I don't really think it matters what you like."

"True, true." I give her the Chandler grin, the one that drops panties at the speed of light. "Thing is, I don't think you liked it either."

She crosses her arms over herself and leans her weight on one gorgeous hip. "So, since I didn't like a bunch of men trying to pick me up, you thought you'd come over and pick me up instead?"

"When you put it that way, I sound like an asshole."

"You said it, not me."

She seems truly put off, and I'm momentarily thrown off my game. Mostly because this isn't at all the game

I usually play. Usually, *I'm* the target. There are too many already willing women to waste time working for one.

Smile and say goodnight, Chandler.

I take a swallow from my drink. The sweetness is so much more tolerable as I imagine licking it off her lips, and now that I've imagined it, there's no going back.

"How about I make it up to you?" I say, totally improvising. "When you're ready to go, I'll escort you out so no one bothers you. Once outside, you can totally tell me to take a hike."

She gives me the same expression she did before—the shocked and fascinated one—and this time I catch a hint of amusement as well. "You're really full of yourself, thinking I need you to help me get out of here."

An unexpected filthy, crass comment about filling her instead flutters on the tip of my tongue, but I push it away. *Play nice.* "I wasn't implying that at all. I'm just offering a service that could be mutually beneficial."

"How would that benefit you?"

"I'd get to be the guy seen walking out with the most beautiful woman in the room." *Yes!* Now my brain's on the right track.

She gives me an incredulous glare, but her icy demeanor has melted. "You American men are such charmers." She takes a sip from her drink, and when she licks her tongue over her bottom lip? Talk about melting. I'm so hot I'm a puddle of molten lava over this girl.

Somehow I manage to remain *charming*. "Oh," I mock groan, clutching my chest as though she's wounded my heart. "You've lumped me with the all the other 'American men.' That's a real low blow."

She laughs, and it's so adorable that I want to sink my teeth into the sound and bite, want to mark it and claim it as mine.

"Perhaps it was a little crueler than necessary," she says, then sobers quickly. "Let me ask you this—is being *seen* with me the only thing you're interested in?"

No, it's most definitely not at all. I'm also interested in fucking her. I'm interested in dragging her into a dark corner so I can feed her my cock. I'm interested in watching her ride me, her petite tits bouncing as she drives up and down the length of my shaft.

And now I *am* hard. So hard it hurts.

I don't answer. Which is an answer in itself.

Damn, I need to get out of here.

I catch sight of the crowd that had earlier surrounded her and use it as my excuse. "Your entourage seems to be returning. I'll let you attend to them." I will myself to turn and walk away, but my feet don't move, and before I know it, I'm leaning into her, so close I can smell her natural scent underneath her floral perfume.

"My offer stands if you want it," I say quietly. "Come and find me. I'll be here."

Shit. Now I've done it. If she has any sense, she'll tell me not to bother waiting around. It's my only hope.

But when I straighten, her eyes lock on mine, and I can't help but think she might be as twisted up over me as I am about her.

"Genevieve," she says, holding her hand out to me.

I barely manage to mask the shock that runs through me when my hand clasps around hers. "Chandler. Chandler Pierce."

Her brow rises in recognition, and for the first time in my life, I'm worried about my reputation. Usually, I wear my name like it's a designer brand. My name gets me things I like. Gets me out of speeding tickets and into the arms of pretty women.

But I've never cared who the pretty woman was—this time I do. This time, I want the pretty woman to be this one. I want *Genevieve*.

Her expression is unreadable, and I can't tell if I've just sealed the deal or if I've blown any chance I might have had.

Then she says, "It's been a pleasure, Mr. Pierce," and turns to greet the gentleman who has just arrived at her side, also carrying two flutes of champagne.

Though she clings to the one I gave her, her dismissal is clear. *Mr. Pierce,* she said. So cold and detached. So utterly unimpressed.

I take the cue and slip away. I should leave the event entirely, but I can't force myself to go. I told her I'd be here, and maybe it's because I really am a nice guy that I can't seem to bring myself to break my word.

Or maybe I just can't bear to let her go yet.

I mingle. Some woman I've fucked in the past drapes herself over my shoulder and introduces her friend who drapes herself over my other arm. *This* is my audience. I could take either of them home right now. Both of them.

But as they fawn, my focus is on Genevieve. I watch as she excuses herself from her admirers. My gaze follows her as she approaches a group of men. She taps one on the shoulder, one old enough to be her father. He puts a finger up, telling her to wait, and I bristle at the gesture because it's rude but also because it's familiar. Just like I didn't like the crowd that had surrounded her, I don't like what this man might be to her. I have no right to care. I've only just met her, and every interest I have in her is carnal. Yet I do care. Very much.

Which is why, when I see her heading toward me a few minutes later, I already know I'm about to say or do something I shouldn't.

Ignoring the women clinging to me, Genevieve looks me straight in the eye. "Does your offer still stand, Chandler? Because I'm ready to go now."

I don't hesitate even a beat. "Definitely," I say, shucking off the women as though they were a well-worn jacket. I slip my hand in Genevieve's. "Let's go, shall we?"

Told you I'd do something I shouldn't. Sorry, Hudson.

CHAPTER TWO

Another thing about me—I'm not immune to falling in love.

The first time was that woman from five years ago, the one that felt like cheating. Gwen was her name. I was nineteen. She was ten years older. It was hot as fuck being with an older woman like that, and perhaps that was confusing. I was just a "kid" and all.

I shouldn't be bitter about it. And I'm not. Not anymore, anyway. She was honest from the beginning. I chased her, and when she relented, she made sure I understood that we were just banging. I got it—I really did.

Until I didn't.

Looking back, I can see the mistakes I made. I let her occupy too many of my thoughts. Saw her too much, too often. The real error was letting myself care, and when she sobbed to me about the man she really loved, a man who'd left her and broken her, I had the white knight kind of noble thought that *I* would have been better. Been a better man to her. Been better at loving her.

She ended up with the other guy, and okay, maybe they're perfect together. And okay, maybe she shouldn't have been expected to tell me her heart belonged to someone else. It was probably immature to feel like she'd been cheating on him while she loved him and fucked me. Cheating on me while she fucked me and loved him. Who can say? What I do know is that when she chose him? It fucking hurt.

I told myself I was done.

I fell in love again six months later.

She was a girl in my business ethics class. Tessa. Three dates in, and I was a goner. Her response when I told her? "*I'm gay.*"

The only bright side was when she told me, "The sex was so good, I got confused." Best compliment ever.

Anyway, two times burned, you'd think I'd learned my lesson.

Nope.

Four months later, I was in love with Bethany. She seemed to be crazy about me as well. I was only twenty, but I pictured us going all the way—two point five kids, a house in the Hamptons, and sex two times a night, even ten years later.

Then she "borrowed" my American Express and racked up fifty-seven thousand dollars before I discovered it. She volunteered to go into therapy in lieu of me pressing charges. I was so crazy into her, I agreed. Which is how she ended up driving off with a handful of my cash in my F12 Berlinetta Ferrari. She ended up crashing it beyond repair. I still miss that car.

I missed her too for a while. Stupidly.

But once my wounds healed, I pulled my head out of my

ass and made myself a new plan, a new mission statement: Do not fall in love.

As most anyone who's had any experience running a business will proclaim—having a mission statement makes decisions one thousand percent easier to make. When a new idea or opportunity arrives, all I have to do is match it against my objective, and then I know whether or not to follow up on it.

Let me demonstrate with a few examples.

Situation: I'm going to Cabo for a week—should I bring someone to spend the nights with or hook up once there?

Response after measuring against objective: Obviously the first option better guarantees I won't be sleeping alone. But romantic beaches? Sunset walks? Sounds like there could be an awful good chance of falling in love. Better choose the latter.

Situation: A woman offers to exchange phone numbers.

Response: What, so I can fall head over heels for her adorable texts and sexy selfies? Kindly decline.

Situation: The redhead with the cute mole wants me to meet her parents.

Response: If I've memorized any of her unique features, I'm already in too deep. Meeting her parents would surely seal my affection. Withdraw immediately.

Situation: There's a girl at the bar that I slept with a month ago—do I say hello?

Response: Hell no. Repeats are a surefire way to trigger an emotional attachment.

Situation: She suggests I go bareback inside her.

Response: Isn't that the definition of falling in love?

See? It works. Using this method, I've established rules

for myself, rules that have protected my heart these past few years, as well as my bank account.

Tonight, with Genevieve, I can't seem to focus on my objective at all, and I have a feeling if I examined my behavior I'd discover much of it has contradicted my don't-fall-in-love goal. I've pursued her. I've let her become too interesting within the space of less than an hour. I've given her too much of my attention, noticing each time she smiles or speaks to another guy, my gut clenching with envy. Any risk management assessment report would mark all of those factors in the hazardous column.

But just because there's a risk doesn't mean the opportunity should necessarily be avoided all together. Right? The best businessmen are willing to venture. That's where the most satisfying rewards are found. And because I'm aware of the danger, I'm more likely to avoid it.

Even I recognize it as bullshit.

It doesn't stop me from escorting Genevieve through the crowd. My skin is on fire through my jacket from the touch of her hand on my arm, and let's not even talk about how badly I need to adjust myself. When I catch her glancing toward the man she'd spoken to just before finding me, I'm already piqued to react poorly.

"Your father?" I ask, feeling nearly insane from the possibility that he isn't.

She sighs. "I look just like him, don't I?"

So he *is* her father. *Thank fucking Christ.*

I use her question as an excuse to study her. "No, you don't. Maybe a bit around the cheekbones. I only asked because the two of you acted so familiar. I worried I'd been flirting with someone who was already taken."

She rolls her eyes, but the spark in them tells me she's not entirely annoyed. "Just because he's my father doesn't mean I'm not taken by someone else."

"Are you?" I challenge.

"No. I'm not."

My instant grin tells her how I feel about this bit of news.

Looking away, she mumbles, "Jesus, I can't believe I'm being so honest."

"You definitely should have lied. What a missed opportunity." I stretch my arm out to hold the door open for her.

"Perhaps."

She brushes past me. The physical contact is intoxicating. Every nerve in my body sits up in attention. Don't even ask what my dick is doing.

"There you are perhaps-ing me again. You have no idea what that does to me."

We take a few more steps before she stops and gives me her full attention, her grey eyes searing into my skin. "All right. I'll bite. What does it do to you?"

"Well. It's a 'maybe'. It's a 'possibly'." I move so I'm facing her. "I'm a pretty optimistic guy, Genevieve. You leave the door open even a crack with possibilities, I'm going to slide on inside."

There's no mistaking my deeper meaning. It's forward and a bit crass, but we're outside the museum now, and soon I'll either put her in a cab or in my car. I so want it to be my car that I'm willing to make the bold move.

Luckily, she doesn't slap me.

She might even like what I'm suggesting, based on the pink blush at her collarbone. As she considers, her tongue swipes across her bottom lip, sending a jolt to the already stiff bulge in my pants, and I'm struck with the sudden strange desire to punish her for it. Spank her pretty ass for making such a sexy gesture. Turn all of her backside red for the ache she's caused my balls.

Holy hell, where did that fantasy come from?

I inhale slowly, trying to release the images from my mind. I've never had such wicked thoughts about a stranger. Part of me is afraid I'll lose all control if I take her home. A bigger part of me is afraid I don't actually care.

Seconds pass, seconds so fraught with tension they feel like an eternity. "Do you have a car parked with the valet?" I ask, eager in her silence.

She shakes her head. "Do you?"

"Yes."

This time she doesn't hesitate, glancing in the direction of the parking attendant. "Give the man your claim ticket then. You can drive me to my hotel."

Relief rains through me. She's only asked for a ride, but *ah, the possibilities.*

Five minutes later, the valet pulls up with my car. Genevieve raises an eyebrow. "A Bugatti?"

I'm so impressed she can name the model that I practically jizz in my pants. "It's the best."

She shakes her head, and I swear I hear her mutter something about rich men and their toys, but I don't respond, too occupied with inspecting my car and then passing the attendant the cash I promised him earlier for returning my vehicle in perfect condition.

I slide into the driver's seat, and when I look over at Genevieve as she buckles her seatbelt, a wave of pure, unadulterated lust rolls through me. I'm very aware that I've trapped her, that she's now defenseless to my whims. Not that I'd take advantage, but goddamn, to think that I could…

I nearly shiver at my own vile thoughts.

Glad she can't know what I'm thinking, I flash her a smile. "So. Where am I taking you?"

"I'm staying at the Park Hyatt on 57th Street."

"Fancy." The Park Hyatt is one of the nicest luxury hotels in New York. That means this girl has money, which isn't a bad thing. Just, the swell of my wallet in my back pocket is usually one of my better attributes. If wealth doesn't attract her, I hope I'm not shit out of luck when it comes to getting an invitation up to her room.

Apparently, I'm transparent because she asks, "Not impressed?"

"Quite the opposite. I'm worried you won't have a reason to be impressed with *me*." Now I'm the one who can't believe how honest I'm being.

"It's a valid worry," she says after a beat, and I can't tell if she's teasing or being blunt. Can't tell if I should prepare for gut-wrenching disappointment or dive into another round of sexy banter.

I concentrate on my driving instead, speeding up before slipping expertly into a tight opening in the adjacent lane.

I'll admit I'm showing off.

"Smashing," she says with a tone that vibrates through my body like I'm a tuning fork.

Then, abruptly, she laughs, and I turn my head toward her, alarmed at the source of her amusement.

"I still can't believe you drive a Bugatti in the city. I

can't decide if that makes you brilliant or as mad as a bag of ferrets."

"Brilliant, of course." Though, with her so close, I feel more like I'm going crazy. "What can I say? I like things that are fast."

"Of course you do."

"You don't?" I raise a questioning brow. "Maybe you don't understand how awesome fast can be." I put my foot on the gas and race down the next block to prove my point.

The traffic light turns red as I approach the intersection, and I ease the brakes. "See? Fast is fun."

"The problem with fast is it's over too quickly."

Is that innuendo? Her gaze pierces into me, and the air around us feels tight and charged, and I'm suddenly certain that I will die if I don't get to taste her tonight.

Even if she didn't mean anything more when she made her statement, I certainly do when I say, "Don't worry. I know when to take my time."

She exhales, slowly, and I swear I can *feel* it. As though she's already in my arms and her breath is grazing every inch of my bare skin. No matter what happens after this, I know she at least feels this…this *attraction*. Or whatever it is.

Her voice is low and sultry when she replies. "You're not talking about cars anymore. But do you really take your time? I'd guess you bolt the minute you're finished." She's so blunt, so direct, and I don't know if it's a *her* thing or an English thing, but I like it.

I also like this conversation we're having. Because we're drawing the lines, and that means the potential for tonight is high. So I answer with a nod, making sure she understands that she's correct in thinking I'll bolt. Because I will.

"That's what I thought." She presses her lips together smugly.

My grip tightens on the gearshift. "Hey. No one cares about the car when it isn't turned on. All that matters is how you handle it when you're in the driver's seat."

I don't add that I fall a little more in love with my Bugatti every time I get behind the wheel, but that's exactly the reason I bolt from women.

Genevieve shakes her head, amused. "Earlier I felt sorry for calling you an American man. But…"

I finish the thought for her. "It's hard to argue with a label I deserve."

She nods as I pull into the driveway of the Park Hyatt and bring the car to a halt. Almost immediately, the hotel attendant opens her door.

She doesn't move.

The tension in the air thickens. It's so heavy, I can't breathe. I can't think.

Genevieve sweeps her head toward me, and electricity sparks between us when her eyes meet mine.

"No cuddling," she says firmly, her voice husky. "No staying the night, and you better have a condom."

I blink, startled by her candidness. "Are you inviting me up, then?"

"Don't act so surprised. Your reputation precedes you. According to the rags, you're quite popular with the ladies. I'm curious to see if your notoriety is deserved." Without waiting for me to respond, she steps out of the car and heads inside.

I hurry after her, stopping briefly to get the claim

ticket from the valet before trotting to catch up with her in the lobby.

"I have a reputation?" I ask softly, coming up behind her. "That's no pressure."

She hits the elevator button and glances at me over her shoulder. "Is it too much for you?"

"Not even a little bit." My answer is eager because *I'm* eager.

"We'll see about that."

When the elevator arrives, we step inside, she selects her floor, and then we move to stand at the back so other people can file in behind us. Silently, I grab her hand, wrapping my fingers through hers.

And there it is. That feeling I love so much. The unspoken awareness that we're about to see each other naked. That we're about to fuck. It's like carrying fire. It's like holding lit dynamite. It's like a bomb about to go off, and every second that passes feels like hours. Every breath I take in and push out feels like lead, and I'm suddenly obsessed with how soft her skin is. Softer than I'd imagined. How soft will she be everywhere else?

At her floor, I practically yank her arm trying to get out of the elevator.

"Left," she directs me, her tone equally impatient.

The walk down the hall is endless, and by the time we reach her door, I'm too wound up to wait even a second longer.

"Hey," I say as she digs in her purse for her key. I'm already stepping closer, and when she looks up, I put my hands on either side of her face, lean in and kiss her.

My mouth is hungry against hers, my lips greedy and

aggressive. Surprised, she takes a moment to react, but when she does, she meets my intensity, and I nearly explode.

God, her tongue, her taste!

With a groan, I press against her. My hands wander frantically, trying to touch every part of her at once. I've never felt so turned on. Never been so blinded with need. Never wanted to be inside someone like I want to be inside her.

And I know, okay? I know that it *always* feels like this when I'm horny and about to bang. Like I've never been this aroused, never been this hard, never been this into a woman. I know this is just hormones and need. I know I'll feel this a hundred times over. Probably feel it again tomorrow, even. With someone else.

But right now? As I kiss and grope and grind against her? Right now, this is the only moment that has ever mattered, the only kiss that has ever affected me like this, and whatever my head says about realistic shit, my body says fucking differently.

It's Genevieve who manages to remember we're still in the hall.

Untangling herself, she pushes me away. "We should go inside," she says, breathless, her mouth swollen and her face flushed.

"Yeah." Dazed, I step away as she works the keycard and shut my eyes tight, clearing my head. I'm on the brink of insanity, just from one kiss. My restraint feels threadbare, and if this is really how I always feel, I can't imagine how I've managed to never go caveman having sex before. Because that's for fuck sure what I want to do now. Want to swing this girl over my shoulder, carry her to the bed, and then beat my chest before devouring every inch of her.

Bring it down a notch, boy. Or seven.

Genevieve opens the door, and I follow cautiously inside. She drops her purse and crosses the room to the dresser. I hang back, trying to cool off a bit before touching her again. With her back to me, she removes her earrings. Then she reaches behind her to unzip her dress. She lets it fall to the floor, and when she turns around, she's standing in front of me wearing nothing but panties and heels.

Holy fucking Christ.

I have to bite my cheek so I don't come right there.

Dirty, filthy ideas flood my mind. Carnal, nasty fantasies. I picture me pushing her against the dresser, my fingers wound tightly in her long hair. I'd yank her head back until she cried out, then I'd pull it harder until she did it again. I'd bite and mark every inch of her creamy skin, starting at her neck. I'd ride her rough. I'd leave bruises. I wouldn't be nice.

Unlike the feeling that I've never been this aroused, these desires actually are ones I've never had before. I've never had these wild thoughts. Never wanted to be brutal in the bedroom, and the things I want to do to this woman, the vile things I want to say to her—they're the kinds of things that might be appropriate for lovers who are well acquainted, but certainly not for two people who've just met.

As inappropriate as they are, they're there, pressing against my brain, begging my body to act. It's tempting. *More* than tempting—the urge is nearly impossible to fight.

But I have to. I can't let it win. This isn't who I am. This isn't what I'm into.

Taking a slow breath, I clench my fists at my side then, as I exhale, I force the vulgar thoughts away. All of them.

When I move toward her, I've resumed control. I'm me again. A nice guy. A gentleman. *Chandler Pierce—the considerate lover.*

It doesn't take long before I'm in my groove. I'm good to Genevieve, just like I'm good to every woman I'm with. I lick at her ears and along her jaw. I lavish her breasts with attention. I kiss and suckle down the pale skin of her abdomen. I bury my face in her pussy and give her two orgasms with my fingers and my mouth.

Later, when I crawl over her and push inside, she's warm and tight and the third time she climaxes, I feel her clenching around my sheathed cock. It triggers my own release.

It's awesome. Like sex always is. Like sex is supposed to be.

I dress quickly after. I clean her up and tuck her in. Pressing a soft kiss to her lips, I tell her I had a good time, and then I leave, just like I promised, just like I do every time.

Her scent clings to me the whole drive home. My body feels hers wrapped around it. My skin still burns from touching her. These lingering remnants of our night will wash away with a hot shower and a good night's sleep. I know this from experience. Lots and lots of experience.

I am a pro at this. I've left many women in many beds, and Genevieve is just another. She's not the first. She won't be the last, and tomorrow I'll have forgotten all about her. It's only tonight that I imagine I still want more.

CHAPTER THREE

A handful of days later, I still want more.

I can't get Genevieve out of my mind. Can't stop imagining being inside her. My dick is practically raw from how many times I've beat off thinking about her.

The thing is—I'm not just thinking about what we did. That wouldn't be so unusual. I've previously had quite a few amazing rolls in the sack that begged to be recreated in my mind later, and who am I to deny those recollections the honor they deserve?

So, yeah. Whacking off to memories is totally standard protocol. I just make sure I don't think about the specific woman too much when I'm in recall mode, you know, to stay true to the don't-get-attached part of my objective. It's generally not a problem.

But with Genevieve, it is.

Her face is etched into my brain. The memory of the silky feel of her skin gnaws at my fingertips. Everywhere

I go, I think I hear her laugh in the crowds around me. Seriously, I'm starting to think I'm going insane.

The worst part is the sexual fantasies. Like implied, I have replayed what actually happened that night a few times—the way her hips bucked under my mouth, the sounds she made when she released. But I'm mostly tormented with the things that *didn't* happen. Things I *wish* happened. Things I wish could happen *in the future*. Things like tearing through her panties and bending her over my knee. Things I can't think about for long without feeling like I need a confessional or a cold shower. Or both.

And it's all day, every day that I'm thinking about her. At the office. When I'm working out. While my mother drones on to me about her latest lunch with the ladies. During the two hours I spend at Hudson's while he shows off the twins—Holden Everett and Brett Evangeline. Even Mina, his three-year-old, can't distract me from Genevieve—and that little girl and I are tight. I'm telling you, there's not a woman who owns my heart like my niece, and yet the sound of her adorable preschooler-speak is underscored with memories of Genevieve's lilting accent, and instead of encouraging Mina to say more, all I want to do is clap my hands over my ears and scream.

In other words, I'm a total wreck.

I know the solution to getting Genevieve out of my head is to find another chick to bang and fast. But she's so present, so vivid in my mind it's like I'm being haunted. There's no way I can begin to entertain the idea of looking for another hookup in this state.

By the time a week rolls past, I'm so miserable that I'm ready to do something drastic to get over this woman. Like make an appointment with Hudson's shrink. Or, worse, track down Genevieve for a repeat.

Problem with the latter? I never bothered to get her last name. And since I never planned to see her again, I didn't take note of her room number. Besides, I was too preoccupied to notice anything in that hallway besides the taste of her tongue.

Ah, that tongue. I imagine it trailing down my skin, lower to places that her mouth never met.

It's this thought that throws me over the edge. I *have* to find her.

And that's how I end up outside Hudson's office on a Wednesday afternoon when I know he's still out on paternity leave.

"Hey there, Chandler," his secretary greets me. "What brings you by my neck of the floor?"

Trish is one of those women who would do anything for me. The way she fawns when I'm in her presence—it's almost ridiculous. She's pretty smoking, too. If she weren't my brother's secretary, I would have nailed her years ago. But we work in the same building, and sleeping with a woman I see every day goes against my mission statement. So instead, we've developed a friendly flirtation that, I think, is pretty healthy. It definitely makes trips to Hudson's office more tolerable.

I unbutton my jacket and perch on the edge of her desk. "Not much. Just been a little cold lately. Figured I needed a little sunshine in my life. Feeling warmer already."

"Stop. You're so good at flattery." She does that thing women sometimes do where she pretends like she's embarrassed by the compliment, but she's really soaking it in.

"You mean I'm so good at truth." And now that I've buttered her up, onto the real item up for business. "Oh, while I'm here. I was wondering if you could get me some more information about that Accelecom benefit I attended last week."

She's already typing into her computer. "Sure. What sort of information are you looking for in particular? The donation list?"

"The guest list."

Trish looks up from her screen and narrows her eyes at me. "Let me guess—she's blonde, blue-eyed, and you just have to have her number."

Actually, she's brunette, grey-eyed, and I'm not sure what it is I have to have from her, but like hell am I admitting to any of that. While I don't think Trish is chatty with Hudson, I'm not taking any chances that she'll slip and mention I've been asking about a girl.

So I focus on Genevieve's father instead.

"Har har." I feign amusement. "Not a woman. A man. About fifty, I'd guess. Distinguished. British. Seemed to be a major big-wig, but I never caught his name." Never even spoke to him. She doesn't need to know.

I stand to move behind Trish as I talk so I can look at the computer over her shoulder. "Maybe you could dig up some pictures from the gala that might match that description, and—"

My words are cut off by what I see, and it's not on the secretary's computer screen but standing right in front of me.

"Genevieve."

"Chandler?"

For a minute I'm not sure if she's really there or if I'm imagining her. That's how in my head this fucking girl is. I can't even tell the difference between reality and fantasy.

But Trish has also glanced up, so I'm pretty sure my ghost is real. I look her over, taking her in. She's dressed for business in slacks and a matching jacket that's open to reveal a white shirt with black trim. Her makeup is subtle, yet her eyes are as sharp as ever. Her dark hair falls down past her shoulders, and it looks longer now that it's missing the waves from the other night. In every way, she's less glam, less "done up".

And damn if she isn't two thousand times more beautiful.

I inhale slowly, remembering I'm in Hudson's office and just thinking my brother's name seems to calm the devil in my dick. When I exhale, I'm ready.

"It's good to see you." I know I should play harder to get—yes, that's a thing guys do too—yet I can't help the smile that forms on my lips. "What are you doing here, anyway?"

She returns my smile—it's more refined and understated than mine, but she's British, and it counts. "Looking for you. This is your office? The security guard said it was on the other side of the building."

Holy shit, she was looking for me!

"Did he?" I mean, he's right. And my office is pretty sweet. It's on the opposite corner with floor-to-ceiling windows, lots of space, and modern furniture.

But I'm not offering to take her there. Partly because, as a rule, I try not to be alone with beautiful women in my office unless we're very clearly sticking to business. But also because there's no way in hell I'll make it across the floor with the semi in my pants.

Besides, as nice as my office is, Hudson's is nicer.

"Why don't you come inside?" I gesture for Genevieve to follow me into his office, making eye contact with his secretary. "Trish, hold my calls, will you?"

"*You're so bad,*" she mouths.

I really am, aren't I? I should probably feel guilty about it. Spoiler: I don't.

"Have a seat," I say to Genevieve over my shoulder as I shut the double doors behind us. I have the same predator feeling I had when she was buckling herself into the passenger seat of my car.

She's trapped. With me. Alone.

And since I'm a betting man, I'm putting a large wager on things getting naughty.

First, the niceties. "Can I get you anything? Coffee?" I ask, crossing the room toward her.

"A little late in the day for that, don't you think?"

Fuck. What time is it anyway? "Scotch?"

"And too early for that." She hasn't taken a seat yet and instead is surveying my—I mean, *Hudson's*—office. "It's tea time, but I don't reckon you have any scones and jam lying around, so I'll pass, thank you."

"Are you sure? I bet Trish could whip—"

She cuts me off before I have a chance to buzz the secretary. "No, please. I was teasing. I'm good."

"You're good," I confirm, nervously. Because I *am* nervous. Because I'm trying to pull off my brother's office as mine, for one reason. For other reasons too. Like, *why-won't-she-sit-down* reasons? And *oh-my-god-she's-so-pretty* reasons.

She's much better at post-one-night-stand than I am it seems, because she's the one to fill the awkward silence that has settled between us. "This is quite brilliant. I'm impressed."

I'm not sure what she's impressed with because I'm a disaster. My mouth is dry, my hands are clammy. Oh, she means the office. Of course. God, I want to just get past the small talk and onto the part where we take our clothes off and start playing Happy Businessman. Are there security cameras in here?

And what did Genevieve just say?

"I'm sorry. I'm having difficulty focusing. I'm too distracted by wondering why you wanted to see me."

"I asked about the square footage, but that's not my business and I should get to the point." She looks so young right now, so innocent. I'd thought maybe twenty-five when I first met her. Now, even in her professional attire, I'd say she's possibly younger.

It makes me feel more predatory. I watch her every move as she paces the room, ready to devour her.

Finally, she plops down in a chair facing Hudson's desk and crosses one long leg over the other. Then she frowns. "I'm not sure how to begin."

I don't understand all she said, but man, do I understand that last bit. Having so little experience with repeats, I'm at a loss myself. Are we supposed to talk first? Just start going at it? Is she going to think this makes us a couple?

Does it?

So many questions. She has to be just as confused as I am.

You know what? This is new, but that doesn't mean

I can't stick to a business model of operation. I'm going full disclosure.

Sitting on the edge of Hudson's desk, I make my declaration. "You don't need to say anything more. I was actually in the process of trying to find you myself."

"You were?"

"I was." God, it's so sexy how she arches her brow like that. Full disclosure for the win. Maybe more of it will get me an even bigger reward. "Genevieve, I'm not usually like this, but I can't seem to stop thinking about our night together. You've taken over my head like a drug, and I…"

I hesitate, not because I'm unsure, but because I'm surprised *how* sure I am. "I can't believe I'm saying this, but I'd really love to see you again."

"Oh." She's surprised too. It's in her body language, in her tone of voice. "Oh," she says again, more acceptant.

Acceptant, but it's not really an answer. "I'm not sure if that's a yes…?"

She sighs, her lips twisting before she responds. Then she says, "Would you be entirely offended if it's not?"

Uh…"What?"

I heard her wrong. There's no other option.

But now she's brushing her hair behind her ear in a way that seems to mean *I'm trying to be polite*. "I had a lovely time with you, Chandler." Because, duh. "But I'm not interested in a date."

Ah! This makes more sense. She's not looking for a relationship. Neither am I—I don't think.

I'll clarify. "You misunderstood me. A date wasn't what I was interested in either. I was thinking more like a replay."

"I didn't misunderstand. I knew exactly what you meant.

I was trying to find a less abrupt way of saying I'd rather not another time, thank you."

Again…"What?"

Her expression is tight. Uncomfortable. Apologetic. "I really didn't mean to lead you on."

"You didn't. Just. I'm confused." Sure I've heard the didn't-mean-to-lead-you-on speech, but not when all we're talking about is getting between the sheets. I swear we're miscommunicating somehow.

I stand and circle to the opposite side of the desk. Placing my knuckles on the surface, I lean toward her. "You're saying you don't want to have sex with me again. Am I getting this right?"

"That's correct."

In a daze, I sink into the chair behind me. "Why?"

"Do I have to have a reason?" My silence tells her that, yes, she has to have a goddamn reason, so after a pause, she continues. "Okay, well, I wasn't that into the whole thing, if you must know."

I don't understand. I tell her, "I don't understand."

"I'm saying it was a good time, but not good enough to want to do it again."

"Not *good enough*?" There's a part of me that can step outside myself and see that I sound like a moron. I hear myself talking. I totally catch the idiocy.

And yet, I can't seem to pull myself together.

It's embarrassing. For both of us.

Genevieve is at least nice about it. "God, this is awkward. I'm so sorry, Chandler."

The way she says my name gets me in the gut. It sounds so damn sexy. Is she doing that on purpose? Teasing me with her off-the-charts sensuality in the same breath that she tells me it's off limits?

No. This isn't what's happening. She enjoyed herself that night. I was there. I know. Like hell am I not reminding her. "You had an orgasm though. You had several."

She shrugs. "And?"

My jaw drops. She climaxed three freaking times from the magic of Chandler "Generous Lover" Pierce. How is this even a question?

She seems to sense my confusion. "You know," she says slowly, as if explaining to a child, "sex is like pizza. Even when it's bad, it's still pretty good."

"That was not bad sex." Irrefutable. Case closed.

She tugs at her hair as she sighs. "Honestly, I'm sure it wasn't. I'm unfortunately one of those unique creatures who never feels satisfied." I open my mouth to say maybe she just needs more orgasms, but she guesses what I'm going to say and says, "No matter how many times I climax. It's me, not you, Chandler. Trite words, but the truth. On the plus side, I'm able to sit here and not be distracted by your genitalia, which seems to be the opposite for you. Looks like I have the upper hand."

"No one who dislikes sex has the upper hand."

I lean back in my chair and cross my ankle over my knee. I'm anxious and worked up, and for the first time I can ever remember, I wish I were able to don the stoic mask that my brother wears so flawlessly. Me, I'm transparent. I'm jittery. My whole body twitches with my distress.

The worst part? I can't let the subject go. "If you knew there was no way to satisfy you, why did you even let me take you home in the first place?"

"Honestly?" She blushes, and it's so hot my balls itch. "I was trying to prove a point to my father."

Holy. No. "You fucked me to prove a point to your father? I'm really not following."

She shakes her head. "Of course you aren't. I'm mucking this up. You see, at the benefit, after I realized who you were, I tried to tell my father that I'd met you. I was hoping to give you both an introduction, but as always, he wasn't interested. He's never very interested in what I have to say. He's one of those men who thinks that women belong behind the scenes of charity functions, or if they must have a career, it should be in fashion or interior design. Definitely not business. Very old-fashioned."

I don't say it, but I can actually relate. My father isn't too impressed with me most days either.

"I'm sorry if you're the type to agree with him," Genevieve goes on, "but, really I'm not sorry, because if you do agree, you're a shallow, closed-minded misogynist who needs to stop being a prat and catch up with the times."

"I'm not. Women should work where they want to work. Equal pay, equal benefits and all that jazz." I sound lame the way I'm falling all over myself trying to impress her.

And I can't seem to stop. "In fact, women should get paid more, in my opinion. They're much smarter than men. More organized. Usually have better ideas too."

"That's really not necessary."

I sense she's biting back a laugh. I really am lame. Kill me now. "I know. I'm sorry. Go on. I'm still not clear on how I ended up in your bed."

Genevieve tilts her head and studies me. "You *are* charming, you know. That had a lot to do with it. And your reputation. I figured if anyone had a shot at disrupting the status quo, it was you."

Now that's what I'm talking about. *Lay on the praise, babe.*

"But also, my father was so dismissive. He acted like he thought it was cute that I had 'made a friend'. Suggested I bring you home for dinner sometime. Needless to say, I was miffed. He'd never dismiss my brother like that, and Hagan wouldn't know a good opportunity if it bit him in the arse. So, out of spite, I let you fuck me."

"That's. I'm." In her short speech, she's dropped so many personal details that I want to latch onto and pursue further.

But there's one that's especially pressing. "You *told your father* I took you home?"

"No. Noooo." She waves her hand emphasizing the degree to which I've got the wrong impression. "It was more of a secret spiteful gesture. I know it sounds silly. It made me feel self-righteous at the time. Anyway, it's backfired because now you also don't seem to be interested in any business talk with me. Which is truly a shame, I might add. I was the top of my class at Cambridge. I have innovative ideas to bring to Werner Media. Accelecom would be such a major coup to have a partnership with, and if you'd just hear me out, I'm certain I could impress you."

"Hold on." I put my hand up to stop her from saying any more. There is shit that needs to be cleared up here and quick. "First of all, I'm already impressed." She's obviously smart as well as classy. I'm so impressed I can't get comfortable in my chair, but mentioning that would probably help her case and not mine.

"Second of all, I am not a misogynist. I'd be more than interested in any idea you might have for Pierce Industries."

I'm already trying to think of places we could use her, and I don't even know exactly what it is she does or what she has to offer. Well, besides the obvious. "But I'm not sure why you'd want to talk to me about Werner Media."

"Because with Warren Werner about to retire, you're going to need someone new at the helm. There's no one currently primed to take his spot."

"Yes, I agree. Just, that's not part of our portfolio. If you'd like me to get you in touch with Warren—"

She folds her arms over her chest and gives me a stern look. "You don't need to be dodgy. You've done well at keeping it under wraps, but I'm fully aware that Pierce Industries owns the majority shares of Werner Media."

"No, we don't." I'm starting to wish we did, but sadly, no.

"Yes. You do. Your brother obtained controlling interest about five years ago."

"No, he didn't."

"He did," she insists, frustration lacing her tone. "Are you really not aware? Pierce Industries has been a silent partner, letting Warren Werner maintain the position of figurehead."

She's so sure of herself, I consider the possibility. I mean, there is a lot that Hudson doesn't tell me. It's a big business, and I've only been working full-time since I finished my MBA last year. So it's feasible that we have deals that I'm not quite caught up on.

If what she's suggesting *is* true, it would explain Hudson's interest in Werner Media forming a partnership with Accelecom. And why he wanted me to make a good impression at the gala.

Actually, it makes a lot of sense.

It's my turn to study her. "How do you know all this?

If this information hasn't been made privy to the public, I don't understand how you know about it."

"Well, I know about it from my father."

"Who's your father?"

"Edward Fasbender."

I drop my leg to the floor and sit forward. "Your father's the head of Accelecom?"

"Yes. Didn't you realize? You saw me with him."

Exactly the man my brother was hoping I'd impress. And I went ahead and banged the guy's daughter. And his daughter wasn't satisfied. This situation is starting to look bad.

I ball my hand in a fist and run it along my forehead. "I didn't realize he was Edward Fasbender. And that still doesn't explain how Accelecom knows about Pierce Industries' silent share majority." The pieces aren't coming together, but I'm starting to sense that when they do, it's going to be even worse than it is now. If that's possible.

"Oh. I see. But of course we know about Werner Media from my stepmother."

"Your stepmother?"

The intercom sounds before she has a chance to answer. Three solid beeps and then Trish's voice fills the air. "Chandler, I thought you'd want to know that Hudson just called and he's on his way up with Edward Fasbender."

Yep, I knew it was going to get worse.

Genevieve bolts up from her chair. "Oh shit. My father doesn't know I'm here. If he finds out, he's going to be mad as hell."

Way worse.

I stand and move toward her. "Then we better get going

before they get up here. Come on. We can slip out to—" I'm about to say *my* office when I remember I'd led her to believe this *was* my office. "To my *other* office."

She seems confused—naturally—but doesn't hesitate when I put my hand on her shoulder to direct her out of the room. My skin feels instantly charged. How the hell can she say she didn't have a good enough time?

Probably shouldn't be worrying about that right now.

I open the door, but instead of moving out, her eyes double in size. "Fuck!" She scurries to hide behind me, urging me to close the door again.

I don't have to ask why because I spotted them myself—Hudson and the man from the gala stepping out of the elevator.

I shut the door and press my back against it. Running a hand through my hair, I will myself to think of something. And quick.

Looking even paler than normal, Genevieve begins pacing and cursing. "Shit, shit, shit!"

There *is* another escape route from this office—the single elevator that leads to the loft above. It used to be where Hudson lived when he was a bachelor. Now I live there, but since my brother doesn't particularly like the idea of me having free rein to just drop into his office whenever I like, he's removed the access key.

As if the loft is the only way I'd drop into his office uninvited.

I also know where he keeps the key. I'm not sure if we have time to grab it, but we can try.

"This way." Grabbing Genevieve's hand, I pull her toward the closet by the liquor cabinet where Hudson's got the key stashed. Then, when I realize we absolutely don't have time to grab the key, cross the room, call the elevator, and get out of the office before my brother walks in, I pull Genevieve in with me and shut the door.

And that's how I end up hiding from my brother in his office closet with the one girl on earth who doesn't want to repeat fuck me.

God, my life sucks.

Did I mention the closet was small?

Really small. Tight. Cozy. So cramped we practically have to press up against each other to fit inside.

Huh.

Maybe things aren't going quite so bad after all.

CHAPTER FOUR

The closet, it turns out, provides exactly enough room for two bodies. We could stand shoulder to shoulder and that would take the entire width. The depth is almost half that. It's only meant to hold a few coats or jackets, nothing more. Thankfully, it's late August, so there's not much in here besides us, a couple of Hudson's spare suits, and a hook with the key to the elevator.

I eye the silver dangling on the wall above Genevieve's head and consider whether we have time to try to make it to the loft after all. Her father and Hudson still haven't entered the office—we'd have heard them.

"Are you sure they'll come in here?" she asks, and I can tell she must be listening for them as closely as I am.

"Not positive. But if they're having a meeting, it seems likely." Which means we should stay put. I pocket the access key anyway. In case we get an opportunity.

She backs up against the wall and sighs. "Why are they using your office?"

I'm a fairly smart guy. I know my cover's blown. The full disclosure tactic worked out all right before, so I just go ahead and admit, "Because this isn't my office. It's Hudson's."

"Why did you say it was yours then?" She's huffy, which I suppose is fair. It's also sort of hot.

I lean on the opposite wall, hands stuffed in my pockets. "I didn't exactly say that it was, if you remember."

"But you knew I thought it was."

I shrug. I mean, she's right, but it's not like rehashing it is going to get us out of the situation we're in.

"Well, that was a nice one, wasn't it? Letting me believe something that wasn't true." She starts to cross her arms over her chest and close herself off but drops them when, I assume, she realizes the space is much too tight to allow that.

Isn't that a shame?

I bend over her, placing my palm on the wall next to her face. "Hey, I didn't know Hudson would be here. And I didn't know he'd be with your father, and I most definitely didn't guess that you'd be hiding from him."

"I wouldn't be hiding from him if—"

The office doors creak outside.

I clamp my hand over Genevieve's mouth, silencing her, and we both perk up, listening to the rustle of the men's movements, praying there's no reason for Hudson to peek inside our hiding space.

"It's not what you intend to do with Werner Media that I'm concerned with," he says, and it sounds like he's passing us by, walking toward his desk, I guess. *"It's how that will affect Pierce Industries."*

"I can assure you, Accelecom has no interest in taking any predatory action against your company. I've conceded to every one of

your conditions, Hudson. Our position should be quite obvious." The voice that responds is British, but I can tell the crisp and formal manner with which the man speaks has as much to do with his personality as the location of his upbringing.

And this is what Genevieve has to deal with as a parent? Damn. It's got to be like being raised by a Hudson. Poor girl.

This snippet of their conversation also confirms what she had said earlier, and I'm intrigued by what else they have to say.

But I'm more intrigued right now by *her*. She smells good, like some spring flower, the purple ones—lilacs, I think. Sunlight slips through the slats of the door, hitting her face, and her gaze is locked on mine. With her delicate features and bewildered expression, she reminds me of a doe, caught under a hunter's riflescope.

My doe. My prey.

You look at me all bright-eyed and trusting like that, and all I can think about is how far I could get my cock down your throat before you couldn't breathe.

Her eyes widen, and I realize I didn't just *think* those dirty, dirty thoughts. I actually *said* them. Out loud.

Oh, shit.

She made it clear that she's not interested. So is that considered…? Did I just, like, sexually assault Genevieve Fasbender in my brother's closet? With her *father right outside*?

There are a thousand ways that this could not be cool. At all.

And yet I haven't let go of her. My hand still covers her mouth. I'm still pressed up close to her. So close that I don't miss that she's not bothered by what I said in the least. Her breath quickens and she peers up at me, her stare intense, wanting, and I swear, I can smell arousal mingling with the scent of her perfume.

"What more can we do to prove good faith?" Edward asks, and I know my brother well enough to guess that he's going to spell it all out for him.

Which means we have some time.

So…should I?

I move my hand off Genevieve's mouth and trail a single finger over her chin, down the slope of her neck. Her pulse trips as my touch grazes across her skin. In response, she arches her neck, swallows, then runs her tongue over her bottom lip, and maybe this is how bad people convince themselves they're not doing anything wrong, but I'm as sure as the hard-on below my belt that she wants this.

Whatever this is. Whatever it's turning into.

Right now I'm just…exploring. Going by instinct. Figuring out what she will and won't let me get away with.

Watching carefully for any sign of rejection, I continue the pathway down her body. She leans into my palm as I slide over the curve of her breast, and it's tempting to stop and spend some time here.

But I'm still a little pissed at her.

I feasted on her tits the last time we were together, and she compared my moves to bad pizza. Like hell she's getting that kind of attention this time.

Instead, I capture the bud of her stiff nipple between my thumb and forefinger and pinch.

Her mouth drops open in a silent gasp. Not the kind of gasp that says, *No* or *Stop*. The kind of gasp that says, *More*.

If I had any doubt, it's erased when a single whisper of a word spills from her lips. *"Please."*

Permission granted. *Score!*

Without further hesitation, my hand slides under the waistband of her pants and inside the silky material of her panties. She's soaked.

Jesus, I thought I couldn't get any harder. I was so goddamn wrong. I'm tempted to pull out my cock and make her play with it. I'm eager for her hands to wrap around the length of my shaft, dying for her to tug and stroke—

But there's not enough room in here to do it the way I'd like her to, the way I need it—with her mouth on me. She'd be on her knees, and I wouldn't be able to see her face. The slats in the door don't go that far down. When she sucks me, I'm going to need to watch every detail.

Notice I said *when*, not *if*. Considering the current turn of events—i.e., my fingers fondling her pussy—I'm optimistic that a blowjob could be brought to the table for negotiation.

Not right now. Later.

Right now, I'm much more wrapped up in what else I can do to her. Wrapped up in what it will feel like when I do it.

She spreads her legs, granting me better access. It's a total green light. I quit my hesitating and press the pad of my thumb to her clit. She's so swollen—I can imagine how sensitive it must be. How hard it must be not to cry out as I touch her.

Suddenly I'm greedy to have her do just that. Never mind that we're trying not to get caught. That fact just makes me all the more intent.

I rub against her again, increasing my pressure ever so slightly. When her eyes glaze and she bites her lip, I double my efforts, stretching my hand so that I can slide a finger inside her without breaking the contact I have with her nub.

This does the trick. She lets out the softest whimper, barely audible, but it's enough.

With my free hand, I press her mouth into the curve of my shoulder and whisper gruffly into her ear. "If you make another sound, I'll stop."

She quiets instantly.

It's fucking hot how quickly she responds. She believes me. Believes that I will stop and is desperate not to let that happen.

She's such a good, good girl.

But now I have to torture her even more because she's so trusting. Curving my finger, I stroke in and out of her, rubbing against her velvety walls, all the while massaging her clit. Her breath hitches. Her wetness thickens and her hips buck into my hand. Still I keep on, caressing and coaxing until she's sweating and squirming and nipping at the fabric of my jacket.

She's nearly there. Another nudge against her sweet spot, and I'm sure she'll climax. I can't decide if it's crueler to pull away now or force her to try to come silently.

She wasn't quiet at all that night in her hotel. I'm not sure she can even do it. I should slowly ease out of her and finish her off when our main priority is not to remain unnoticed. That would be the nice guy move.

But I don't want to be the nice guy. Not anymore.

Wrapping her hair in my fist, I yank her head up so I can see her eyes. Then, sinking my fingers deeper inside her, I hit her where she wants it—where she needs it—and send her over the edge.

"*Shh*," I mouth in warning as her face crumples into the most beautifully tormented expression I've ever seen. She trembles against me, her entire body shuddering with the wave of her release. It's awesome. Not awesome like the word that's thrown around in everyday generic vocabulary but in the true definition. Awe-some. As in, inspiring awe. As in, *damn, I'm awed.*

Distracted as I am watching her, I keep up the job. I'm merciless, even, stroking and coaxing her until she's completely drained, until she's given me every last drop of her orgasm. Until she's limp in my arms, her breathing ragged, her skin glowing with a fine sheen of sweat. She's spent.

And me?

Shit, I'm only getting started.

CHAPTER FIVE

Genevieve clings to me, even after she can stand on her own. She keeps her gaze averted, but I can't stop staring, can't stop taking in every single observable detail in the thin streams of sunlight. Her mascara is slightly smudged, her hair tousled, her breathing shallow.

And she suddenly seems so slight and small.

When I first noticed her at the gala, I was drawn to her strength and confident detachment. In this moment, her beauty is in how she's fallen, how she's folded into my arms, how her fingers dig into the sleeve of my jacket, like it's a lifeline. She's not a fragile woman in the least, but there's a delicacy about her right now. An elegance that she likes to keep private. I wonder how many people she's let see her like this.

After a minute, she remembers herself, and her head pops up, her eyes fluttering to meet mine. Now that I have her attention, I bring my finger to my mouth and suck her wetness from my skin. I tasted her the other night, but this simple gesture is so sensual and erotic that I swear she tastes better today.

Her eyes spark, and my dick jumps as though it's connected to her gaze with jumper cables.

Not that it needed the extra jolt. I've been hard as steel the whole time we've been in the closet, and when she cups her hand around my bulge, silently asking for my permission, I practically burn from the contact.

"Don't," I hiss, and her expression says she's confused.

Honestly, I am a little too. Because I fucking *need* her.

But not yet. Not on these terms, and thank Christ it's only a few seconds later when I hear Hudson say, "*My chief financial advisor can show you the projections she's put together. Her office is just down the hall. Let me walk you over.*"

I put my hand on the knob, and the instant I'm sure that Hudson and Edward have left, I fling the door open. With Genevieve's hand tucked in mine, I pull her to the elevator, push the button, and tug her inside after me when it opens.

"Where are we—"

I cut her off. "Don't talk."

Her jaw closes, drawing her mouth into a tight line. I'm not sure I can quite articulate why I want her to be silent. Because I'm near sensory overload. Because I don't want her to break the mood. Because I'm too focused on my agenda at the moment to be disrupted. Maybe it's all of that or something else all together. I don't know.

What I do know is that I love the way she's obeyed me. Without question. Without comment.

It does good things to the buzz in my veins. Good, good things.

At the elevator, I insert the access key, and after a short

ride the doors open to my loft. Genevieve walks out beside me, and before she's taken two steps, I have her pressed against the wall. I kiss her thoroughly, roughly. My tongue swipes across her teeth. My hands wander up. Soon, I'm helping slip off her jacket.

Again, she reaches for my crotch, and damn, I want her to touch me, but I want it with her mouth. I want it so badly I can barely speak, can barely think straight. I step back and start working on my buckle. "Shirt and bra off," I say gruffly, and it sounds like an order.

Hell, I guess I mean it to be one, too.

And god bless Captain America, she complies.

By the time I've gotten my pants undone, she's naked from the waist up. My eyes eat her up, greedily, as I lower my boxer briefs just enough to draw out my rock-hard cock. With one hand on her shoulder, I nudge her down to her knees.

"This ends the minute you say stop. If you can't talk, pinch me." Because in about two seconds, I don't expect her to be able to say a thing.

In fact, I'm so impatient, such an asshole in my lust, I don't wait for her to respond before saying, "Open your mouth," and the instant her jaw drops open, I step forward and thrust inside.

I mean, thrust. Completely. As far as I can go. No hesitation. No going slow. None of this foreplay-take-your-time bullshit. I am that shithead who sees a hole and shoves all the way in.

Jesus.

And all that is holy.

There are no words for how good it feels to have her

lips around me. My head is practically touching the back of her throat, her tongue flat against the bottom of my cock. It's everything I'd imagined and more.

I draw out, slowly so I can feel everything. I pause to let her catch her breath.

Then I drive in again.

Her cheeks hollow as she presses them in against my length. She swirls her tongue, and it feels like she's licking me everywhere at once. Like she's a whirlpool around my dick. Goddamn, it's so good. So hot.

Especially the way her tits bounce as she moves her mouth up and down my length. My eyes are glued on her breasts. I alternate between imagining that my cock is sliding between them and imagining my fingers tweaking her nipples, so hard she cries out. Mostly I just like staring at them, fully ogling her. It's so dirty and filthy and me-centric. She's getting no pleasure from this. It's all about me.

God, I'm a douche.

But then I catch her gaze. Her eyes water as she looks up, adoring me. Idolizing me. Wanting to please me. It's almost spiritual, and all I can think is no wonder man decided god wanted to be prayed to, because being prayed to is fucking awesome.

So awesome that I lose control.

Or rather I go into hyper-control. The kind of control I've seen in other people in business and boardrooms—not ever in me. The kind of control I've only ever aspired to. Hyper-control like my brother who micromanages and supervises every transaction. That's what I do to Genevieve. I cradle her face and hold it exactly where I want it and then I just…let go. I pound into her. I take advantage. I use her. She's not doing it to me; I'm doing it to her. She's not sucking my cock; I'm fucking her mouth.

Her hands curl around my calves, steadying herself, and I try to pay attention to the way she grips me. Try to notice whether or not she means to stop me.

But I've got to be honest—I'm so into how good this feels that she'll probably have to pinch me hard enough to break skin to get me to notice anything else. If she does, I'll stop. I don't know how, but I will. That promise is the only way I can live with myself as I push in again and again and again. Mercilessly. With total abandon.

"I'm going to come down your throat now, Genny. That's all the warning I'm going to give." Because that's as long as I can manage to hold out, and almost as soon as I've said the words, I'm there, exploding, shooting down her throat in long thick spurts. My hands are still clamped so tightly on either side of her face she has no choice but to take it.

And she does, she takes every drop, every bit of what I give her.

It's the best blowjob anyone's ever given me.

Except, it was more taken than given. And the second I've finished spilling inside her, the realization fully rushes over me.

Oh, god. What have I done?

Flooded in guilt, I can barely look at her.

"I'll be right back," I say and make a dash for the bathroom. I clean up quickly, tucking myself away when I'm done. Then I scrub a hand over my face and brace my other on the countertop.

Leaning over the sink, I stare at myself in the mirror.

"You're an asshole," I tell my reflection. "Whatever she accuses you of, you deserve it because you just raped that woman's mouth. She didn't say yes. You just took what you wanted. Happy?"

Worst thing is I *am* happy. Even tainted with regret and shame, I still really enjoyed it.

Asshole is too nice of a reference for what I am.

I heave a sigh as I wet a washcloth. I need to clean her up. Need to apologize, even though assault isn't something you can just say sorry for. I need to try to make amends even as I'm certain that I'm going to hate myself for this for a long, long time.

And what if she presses charges?

I can't even think about that. I'd deserve it, but I can't think about that shit.

After several deep breaths to psych myself up, I venture back out of the bathroom. I keep my head down, staring at my shoes, unable to look at her.

"Genevieve…" I trail off. I don't know what to say next.

I brave a glance in her direction. She's on the floor, her back against the wall, her legs splayed in front of her as though she were a ragdoll that was thrown across the room and this was how she happened to land.

I did this to her.

Fuck! What the hell is wrong with me? After violating her downstairs, I follow it up with this?

But then I study her face—really study it. And the expression she's wearing doesn't say traumatized. It's a much more familiar look, one I've seen on plenty of women in the past.

Holy shit!

"You liked it." It's not a question because I'm sure of the answer.

Still, she confirms. "I liked it."

A roller coaster of emotions rumbles through me. I'm overwhelmingly relieved. And surprised. And delighted. And a little confused.

Also, I'm cautious. "Are you going to make a pizza comparison now?"

Her lips creep into a smile. "Better than any pizza I've ever tasted."

"Good. Good." I mean, pizza is still a lame correlation, but it was good sex, and I'm just glad she knows it this time.

Which begs the question…

I cross to her and squat so I can wipe at her mouth with the washcloth. "What changed?"

I'm desperate to know the answer. Because I'm pretty sure a lot of what I just did to her would have been considered rapey if whatever it was that has obviously changed hadn't changed.

Though, as much as I want to know, I have to confess—it's difficult to concentrate when her breasts are so near and so naked. A fantasy forms in my head of her tits covered in my jizz. It's mind-blowing to think about. Sure I've given a pearl necklace or two in my time, but I've never wanted to see a woman bathed in my cum like I want to see Genny.

I'm so distracted by the image that I almost forget what I'd asked when she responds. "Are you going to make me talk about it?"

I pull my eyes up from her naked breasts to answer. "I think you'd like it if I did. You like to be bossed." Somehow I make it sound like a statement, but it's most definitely a question. I'm still feeling out this thing that happened between us, trying to come to grips with what exactly we both liked about it.

Seeming to understand my need, she answers, "Yes."

Which is awesome, because I liked bossing her. I liked it a lot.

I boss her again now. "What else?"

She looks away before answering. "I guess I liked it when you pinched me. And maybe when you pushed me to my knees. I really liked the way you held my head while you…" She blushes and her skin goes pink from her cheeks to the tips of her nipples.

"You like it rough."

The tentative way she nods tells me she's just working this out herself.

Well, that makes two of us. Because I had no idea how thrilling it could be to dominate a woman. Like driving on a clear night down the highway in my Bugatti. It's a rush like no other—handling something as it moves that fast. Feeling it respond.

I brush my hand across her face, tracing the crimson in her cheeks. "I liked when you opened your legs for me, and I didn't even have to tell you."

"I liked how you didn't let me speak."

"Which time?"

"All of them."

God, she's perfect.

I stand and hold my hand out to her. "Come here."

She lets me help her, and as soon as she's on her feet, I capture her wrists and bring them above her head, pushing her back against the wall. After shifting my grip to one hand,

I use my other hand to trace my thumb across her bottom lip. It's plump and swollen from the way I made her take me. It's such a fucking turn-on, I'm already getting hard again.

"I've never been like this with anyone before," I say, sticking my thumb between her lips.

She tightens her mouth around me and sucks, sending electric shocks down my arms and thighs and to my cock.

I pull my thumb from her lips slowly, prolonging the hum of desire in my veins.

"I've never been like this with anyone either," she says, and I'm as glad as if she'd told me I'd taken her virginity. "I've imagined it sometimes, but I've never had the courage to ask a guy to try it out."

"If you had to ask, it would be beside the point."

"Well. Yes. Exactly."

Unlike her, I haven't thought about it. But *I get it.* It feels natural. Right. The way I want to make her bend to me again and again—it's like a second engine I've just discovered. An engine that's fully tuned and raring to go.

The possibilities of future trysts stream through my mind as I gather her clothes. Silently, I help her put them on, the whole time thinking about the next time I get her undressed, thinking about her wrists tied behind her back with the sleeves of her blouse. Thinking of the cups of her bra pulled down, propping her tits up for my exploration.

And it hits me. "I have to see you again."

She takes a shaky breath in, and I'm sure that acquiescence is on the tip of her tongue.

Except then she turns away.

"It's not a good idea," she says matter-of-factly, bending

to get her jacket. She's careful to keep her distance and avoid my eyes.

"Uh, what?" I totally did not expect that response.

She straightens and forces her eyes to mine. "I said it's not a good idea. It's not. So we had our fun, but we're done now."

"Bullshit." No fucking way is she getting away with that. She must want me to convince her to change her answer.

She shakes her head, her mouth drawn down sullenly. "I have things that I want—things that aren't you. Things like my job. My father already doesn't take me seriously. Spending time with you will look like I'm using my body to get what I want at Werner Media, and that won't help prove to him I'm actually qualified."

"Your father doesn't have to know. In fact, he shouldn't know. Because that's just..." I don't have kids—obviously—but I have a niece, and there's no way I ever want to hear about her having sex with someone. "That's weird, is what it is. Besides, maybe I can help you figure out a way to get him to listen to you."

She squints at me. "And how do you plan to do that?"

"I haven't gotten that far. We should talk about it over dinner." I wink, which is maybe a little much.

"Not happening."

Yeah, definitely should have foregone the wink.

I grab the edge of her jacket and pull her to me. Clasping my arms around her waist, I kiss her forehead. "Come on. Imagine it. Us, exploring this thing further. Pushing boundaries. Discovering what it is that we really want out of a sexual encounter. Together. Are you imagining it?"

"Maybe."

I bend to study her features. "You are. I see it in your eyes."

"Imagining doesn't mean considering."

Damn, I love her creamy European complexion—it's the best tell, her every emotion showing up scarlet on her skin.

She knows it too. She twists out of my embrace, trying to hide her face, but I catch her from behind and wrap my arms around the bottom of her breasts.

"You are so considering it," I say, pressing my mouth to her ear. "Let me help you with your decision by giving you this little bit of information—the things I want to do to you? The ways I want to fuck you? The nasty things I want to whisper to you? We haven't even scratched the surface."

"Chandler…" she says with a shiver.

"See me again, Genny." Without letting her go, I twist my torso around so I can watch her face. I have her physically gridlocked, and when she tries to push my arms off, I only tighten my grip.

She struggles, and Jesus, does it make my boxer briefs feel tight, and it also makes me wonder once again if I'm doing the wrong thing, crossing a line. Mixing up my desires with her consent.

She lets out a frustrated sigh. "You need to let me go. Please."

"First, say you'll have dinner with me tomorrow."

"No." She isn't budging.

Neither am I. "Tonight, then."

"I have plans."

It could be just an excuse, but I'm suddenly jealous

wondering who her plans are with. "Are you playing hard to get?"

"I don't need to play—I *am* hard to get. Now let me go."

But I don't want to. Which is fucked. I mean, who the hell am I, and what the hell happened to my standard protocol?

It's gone out the window, obviously, because I'm holding her tight. "Say you'll go out with me first. You know you want to."

"No. I really don't." She pushes against my arms, and I don't let her go, but I twirl her around so I can face her. And then I really look into her eyes, and I see that she's serious. Dead serious.

Fuck. Did I just read her totally wrong?

I let her go. Reluctantly.

"Thank you." Her lips purse, and she won't meet my eyes again. She nods toward the door leading to the hall elevator. "I don't suppose I should leave the way I came. Will that get me out of here?"

"It will." I try once more to woo her. "If you're sure you really want to go." Yes, I give her my charm-your-panties-off grin.

She rolls her eyes and moves toward the door.

I follow, confused. Because I have no idea where I went wrong in the last few minutes. Didn't we just have amazing sex? Didn't we both say we liked it? And then, did she just turn me down for another repeat?

I really don't understand.

So I ask. "Before you go, can you tell me what just happened?"

She stops to look in the mirror by the door, straightening her tousled hair while she answers me. "What do you mean?

We fooled around. It was better than the first time. And now I'm leaving. Does that about sum it up for you?"

"Well…" No, it doesn't. Because there has to be something between the "better than the first time" and the "now I'm leaving". It just doesn't make sense.

She seems to guess what's going through my mind. "What? Did you think this made us a couple or something? You can't be a stranger to the term sex-without-strings."

Ouch. Is this what it feels like to be on the other side of that line? 'Cause it kind of sucks.

I play it cool though. Or I try to. "No. I'm not expecting that we're a couple now. Of course not. Sheesh." Okay, maybe the thought crossed my mind.

"Good. We're on the same page then."

"Right." Except I have no idea what that page is. Is it a page where we still get to see each other and bang? I don't want to be on any other page than that.

Somehow it seems that's exactly *not* the page we're on, because next thing I know, I'm holding the door open for her as she leaves.

The air crackles around us as she passes me, and I swear she feels it because she narrows her eyes and glares at me. As if the electricity between us is *my* fault. "Nobody calls me Genny," she says, her voice terse, before bustling off to the elevator.

"*I* do," I call after her triumphantly, like that somehow makes me victorious over this situation that I'm pretty sure I actually lost. I don't even know why I started calling her that. It just came out in the heat of the moment, but it rankles her and that makes me like it. A lot.

Right now I feel like it's my only weapon against

her. My tiny little squirt gun against her death ray. I'm so obviously out of my league with this woman. That hasn't happened since…well, since Gwen. I didn't even know it was still possible.

For some reason that just makes me want her more.

CHAPTER SIX

Genevieve leaves me at a loss. I want more of her—*need* more of her—but with no idea how to go about *getting* more of her, I decide to try to put her out of my mind for the rest of the day. Besides, I really should be working. There's a pile on my desk and a phone call with the finance department that I've been avoiding.

First, I head back to Hudson's office to return the key. I should take the hall elevator and enter through the front doors like a polite person, but what would be the fun in that? I definitely go down the way I came.

He's sitting at his desk when I arrive. His jaw tenses and his eye twitches, telling me he's irritated but not really surprised. Which isn't remarkable—I wouldn't be shocked to find out he'd known I was there the whole time. That man misses almost nothing.

We don't say anything, but I whistle as I head to the closet, because I'm an asshole like that.

"I'm going to find a new hiding place, you realize," he says behind me.

"Or you could just leave it there and trust that I will only use it when absolutely necessary." I continue with my task, opening the closet and hanging the key back on its peg. I'm not sure whether it will still be here the next time I look. It could go either way. Hudson isn't very predictable.

Like, I don't predict when he asks, "Do you want to tell me what you were doing holed up in my closet with Genevieve Fasbender?"

I close the door again and turn to face him. "Not particularly." Though a part of me is gleeful that he knows. Getting caught with a woman is like getting to brag without being a bastard. It's a definite win-win. "Do you want to tell me about Pierce Industries' controlling interest in Werner Media?"

He pauses for a beat. "Not particularly."

It feels like it might be a dismissal, but shit, I don't need invitations. I saunter over to the chair facing his desk—the one that Genny sat in earlier when she told me our sexcapade was like bad pizza.

I'm still shaking my head. Though, after the amazingness that happened between us today, even I'd say the previous banging was only mediocre.

Whoops. Need to stop thinking about her before this conversation with my brother gets awkward.

"It's not the same," I tell him. "Me not telling you about Genny is because the matter is personal. You not telling me about our holdings is…well, I don't know what it is. It's just uncool. I'm just as much of an owner of this company as you are."

He raises a brow because he actually holds more stock in the business than I do.

I correct myself. "Not *just as much* in terms of percentages owned, but *just as much* as...you know what I mean. Stop being a dickwad and give me some answers, will you?"

I prop my legs up on his desk and cross my ankles just so I can be rewarded with another typical Hudson scowl— and I am. God, this could be a drinking game. What fun.

"You're in charge of our Midwest holdings, and this is a subsidiary holding." Standing, he reaches over and knocks my feet to the ground. "But I suppose there's no reason to keep it a secret now."

"But there once was?"

"There was." He loosens his tie as he crosses the room to his liquor cabinet. "I purchased the shares through another company that we own so that it wouldn't be easily connected back to me. I wanted Warren Werner to believe he still had the majority shares."

I swivel in my chair to look at him. "Why would you want that?"

"So I could blackmail his daughter."

Well, damn. Definitely didn't predict that. "I think I'm going to need a drink."

"Already ahead of you." He holds a tumbler of scotch out in my direction. I move to retrieve it and take a solid swallow before plopping down on his couch.

Hudson pours another glass for himself and sips it in a much more gentlemanly fashion. "I'm sure you remember that Celia Werner and I used to be close."

"Right." There's eleven years between Hudson and me, so I'm a bit in the dark to what happened with him in his college days, but I know the highlights. "You were practically engaged. She was pregnant with your baby, wasn't she?" I ask the question before I realize that bringing up her miscarriage might not be the nicest thing.

But I'm immediately glad I did when Hudson says, "I *claimed* it was mine. It wasn't."

This is news. "Whose was it then?"

He shakes his head. "Now that is not my secret to divulge. Nor has it any bearing on this story except to illustrate that Celia and I have had a very layered relationship. A lot of water that's passed under the bridge. A lot of betrayals. There were reasons I did what I did and reasons she did what she did, but ultimately, I was to blame for a great deal of…of the *issues* that existed between us. Nevertheless, she took it too far when I started seeing Alayna. She harassed us. Threatened us. Bullied Alayna."

Though he hasn't divulged specifics, his speech is uncharacteristically revealing. I'd suspected Hudson was at the center of the rift between our families, but I'd never expected him to outright claim responsibility.

I'm intrigued.

But I know my brother well enough to know he'll only tell me what he wants to, no matter how much I poke. So I tread carefully, asking the question I think he's most likely to answer. "She bullied your wife? Like, what did she do, exactly?"

He moves to sit in the armchair across from me. "The details are irrelevant now. All that matters is that Celia got out of control, and I became convinced that the only way I could ensure she wouldn't continue to wreak havoc in our lives was to have something over her head. So I purchased majority shares in Werner Media, but allowed Warren to remain the figurehead—"

"And told Celia you'd take away his control if she acted up again," I finish for him. "That's actually pretty slick."

"I'll take that as a compliment."

He should, because I'm impressed. But as I keep thinking about it, I see the current dilemma. "Except now Warren's retiring and you don't have anything to hold over Celia's head, do you?"

"No. I don't." He raises his glass toward his lips and takes a sip. "But that is most definitely a personal concern and not a business concern."

I beg to differ. "What happens with Werner Media seems to be a concern for both of us. For our business."

"And I'm taking care of it. Hence the reason I've been interested in Accelecom. Warren is still unaware that I hold controlling interest, and I'd prefer to let him designate his replacement without ever finding out. But he wants it to be Edward Fasbender. Obviously, I'm opposed."

"Right." I'm actually not sure what's obvious about his opposition, but I decide to play along. I've learned that sometimes the only way to get Hudson to divulge information is to pretend I'm in the know. It's got a fifty-fifty success rate, but it's better than any other odds with the man. "It's a shame, though. Accelecom could bring a great deal to Werner Media."

"I know this. It's why I met with him today. I'm looking for an ideal compromise."

I'm suddenly annoyed. Annoyed that I've been kept in the dark, but even more annoyed that my brother obviously doesn't trust me to help him get through this sticky situation.

With one giant gulp, I finish my whisky and set the glass down on the table beside me. Leaning forward, I rest my elbows on my thighs. "That sucks, Hudson. You have a lot on your plate right now. You should be at home with your wife and children. You know what would be awesome? If you had someone you could rely on to take your place in these negotiations." Sitting up, I give him a dramatic wide-eyed expression. "Oh, wait! You do!"

He hesitates. "Chandler...I appreciate the offer, but this is not a situation that you need to worry yourself with."

"Because you want to be Mr. Micromanager and make sure it all works out the way you see best. I can handle more than just managing a couple of corporations based in Iowa. Has it ever crossed your mind that, although you might not agree with my methods, I might be perfectly capable of attaining the same outcome?"

"No, it hasn't."

Jesus, sometimes I could just choke him. "Well, consider it. Asshat."

"I'm not going—"

He's interrupted by Trish's voice over the intercom. "Mr. Pierce, your wife is on the line for you."

Hudson stands and crosses to the desk where he pushes the button on his phone to respond to his secretary. "Thank you, Patricia." He glances at his watch, which makes me glance at *my* watch—it's just after five. "Go ahead and head on out. I'll lock up."

"Sure thing, Mr. Pierce."

I stretch out on the couch, my hands laced behind my head and propped up on the arm so I can watch as Hudson clicks off the intercom and picks up the receiver.

"Alayna," he says, sinking into his chair. "I'm sorry. I meant to be home before now. I got caught up. Have you gotten any sleep?" He pauses for her response, and I can imagine that as a mother of two newborns and a preschooler, the answer is no. "Can Roxie take Mina to the park while Jenn takes the twins for a little while so you can get a nap?"

Another pause, and I realize that my sister-in-law isn't the only one who isn't sleeping—Hudson looks terrible.

"Yes. I know, precious," he says now. "It's not easy. But I have to go to that awards dinner I told you about. Maybe I could send Chandler home to entertain Mina."

"Or you could send Chandler to the dinner in your place," I prod, unconcerned that he'll now realize I've been listening to his conversation. Also unconcerned with that stack of work I'd meant to get to. It can wait another day.

"Right. It's not the same. I understand." He glares up at me, and based on the tightness in his jaw, I think I might actually have won. It almost makes up for my previous loss with Genevieve.

Okay, not almost. Not even close. But it's something.

I sit up, my brows raised.

"Tell you what," he says to his wife. "Give me a few minutes to shift things around. Then I'll be yours for the evening."

Uh, wow. Not sure how that happened, but right on.

He hangs up, and I cross back to the desk.

"So what is this dinner thing I'm going to, anyway? Please don't tell me it's black tie."

"It's black tie." Ignoring my groan, he digs in his desk and retrieves an invitation that he hands over to me. "It's the Annual Award Banquet for Advances in the Media. While

I don't want it made known that I'm talking to anyone else in the industry, I've arranged to be seated next to Nathan Murphy tonight. He's a key player at Mirage. I'd like you to take my place at the dinner and use the opportunity to feel out what Murphy could bring to Werner Media."

It's hilarious how quickly he's changed my idea into his own. But whatever. It's something.

He stands and why do I have the feeling it's because he wants to take a power stance? "It's critical that you keep this on the down-low. Do you think you can manage that?"

I want to roll my eyes. Instead, I study the paper in my hand. "The invite has a plus one."

"Do *not* bring a plus one." There's that scowl again. I'd be drunk if I'd been taking shots. "I need you at your best tonight. No distractions."

"Stop worrying, bro. I got this." Before he can change his mind, I pocket the invitation and head out the door, calling over my shoulder, "You won't regret it."

"I already do," he mutters behind me.

I'm facing away, but want to bet he's scowling? Life is good.

• • •

The Broad Street Ballroom is in the Financial District, and by the time I'm dressed and get down to that part of town, the dinner is just about to get started. It's perfect timing though, because I walk in behind a familiar gorgeous, leggy brunette.

Man, my luck just got a whole fuck-lot better.

I follow Genevieve without making my presence known.

So this was what her plans were for tonight. It totally makes sense that she'd be at the media awards.

I distract myself from the idea that she might have a date with how hot she looks, even from behind. Her hair is pulled into a thick knot at the base of her neck. Teardrop jewels dangle on silver chains from her ears, a nice contrast to the dark brown of her tresses. Her shoes are strappy, high-heeled, mixed metallic sandals that lace up her toned calves.

The best is her outfit, though. She's wearing a black trapeze dress that falls unevenly along her mid-thigh, and all I can think about is how easily that style lifts up, how little work it takes to get underneath.

(Yes, I know what a trapeze style is. I wasn't kidding about learning fashion basics from my sister. Did I mention she used to use me as her model to practice her design skills? I picked up a lot along the way. I mean *a lot*.)

Genevieve pauses, and I duck back as she looks around. She's definitely waiting for someone. Imagine my relief when I see her father walking toward her.

Though, there's also a younger man at his side. A tall, broody looking gentleman. Exactly the kind of guy who gets the eyes of the prettiest girls in a room.

I immediately hate him. Obviously.

"Genevieve, what are you doing here?" Edward Fasbender seems both surprised and irritated to see his daughter. "I specifically told you I didn't want you interfering."

Her spine straightens, and I feel the air bristle. "And then you brought Hagan?"

Hagan. Her brother she'd mentioned earlier. Yeah, now I don't hate him, but he irritates me for another reason—namely, because he's competition for her with her father, and though I don't know a lot about her yet, I know that she's better than this asswipe.

Maybe that's an unfair judgment. But I know what it's like to have a holier-than-thou older brother.

And then he says, "Sucks to be you, doesn't it?" and I reinstate my first opinion. Hagan Fasbender is definitely an asswipe.

"Very professional," Genny says, and I give her points for refraining from the name-calling I've resorted to in my head.

Edward ignores the exchange between his offspring. Placing a hand on her shoulder, he says, "Thank you for stopping by, but there isn't a spot for you, princess. Why don't you go join your stepmother at the nail salon?"

Jesus, he's patronizing. My hands curl into fists and I can't express how much I want to slug him.

But then I have another idea—a better idea.

I step forward and slip my arm around her waist. "She's here with me, actually. As my date. Aren't you, Genny?"

"Uh." Startled, she squints up at me, and for a minute I think she might not play along.

Then she smiles. Tightly, but it counts. "Right. My date."

Edward drops his hand from her shoulder but narrows his eyes in my direction. "And who are you?"

It's okay. I'd be predatory about her if she were my daughter, too.

Thank fuck she's not.

I extend my hand in his direction. "Chandler Pierce."

"Ah, the younger Pierce." The glance he throws his son is the kind I'm used to getting—the one that says, this man isn't as important as his brother, but he's still important; better kiss up.

I usually hate that glance. Tonight, I'm using it to put this turd in his place.

"Younger, less-exhausted," I say. "I've been filling in for Hudson as much as I can. I was at the gala the other night. Your daughter meant to introduce me to you then, but it seems you were otherwise occupied."

In other words, she's the only reason I'm giving you my time right now. Get the point, buddy?

His expression says he gets it.

He's about to fall over himself in flattering me—I know the drill. I don't let him get that far. "Perhaps we'll have the opportunity to speak some time. Right now, I believe they're starting to serve our meals." I turn toward my pretend-date. "Genevieve? Shall we?"

"We shall."

With my hand still on her waist, I nudge her away from her father and her stuck-up suit of a sibling.

"Goddamned narrow-minded tosser," she mutters as soon as we're out of their earshot. She stops walking to complain. "I can't believe he brought my brother to this event. Hagan's only interested in how many skirts he can get under in a single trip to the States. He collects sexual encounters like some people collect passport stamps."

Ah, huh.

"I think I know the type." I mean me. Hagan and I are cut from the same cloth, it seems. Realizing that, I stand behind my earlier harsh thoughts. I'm definitely an asswipe as well, especially with the speed I go through women.

Though I've barely noticed any other skirts since the one on my arm walked into my life.

Which is probably why I'm only just now realizing that I can't actually have dinner with Genevieve. The reason I'm here in the first place is to feel out her competition. There's no way I can do that with her at my table.

Just, how do I break the news to her?

"And you!" she exclaims suddenly in a tone that makes me think she'll take the news just fine. "Are you happy now? You wanted me to agree to a date so badly, you must be happy as a clam that you've trapped me into one. You probably followed me here tonight just so you could find your opportunity."

"What?" I'm floored by her turn of hostility. And I'm more than a little perturbed. "Let's just get one thing straight right off the bat. I did not follow you here. You think I only have you as an item on my agenda? I do *work*, you know."

"Really? Doing what? It seems that mostly you just stand around looking pretty."

It's probably not a good time to mention the trading company I manage in Iowa because, well, it's in Iowa.

Besides, she's kind of not far off from the truth. Not that I stand around looking pretty—though, I *do* look good, if I say so myself—but that I don't actually seem to have a lot of responsibilities at Pierce Industries. Something that's been bothering me more and more as of late. That's a matter to take up with Hudson. Eventually. Not now.

Right now, my focus is on Genevieve. "For your information, I'm here not because of you but because of my job. My *job*. I have an important tête-à-tête on the menu." So there.

She laughs. Actually laughs. "*Important tête-à-tête.* Well, aren't you fancy."

"Laugh all you want. I'm glad I can be the source of your amusement." Is it weird that the more she mocks me, the more desperate I am to win her over?

But like I just told her, I'm not here for her. I'm here for Hudson. For Pierce Industries.

I force myself to stay focused on my agenda and pause to scan the room, orientating myself with the layout so I know where I'm going. "I believe that's my table right there." Nate and his date are seated there already. "Do you need me to put you in a cab before we part ways?"

Her jaw drops. "And now you're abandoning me?"

"You mean, you *want* to stay for dinner? You just got mad at me for trying to make this a date, and now that's exactly what you want this to be?" Is it totally bad if I kind of want her to want the date? "Which is it, Genny?"

Her eyes flare, I think as much from the nickname as anything else. It's absolutely adorable.

It's also absolutely confusing. *She's* confusing.

"This is not a date," she hisses. "I didn't want or need to be rescued, but now that you've created this situation, you have to follow through. What will my father think if I suddenly disappear from tonight's event? I can't let him win."

Yeah, I totally get that.

And shit, now we are in a serious dilemma. I can't do what I've set out to with her along. "Maybe he won't notice if you slip out," I say.

Except then I realize that he totally *will* notice if his daughter goes missing and, more importantly, that she isn't the only deterrent to my evening's agenda because two other people have just arrived at the six-person round where I'm supposed to be sitting, and fuck if it isn't Edward and Hagan Fasbender.

Looks like it's going to be one of those nights.

CHAPTER SEVEN

There's no way Hudson knows that the Fasbenders would also be sitting at his table. Not when he's told me to keep the discussion with Nathan Murphy on the down-low. I have half a mind to text him right now and tell him the whole plan is off.

Except I'm not a quitter.

Also, I don't want him to give me any reason for cutting the night short. I'm fucked in the head for feeling this way, but I'm actually kind of excited about having an excuse to spend a whole meal with Genny, and yes, I do take the excuse to let her stay. My assigned task is already hindered by her father. I might as well let her hinder it too.

We sit and make the necessary introductions. Nathan is younger than Edward by about ten years and doesn't look as comfortable in his tux as the Englishman. His wife is young and mousy, and either extremely shy or extremely bored, considering the amount of effort she puts into the table interaction.

To be honest, the early conversation has me stifling a yawn myself. It's mostly business gossip specific to the media world, a world I know very little about since I've only learned today that our company owns shares in the industry. Though I look for opportunities to add to the discussion, I can't find any.

Genevieve is equally quiet beside me. From the furtive glances I've cast in her direction, I've noticed her lips are drawn tight, and I decide she's biting her tongue. Whether it's because she's bristling over her father's earlier remarks or because she's pissed she had to lean on me for help, I don't know.

Honestly, it's probably a little of both.

It gives me smug satisfaction. So much so that I feel totally comfortable stretching my arm out along the back of her chair. God, the way she glares at me. If I thought following the conversation was hard before, it's even harder now. And I do mean *hard*. I wish I knew what it was about this girl that makes me so completely turned on and intrigued. The mystery confounds me. I'm as far from understanding her as I am from getting what Hudson's sent me to this dinner to do.

By the time our salad course is being cleared, I'm antsy. My leg is twitching under the table, my arm tingles from where it brushes against Genny's shoulder, and I still haven't found a way to talk covertly to Nathan Murphy when, miracle of miracles, he opens the door for me.

"Any special reason Pierce Industries is representing tonight? Are you guys finally looking to enter the playing field? With the innovative direction you've gone recently in the tech world, I wouldn't be surprised to find that you were."

Genny straightens in her chair beside me, and I feel all three pairs of the Fasbenders' eyes move toward me.

This is probably when I should really be feeling the pressure, but it's just the opposite. Even though I know nothing about the topic, I'm excellent at improvisation. "Haven't got anything planned that we're ready to announce," I say, "but I'm interested in your observations. What sort of role could Pierce Industries take in media?"

I direct the question to Nathan—it's the perfect opportunity to feel him out like I need to.

Except it's Hagan who jumps in with an answer. "Easy. Network ownership. You already have the people and talent to start your own programming in either a cable situation or something competitive with Netflix and Amazon."

I hate to say it, but Hagan Fasbender isn't exactly the dummy that his sister wishes he were.

His father nods. "All the subscription-based services are focused on entertainment. Pierce Industries could bring news and business programming to the market."

So Dad's also a smart one. The two of them piggyback on each other for the next several minutes expounding on their ideas. They've obviously thought a lot about this. Their thoughts are well-researched, and it's not exactly uninteresting.

Okay, it really is. Partly because the male Fasbenders aren't the ones I want to hear from but also because everything is uninteresting next to the female sitting at my side.

She's particularly interesting, I realize, when her mind is at work. After listening to her father and brother ramble on and on, she seems to lose her resolve to keep silent and pipes in with her own opinion. "Yes, that's one possible avenue of expansion," she says, shaking her head dismissively. "But it's so narrow in its focus. Pierce Industries has the capability of much loftier objectives, like laying down Internet connections that are on par with Google Fiber."

"Lofty goals are fun until you have to pay the bill. Remember that, Genevieve." Edward follows up his patronizing remarks to his daughter with an apology to me. "She's straight out of school. Hasn't had a lot of hands-on yet."

Perhaps it's because I'm also straight out of school, but I think her plan is really intriguing. "That's smart, actually. It will take years for Google to spread throughout the nation. There's definitely an opportunity to step in there. It's not like Pierce Industries can't foot that kind of endeavor." Particularly if Pierce Industries comes out of the dark on its affiliation with Werner Media.

The men at the table take a completely different approach to the idea once I've affirmed it, adding supporting commentary and looking on like I'm a wizard of some sort. It's pathetic. Genny gives me a confused smirk, one that says she's not sure if she's grateful for my words or irritated.

It's so sexy and such fun tormenting her that it makes me want to say more nice things about her ideas. Makes me want to pursue the subject further. Makes me want to lean over and nibble on her earlobe, but that's probably not the best move I could make.

But laying network fiber…there are so many interesting directions to go from here, and I'm curious whether we could come up with a vision to share with my brother. The wheels start turning.

Until I yank them to a stop. It's a good idea, but I'm here

to find out what Nathan's good ideas are. And so far I've heard practically nothing from the man.

Despite being even more attracted to Genny now that I've seen glimpses of her brain, I refocus on Nathan. I try several more times to pull him back into the conversation, but he seems more interested in listening. Maybe he's not as innovative as Hudson thinks he is. Or maybe he's just not as eager to brag about his ideas.

But then there's a lull in the conversation, and it's Nathan who breaks the silence. "Warren Werner's receiving the Lifetime Achievement Award tonight," he says. "What do you want to bet he names his successor in his speech? There's a rumor you're in line for the job, Edward."

Edward answers modestly. "If I truly am, Warren's not announcing it tonight. Because I've been made no such offer."

"Oh really?" Nathan's eyes widen. "Then the job might still be open. Whoever gets it is a lucky bastard. Imagine being able to helm that company. The magic that could be made. I would die to get my hands on that position."

Ah! Then he *is* interested. I shouldn't have doubted Hudson—his instincts are almost always good. Not that I'm ever telling him that.

But now things have gotten interesting.

Here's the score—everyone at the table except Nathan and his lovely wife knows that Warren won't be naming his replacement tonight—or ever, if Pierce Industries doesn't approve. And pretty much everyone at the table (except Nathan's lovely wife) is vying for the spot. Which means everyone at the table (including Nathan's wife because I've given her the Chandler grin more than once) is looking at me.

Gotta say it's a pretty empowering position to be in. Damn, sometimes being a Pierce is pretty fucking bomb.

With the table as my court, I lean back in my chair and ask, "Which direction would you take with Werner Media, Nathan?"

Genny kicks me under the table, and when I glance toward her she mouths, "What are you doing?"

"Making conversation," I mouth in response and turn back to Nathan.

"But…" Genevieve's hand falls to my upper thigh. My upper, upper thigh.

My head whips back toward her, and before I can second guess myself, I lean in and whisper, "A little higher and you'll know exactly how much I've been thinking about what's under your dress."

I glance down at her lips, which have parted. She swallows.

And now I'm remembering what it felt like when she swallowed around my dick.

Puppies! Kittens! Nathan Murphy in the boardroom with Hudson!

I manage to get myself under control and direct every bit of my attention on Nathan and not the blushing beauty next to me. Definitely not thinking about the inappropriate comments I just made to her.

I almost don't notice when she politely excuses herself from the table.

Okay, it's a lie. I totally notice.

"Excuse me. Too much wine," she says. Which is clearly

untrue since she's barely touched the cabernet in front of her. I'm convinced I flustered her.

I'm thoroughly pleased.

While she's gone, I find it easier to concentrate, and somehow Nathan and I manage enough of an exchange for me to solidify his interest and mentally mark him as a possible candidate for the job.

Genny returns a few minutes later. After she sits, she moves her hand to mine under the table. I eagerly grab at it, desperate to feel her skin under the caress of my thumb, but she doesn't let me hold it, pulling away after she drops something in my palm.

Something rough. Something flimsy. Something familiar.

I'm smart enough to not bring the material out into plain sight, but I'm too much of a guy not to look. When I'm confident no one's watching me, I sneak a peek, and sure enough I'm holding a pair of black lace panties.

As discreetly as I can, I tuck the souvenir into my pocket. I'm biting back a grin when I next glance over at her. A big, big grin. And a semi, but that one's easier to hide thanks to the whole I'm-still-sitting thing.

Her smile in return is tight. "You wanted to know," she says softly. Cruelly.

Wanted to know what was under her dress. Yes, I did say that. Though I was more interested in the part that doesn't come off. The part that the panties were covering.

Jesus, she's not wearing anything now.

I am officially never going to make it through this meal.

"What was that, princess?" Edward asks, and it takes me a second to realize he's heard what Genny just said. I'm beyond glad the question isn't directed at me because I'd have no idea how to answer.

Thankfully, she's on top of it. "Chandler has a headache," she says, patting my leg. "He just gave me a miserable look, and I asked him if he wanted to go."

Oh, that's good. *Want to go* does sound like *wanted to know*.

He buys it. "Sorry to hear that, Chandler. You do seem a little pale."

Probably because I'm still in shock about the gift she's brought me. And more in shock that she's doing this to me on purpose. Throwing me off my game for...what? Spite?

"I'm fine. Probably just low blood sugar." Or rather all the blood running to the wrong part of my body. "I'll feel better once I finish eating, I'm sure."

Except, try as I might, I'm no longer interested in eating. Not food, anyway. The only thing I want to feast on is half a foot away, bare under a small skirt of thin material. I barely tasted her today, and all of a sudden it's the only taste in my mouth. The only taste I want more of.

Especially when she's playing it so cool. I totally want to knock her off that throne. Want to show her I can get to her the way she gets to me.

I am smart enough to realize that the worst thing I could possibly do at the moment is reach over and stick my hand up her dress. I know this.

But it's all I can think about.

I pick at my food. Conversation gets harder to follow. I say less and less because of it. At one point, I swear I hear Nathan say, "She's good and wet."

Luckily, before my eyes pop out of my head, I realize

he really said, "She's a good bet," in reference to a stock exchange he and Edward are discussing.

Then dinner is cleared and coffee is served and the lights dim for the award ceremony, and I find that now that I'm not pretending to eat, I no longer have anything to occupy my hands. So it's not really my fault that my fingers find their way over to her lap. And under her skirt.

Her eyes widen. Her mouth drops. But she doesn't brush me away. She could easily, too, without anyone seeing. And she doesn't.

So my hand rests there. Rests on her silky soft thigh, and I think for a minute that this is enough, that I don't need more.

But I'm kidding myself.

Then she parts her legs slightly, and maybe it's not an invitation, but it definitely seems like one and how can I know without taking the bait?

Slowly I climb higher, higher, past the natural swell of her leg, to the place I want to be most. My finger brushes against the lips of her pussy, and her breath hitches. I scan the others at the table, then, when I'm sure no one noticed, I make a second pass. This time I continue down to circle the rim of her hole.

And yes. She *is* good and wet.

Damn, it's amazing.

Paybacks are a bitch though, because not only am I rock hard, but next thing I know, her palm is cupping my groin. She squeezes, and god, it's all I can do not to let out a moan.

That's it. I'm going in. I slide two fingers inside her opening. She's so tight, so perfect. I want to be in farther. Want it to be my cock inside her. I turn so I can get a better angle.

Suddenly, our gazes crash into each other, and I know from the look on her face she's had the same epiphany I've just had—we're groping each other *in public*. Where who knows who could see.

She stands up and braces the teacup she's just knocked from rising so quickly. "I've…got to go," she says hurriedly then takes off.

"I'll make sure she's okay," I say, following right behind.

It's such an obvious exit. But who the fuck cares anymore? Everyone else was so enthralled in the awards, I'm not even sure they remembered we were there.

I keep my eyes pinned on Genny as I wind around the tables. She heads to the bathrooms, and for a moment I feel defeat when I think she'll disappear into the ladies' room.

But she passes it. And goes instead to the single-family bathroom beside it. I'm practically on her heels, but I freeze several feet away. Does she want me to go in after her?

I want to go in after her.

If the door's unlocked, I decide as I head toward it, then it's an invitation. I reach for the handle and turn it…

The door clicks open.

She's facing me when I walk in, as though she were waiting. I lock the door behind me, and with two steps, I have her backed up against the wall.

"You are such a naughty, naughty girl." I'm already pulling at my belt.

"And you're an arsehole," she says breathlessly, her eyes darting from my lips to my eyes and back again.

"I was only acting defensively. You're the one who was naughty first."

"Because I took off my knickers?"

Yes, because of that. Also because she's the one undoing my belt. She's the one unzipping my fly.

And I'm naughty too. I'm naughty because I help her find what she's looking for, drawing out the steel rod that has taken residence in my tuxedo pants.

She rubs her hand over my head and meets my eyes. "Tell me again why I'm so bad."

I lift her legs up around my waist and rock forward so she can feel my cock against her bare pussy. "Because you did this. You gave me this."

I pull out a condom from my wallet, and she wriggles against me as I suit up.

"Seems like we're even since I'm dripping." Her hands grip the handicap railing for support.

Good. She's going to need it.

"You're not dripping nearly as much as you're going to be." I dig my fingers into the lush skin of her ass, position my cock at her entrance and slam inside.

We gasp in unison.

She's snug and hot, and I feel like a jackhammer the way I can't stop pounding into her. Relentlessly. Without mercy.

"You wanted this, didn't you?" I know she did, but I want to hear her say it. "You were such a naughty girl because you wanted me to come in here. In you."

She nods her head, but she's already tightening at orgasm's edge, and her lids are closed and her chin is tucked into her chest, and I'm frustrated because I want her to look at me. Want her to answer in words, while she's looking me in the eye.

I raise her higher until her ass is braced against the handicap bar. Now my hand is free, and I grip her jaw and jerk her chin up. "You look at me when I'm making you come, Genny. Do you understand?"

She's staring up at me now, but she answers again with just a nod.

"Words. Tell me in words how much you wanted this." I'm desperate to hear her say it, and it's only partly because I need the reassurance. The other reasons are less easy to put a finger on. They're more base. More primal. I need her to say it because, in this moment, I'm half-caveman and crazed with lust.

I need her to say it because I know when she does, it's going to be the sexiest sound I've ever heard.

Her expression twists into anguish, her eyes water, and she's so fucking beautiful like this that I don't know what the hell I'm going to do if she tells me that she didn't want this because, Christ, I *can't* stop.

And she still hasn't answered me.

I tilt her chin up harder and move my face inches from hers. At the same time, I press my pelvis forward so that I rub against her clit each time I drive in. She grows tighter, but like fuck am I letting her come before she responds. "Answer me, Genny. Tell me that you played with me out there because you wanted to be fucked."

"Yes," she says, panting. "I wanted to be fucked."

"And you wanted me to touch you. Under the table. So you took off your panties and taunted me."

"Yes. I wanted you to put your fingers inside me."

It's my turn to nod. Because I'm speechless. Hearing her breath ragged, her voice thin from exertion—it really is the sexiest sound I've ever heard.

With her chin still pinched between my thumb and forefinger, I stare down at her open mouth. Then I lean down and suck on her lower lip. "Good," I tell her before slipping my tongue along hers. "You're so, so good."

All of it is so, so good. Every last piece of this moment is perfection.

She orgasms first, but I'm right behind her, spiraling so hard and so fast I can't hold her anymore. I let her go, keeping her caged against the wall. My legs are shaking; my vision is black. I press my forehead to hers and gulp in air like I've just finished running a mile at a full sprint.

When I'm calm enough to speak, I wipe at her smudged mascara with my thumb. "Are you all right?"

"Yes," she sighs, her eyes closed.

Then, suddenly, her body goes rigid and her lids fly open. I step aside when she nudges me off of her. She crosses to the sink and examines herself in the mirror. "Jesus," she mutters, sweeping her fingers along the lash line under her eyes. "What did we just do?"

I turn and lean against the wall, not quite ready to stand by myself. "Uh, do you need an instant replay?"

An instant replay. I practically feel myself getting hard again thinking about it.

Genny rubs the remnants of lipstick off her mouth, washes her hands, then crosses to the door.

"I'm going out first," she says over her shoulder. "Give me at least five minutes before you follow."

Not a problem. Because I need at least five minutes to recover. When I can move, I cross to the mirror and echo her previous sentiment. "What the hell did we just do?"

She's still not in her seat when I return, which is odd since I waited a while before coming after her, but maybe she really went to the bathroom this time. Or maybe she saw someone she knew. I glance around and don't see her, which makes me unexplainably anxious.

I wait until the current speaker sits down before leaning toward Hagan. "Do you think Genevieve is all right?"

He blinks a couple of times as though he needs a second to remember who I'm talking about. Then he says, "Oh. She came back while you were still gone and said she wasn't feeling well. Sorry. I assumed she'd already told you."

"Ah, no. I didn't get that." Had she said something that suggested she was leaving? Did I miss a cue?

I sit back in my chair, now more anxious than ever. What is it with this girl? Twice today I've had sex with her, thinking it was pretty damn fantastic, and twice she's blown me off afterward. Am I seriously so twisted up about her that I don't realize she's not having a good time?

No. Impossible. She wanted it. She told me she wanted it.

This time I'm not waiting a week to chase her down. If she's going to compare this experience to something banal and everyday like pizza, I need to hear it tonight.

I wish I had her number, but because of the way she took off, I'm pretty positive she wouldn't respond to a text anyway. Besides, this is face-to-face subject matter.

So, once again, I lean over toward her brother. "I should send her some flowers. I know where she's staying. Do you have her room number?"

Sucker gives it to me without a second thought.

I mean, it's not like I'm going to do anything terrible with the information. Maybe I'll even really have flowers when I show up there later on. We'll see.

CHAPTER EIGHT

I end up foregoing the flowers.

Mainly because by the time the awards banquet is over, it's after eleven and I don't want to take the time to find a bouquet in the middle of the night. Anything I located would be shit leftover that didn't sell during the day, anyway. Genevieve deserves more than that.

She deserves more than me standing at her door empty-handed, too, but if my gut is correct, all she really wants is for me to show up. And I have.

The *Do Not Disturb* sign is up, but I decide it doesn't refer to me and knock quietly. A minute later, I hear her moving on the other side of the door, looking through the peephole, I assume.

"What are you doing here?" she says, irritation lining her tone, though I'd guess that half of it is put on.

Or at least I hope that it's put on.

"You left," I say, not wanting to have this conversation in the hall.

"Don't you know it's rude to show up at a woman's room uninvited?"

I smile tightly at the scowling couple that passes by. Another two minutes out here, and I'm going to get reported for harassment. "Genevieve, please. Let me in. We need to talk about what's going on between us."

"Whatever is going on between us needs to stop. You should go."

I'm conflicted. Her words say one thing, but I also hear her subtext. It matches much of what's going on inside me—confusion, excitement. Maybe a little bit of fear.

Okay, more than a little bit.

And maybe I'm making it all up, and she doesn't really feel the same way I do. I lean my head against her door. "Do you really want me to go?"

She's quiet, but I sense her there, on the other side of this barrier, and I want her more than ever. "Tell you what." I pray I don't sound like I'm begging, even though I kind of am. "You let me in and explain what happened tonight, and then I'll go. I think I'm entitled to that much, don't you?"

There's another beat of silence.

Then the deadbolt clicks and the door swings open. There she is, her hair down and damp from a shower, her face freshly scrubbed, wearing nothing but pajama shorts and a tight tank that perfectly outlines her tits.

She's so beautiful, it makes my stomach hurt. Or higher than my stomach, somewhere in the middle of my chest, a pinching feeling that makes me feel both a little sick and a little amazing.

"Come on in then," she says, sweeping her arm out in

invitation. As I step past her, she adds, "But keep you bits in your trousers, please."

Jesus, she sounds like my brother.

I move into the room, giving her space. "I will keep my pants zipped, as long as you promise never to refer to it as a *'bit'* again. *Monster* would be preferable. *Lord* could work. *Great Big Dick of Amazingness* would earn lots of points with me."

She folds her arms across her chest and smirks. "Do I *need* points from you?"

It's a tad embarrassing how transparent my interest is. But I own up to it. "No, you really don't." I unbutton my jacket and turn toward her, my hands in my pockets. "It seems like I need points from you."

Her shoulders relax slightly. "Don't be charming."

"Or what?"

"Or we'll end up with your bits back out of your trousers. Excuse me," she says, correcting herself. "Your *Great Big Dick of Amazingness.*"

I can't express how happy it makes me to hear that phrase come out of her sexy little mouth.

It's a relief, too, that she's obviously still interested in my Great Big Dick of Amazingness. I sprawl out on my side on her bed, all suave-like. "And that's a problem because?"

She throws her hands in the air and starts to pace the room. "Because I don't have time for you! You're an obstacle on the path to my dream career. A distraction. Tonight, I should have been on my A-game. I should have spoken up and given my ideas instead of letting my father and Hagan take all the limelight. You know that subscription service idea? It was mine originally. Hagan ran with it after I mentioned it in passing. I should have taken credit. It's still got merit but too small in scope, as far as I'm concerned."

I take half a second to bask in her acknowledgment that she's into me. I'd like to spend more time on the topic, but that's not what she needs from me. So after I get past my ego, I mentally make a note to tell Hudson about the subscription service before Hagan has a chance to claim it as his.

Propping my head up with my elbow, I consider what else she said. "Now you've learned that you should hide your cards in front of others. And you did, for the most part. That's smart. Sounds like A-game to me."

"Except that wasn't my reason for keeping silent." She continues to wear a path back and forth across the room. "I was too wrapped up in thoughts of you to even think of that."

This time my ego speaks before I can silence it. "Thoughts of me?"

She ignores my interruption. "And then you whispered those crude words. How was I supposed to think strategy after that? Do you not realize how important this opportunity with Werner Media is for me?"

Actually, I hadn't really thought about it. I wish I had, and I want to rectify that now.

Before she crosses by the bed again, I stand up and pull out the chair from the desk. "Can you sit please? You're making me dizzy." Actually, her pacing is adorable, but it's keeping her wound up, and I want her calmed down.

She stops short in front of it. "Fine." With a reluctant sigh, she sits.

I move around to sit on the edge of the bed, facing her.

"Okay. I'll admit that I did encourage some bad behavior. I take full blame for speaking inappropriately." I don't remind her she'd started it by practically grabbing my goods. "I do not take the blame for you taking off your panties, however—"

She shoots to a stand. "I knew you were going to bring that up. I make one bloody mistake, and you're throwing it back in my face. That's your fault too, you know. It wasn't like they were doing any good anyway. They practically melted off the minute you showed up looking like a crumpet in your black tie."

"Crumpet is a good thing, right?" There's that damn ego again.

And now she's resumed pacing.

"The point is that I have spent years focused on nothing but earning a place at Accelecom. All of college, my postgraduate work, my entire twenty-three years of being alive, has all led to right now. To this opportunity."

"Sit down, and we can talk about that."

She sits and crosses one leg over the other, bouncing the top one in a frantic rhythm. "Talk about what? How I've managed to go from no libido to hyper-drive in the course of one day? How I don't recognize myself anymore? How I'm more caught up in when you're going to touch me again than in what I'm going to do to get Accelecom this job?"

Again, she springs up from her seat. "Talking to you doesn't help. It just makes it worse." She's back to pacing and fretting. "I was fine after that first night. One-night stands are supposed to be one night for a reason. Then, today, you had to muck it up by being charming and amazing with your monster dick. This is your fault! Every bit of it."

"Genny. Sit down." I'm as surprised as she is at the command in my tone.

Needless to say, it works. She sits.

"If you can't stay put, I'll tie you to the chair." Damn, where did that come from?

"Ha. I dare you."

Uh, did she really just *dare* me? Because that's some bullshit if she thinks I can ignore the underlying invitation, and suddenly, I not only want to see her tied up—I *need* to.

Without explanation, I stand and start stripping my belt from its loops.

"Chandler!" Her exclamation seems to be as much thrill as admonishment.

"Don't worry. Monster's staying put," I assure her. "But so are you." I circle around her, assessing. The easiest would be to strap her torso and arms to the back of the chair, but I'm not sure the belt is long enough, and besides, her hands would still be free.

"Give me your wrists," I say after a minute. Surprisingly, she does so, reaching back around the sides of the chair.

Admittedly, I have no idea what I'm doing. Here's to faking it.

I wrap one wrist in the leather, threading the strap through the metal buckle and pulling it tight. Then I weave the end through the middle slat of the chair and around her other wrist before looping back to where I started. There's enough length to do it one more time.

When I've finished, I pull on her wrists, and shockingly, they're secure.

Pleased with myself, I move back around to face her, and wow. I'd really meant it when I'd said I'd keep it in my pants, but all of a sudden I'm regretting making such a promise because she looks good.

And since my crotch is not too far below her eye level, she notices what's going on down there. I swear to god, she bites her lip. Like that's going to help.

Actually, it kind of does. Now we're both aroused, but I have the upper hand.

I adjust myself and settle on the bed facing her. "Okay. Now let's talk." I lean back on my elbows, partly because I'm a giant narcissist, and I want her to have a full view of my hard-on. Also partly because the position gives *me* a perfect view. With her arms behind her back, her tits protrude like fruit ripe and dangling. It's all I can do not to eat her for a midnight snack. "This having you tied up, though, is quite spectacular."

"Oh, Jesus. Do you have to ogle?" She feigns disgust.

Trust me—she's feigning. I know.

"Shut up," I tell her, reaching my foot out to wrap around the leg of the chair so I can pull her closer. "You like it. Your skin gets splotchy and pink when you're turned on."

Her blush deepens. "But that's the problem, Chandler. You *do* turn me on. And I don't have time for this. I don't have time for *you*."

"You don't have time for me because I'm a distraction," I say, validating what she'd said earlier. "But what if I can also help you?"

"How?"

I work my jaw back and forth as I consider. "We've already determined it was good to keep your ideas to yourself tonight. And what you did share was quite excellent."

"My father doesn't think so."

"So your father is never going to steal that angle. It's not good for his company, anyway. It's only a viable plan for a bigger corporation like Pierce Industries. Luckily, someone who matters heard the idea and thinks it's really innovative." I wink.

She furrows her brow and frowns. "Who? Nathan Murphy?"

"No. Me." *Duh.*

Irritating woman that she is, she laughs. My ego shrivels back in on itself, and I can't decide if I want to choke her or kiss the fuck out of her.

Maybe both.

"You know what? Suck my dick." I adjust myself. Again.

"I'm sorry," she says, recovering. "You just. You didn't even know you owned Werner Media until I told you."

"True. But it's my brother you need to win, right? I have pull with him."

"Do you?" This time she's not making fun—she's sincerely asking.

"Yes. I do." I think. Maybe. "He's the one who sent me to that dinner tonight, you know." I'm trying to convince myself as much as her.

"And you spent it trying to get to know Nathan Murphy." Realization crosses her features. "Oh! Are you courting him?"

"Give me your foot," I say, trying to distract her from the question but also just needing to touch her.

"You *are* courting him!" she says, obliging me with her foot in my lap.

I sit up and take it in my hands, massaging my thumb into the ball. Her feet are dainty, but her skin is calloused and tough, and because it's something new and interesting about her, I find it hot as hell. "Were you a dancer?" I ask.

"I'm a runner. My feet are gross. Now tell me about Nathan Murphy."

"I think they're sexy." I bend down and draw her big toe in my mouth to prove it.

She tries to pull it away, but I don't let her.

"Nathan. Murphy." She attempts to make it sound like she's frustrated that I haven't told her, but the way her breathing has quickened and the way her eyes have gone dark and liquid, I can tell she's also just frustrated from this foot rub.

I, however, pretend like sucking on her bits is no big deal.

Spoiler: It is. I'm fucking lead.

"I'm not at liberty to discuss Nathan Murphy," I concede. "But I am at liberty to tell you that I will speak highly of you to Hudson. Is that what you want?" Carefully, I raise my eyes to hers, a little unsure what I'll find when they meet.

Confusion. Excitement. Fear. That's what I see. The same things I heard in her voice earlier, and it's like her gaze is a mirror of all the ways she makes me feel.

Oh, but we're talking about work. Yes. Right.

"I don't know what I want anymore," she says, sighing, and I pretend that it's mostly from what my thumb is doing to the bottom of her foot.

"Yes, you do. Tell me."

She chews on the inside of her lip while she thinks. "I want to follow in my father's footsteps. I want him to bring me on as a major player in his company. I want Accelecom to merge with Werner Media, and I want to have a position where I can implement progressive concepts and take the industry in a new direction."

I nod, encouragingly, despite what I'm about to say. "I hate to break it to you," I set her foot down and reach for the other, "but I don't think I'm the one standing in your way of your ambitious goals."

"I know. It's my father. And Hagan." She sighs again, and this time it's complete discouragement. "He's actually a really smart guy, even when he acts like a prat. It's just frustrating that my father only sees *his* achievements and only hears *his* ideas."

"Yeah, that is frustrating." The thing is, I get it. "Not that I know what you go through exactly, but I do know a thing or two about being in a sibling's shadow."

She tilts her head and stares at me. "I imagine you do. At least you don't have your gender working against you."

"You're right. I can't know what that's like, but I have to say, I kind of even live in the shadow of my sister. She was pushed and supported and championed through her entire life."

"And now she works in fashion? A 'female appropriate field'? Not the same."

"Well, yes, but she started off in business. Mom and Dad groomed her to take a seat at Pierce Industries, just like Hudson. And gender is still at play because, when she decided to do something else, they didn't bat an eye. Do you know what they'd do if I didn't want to work in the family business? I doubt they'd be so understanding."

She frowns. "Do you not want to work in the family business?"

"No. I do. I like the job." I like it more than I let on,

actually. I love the adrenaline and the maneuvering and the ideas. It's as thrilling as driving my car fast when I'm up in the country. Don't even ask how many tickets I've gotten—I can barely count. Thank god I'm in with the traffic judge, or I might not have a license.

But it's also frustrating. The job, not the tickets, though those are a pain in the ass too. "I'm trying to say that I've also encountered expectations revolving around gender. And I've been discounted and overlooked. My family doesn't take me seriously. I'm just the baby. The cute one. The spoiled one. The one who gets everything handed to him. Sometimes I think everyone just expects me to be Hudson's lackey forever. My father acts like I'm a joke. My mother probably hopes I'll marry well—probably assumes I have to, unlike my brother who was elite enough to fall for who he wanted. Marry well, breed, and learn how to play a good golf game. Those are my prospects."

She pulls her foot away to kick my chest. "Stop it. Your family sees you as more than that."

I shake my head. "Why would they? I don't head Pierce Industries' top accounts. Anything innovative I've brought to the table has usually been dismissed. The only press write-ups I've ever received have remarked on my social life rather than my business efforts. I don't know why they'd expect me to amount to much more than that." This is all stuff I've felt for as long as I can remember, but I've never told anyone. It's odd sharing it now with Genevieve—she's someone I should be trying to impress. She doesn't need to think that I'm a loser.

Strangely though, when I tell her, she doesn't make me feel like I'm a loser. "That's absurd," she says. "I've spent very little time with you, and I already know you're more than that. You're quick and witty, good under pressure, can improvise in sticky situations. Those are skills that can't be taught. You either have them or you don't."

Our eyes meet and though I've looked at her like this before, this time it's different. This time her gaze pulls at something in my chest. Makes me feel like I'm exploding and crumbling in on myself all at once.

If I were as fair and as prone to blushing as she was, I'd be bright red right now.

I duck my head. Focus on massaging her ankle. Tease her instead. "All these nice things you keep saying about me. It's like you like me."

"Oh, sod off."

"Look, you can admit it. We just discussed how liking me is actually *not* a problem. I'm not going to get in the way of you and your goals. In fact, I'll help you as much as I can."

"Helping me work off my frustration in public bathrooms is not what I need right now."

"No, *princess Genny*." I use her father's nickname mixed with mine just to poke at her. "I'll help you with Hudson."

Shit. What am I saying?

I have no idea why I keep offering Hudson as a token of my affection. I already know he's not keen on Accelecom, and I'd be fooling myself to think that the ideas brought forth by a twenty-three-year-old woman—yes, gender does matter in this business—will be enough to persuade him to take another look.

Yet when she asks, "Got any plan how to pull that off?" I wrack my brain for a solution.

"Actually, I do." I rest my hand on her ankle and lean forward. "Remember that date I want to take you on? That's happening. I want to see you bright and early on Saturday."

"Oh, no. I'm not going out on a date with you. I already told you that a mill—"

I cut her off. "It won't actually be a date." Well, it will be as far as I'm concerned, but anyway. "It will be an opportunity. I'm taking you to my parents' vacation home in the Hamptons for the weekend. They're having their annual end of summer/Labor Day party, and this year it's also where Hudson and Alayna are presenting their new babies to their friends and family. It will be a perfect chance for him to get to know you on a personal basis." It's brilliant. I can't believe I thought of it. "If we play our cards right, we might even be able to steal him for a few minutes of business talk."

She squints at me, hesitant. "You're sure your brother won't mind?"

"No, he loves business talk no matter the time or location. Even when he's not working, he's working."

She delivers a kick that lands awfully close to my family jewels. "I meant, are you sure he won't mind me intruding on your family's holiday?"

"You won't be intruding. You'll be coming as my date." And, yeah, that's the real impetus behind this idea. Sure, I want her to get what she wants with her career, but I also want her with me. I want her to meet my family. I want everyone to meet her.

"*Chandler Pierce's date.*" She tilts her head like she's mulling it over. "Will I be photographed in the rags?"

Let me pause to say that I've had pictures taken with many women. Many, many, many women. It's not a big thing.

But at the mention of being photographed with her? I'm into that. I'm so into it, I'll hire my own photographer if that's the only way to make it happen.

Problem is, I don't think she feels the same. Luckily, for her, it's not an issue. "There won't be any media at this. It's low-key. It's family and close friends."

"So I'm only posing as a date in front of them? I guess that might be acceptable."

I ignore the disappointment that she doesn't want to flaunt a relationship that doesn't exist between each other the way that I do and remind myself that this is just the first step in winning her over. Maybe. Hopefully.

"But fair warning—there will be a lot of people at this thing. We might not get to talk to Hudson. If that's the case, are you going to blame me for distracting you from your career goals?"

She raises her chin, and if her hands were untied, I imagine she'd put her hand over her heart—is that something Brits do too? "On my honor, I will not."

"Then it's a date."

"But not *really* a date."

"Exactly." Or not exactly at all, but it's fine.

And then, because it seems like it's been forever since I've sampled her, and because she looks so perfect and vulnerable bound to the chair in her skimpy pajamas, and just because I want to and I'm not sure she'll ever give me the opportunity again, I stand slightly and kiss her.

Somewhat surprisingly, she responds eagerly, her lips matching me as I keep kissing her. And keep kissing her. My hands tangle in her hair. I get aggressive. I nip at her lower lip. I swallow her taste. I fuck her mouth with my tongue.

I pour everything into this kiss, and all I can think about is how, despite being so hard my balls hurt, I just want to keep kissing her and kissing her. And kissing her.

I'm pretty sure this has strong implications for what kind of feelings I'm developing over the girl. Feelings that scare the fuck out of me. Feelings that make me want to do naughty, terrible things to the girl tied up beneath me. Feelings that are more instinctual in nature than emotional.

A blaring alarm in my head says I'm not ready for this. That it needs to stop. That I should pull away and leave before this relationship gets out of hand.

The twisting in my gut says I'm too late. It's already out of hand.

And if it's happening anyway, I might as well stay.

Right?

CHAPTER NINE

With her hands still bound behind her, I tilt Genevieve's chair back against the desk.

She gasps, the movement surprising her. "What are you doing?"

Honest answer? I don't know anymore. I don't know at all.

I test how secure it is, which is pretty darn secure. "Remember all you have to do is say stop and I will. You understand?"

She nods, but her expression is unsure. "That doesn't tell me what you're doing."

I consider explaining but have no idea what I'd say. This is instinct I'm going on right now. "Do you want me to stop?"

Her eyes widen, but her mouth clams shut.

"That's what I thought."

Tucking my fingers around the waistband of her shorts, I pull them down along with her panties then toss them on the bed behind me. Then I stand back to survey her because, goddamn, if I've ever seen anything this hot, I don't remember it. Her hands tied, her breasts pushing forward against her tank top, her long limbs hiding the sweet treasure of her pussy.

I nudge her legs apart, and let me tell you, Genny has a treasure of a pussy. One of the prettiest I've ever seen, and yes, there are pussies that are prettier than others. Trust me. I can't explain what makes one nice to look at and another not, but I'm telling you—hers is a wonder. Her dark hair is trimmed into a landing strip, contrasting nicely with the pale white skin of her inner thighs. And her hole is tight and inviting. Like it's begging to be plundered with my fingers. Or my cock. I'm even having fantasies about sticking a dildo in her, and it's not usually my thing to put other objects in places my body yearns to be instead.

Genny though—nothing is usual about how I'm obsessed with her. All I want is to watch her writhe. Want to see her come apart at the seams. Want to know I'm the one making her feel that way.

From her shallow, anxious breaths, I'd say she wants the same thing.

Eyes fixed on the prize, I kneel down and start to feast.

She tastes incredible. I've tasted her before, but each time I do, it's better than the last. Like I forget just how good her scent is, how good her flavor is on my tongue, because how good can pussy actually be? It can't possibly be as amazing as I remember.

And yet it is. *She* is. She's amazing and delicious, and even though I endeavor to bring all my women to orgasm,

I've never wanted to pleasure one as completely as I want to pleasure her.

With my hands hooked under her thighs, I spread her wider, licking up and down her folds in long strokes, teasing her before I zero in on where she wants me. She moans. She squirms. I do it again—long sweeps up and down, then I stiffen my tongue and lap at her bundle of nerves. I suck her clit until it's so swollen that it throbs in my mouth.

She comes long and hard. Twice. By the time I'm working her up to her third, she's shaking and writhing and I'm drowning in her wetness but I won't stop until she's thoroughly spent, until she can't even think straight.

"It's too much," she pants. "Chandler, I can't. I can't."

She tries to wriggle off of the chair, but my impromptu binding seems to be holding pretty well.

I replace my tongue with a finger so I can respond. "You'll take as much as I want to give you. Now shush up and take it, or I'll have to give you even more."

She shakes her head. "No. No more. No more. Please."

But she hasn't said *stop*. I know I don't have to remind her that it's the word she needs to speak to end this—I'm certain she remembers. I'm also certain she won't use it. I'm giving her too much, but it's exactly what she wants.

And it's exactly what I want.

In fact, I think we both want more. "Stop struggling. Or I'll…." I trail away, not sure how to finish my statement. "Or there will be consequences." No idea what consequences, but it feels good to say and I'm determined to see my threat through.

I return my lips to her soaked pussy and suck her clit into my mouth one more time.

"Will I be punished?" she asks, her thighs quivering. That's the last thing she manages to say before the very word sends her into an orgasmic tailspin.

I'm minutes from my own release, and I haven't even touched my dick yet. That's how hard I am. Hard and desperate, so even though I'd love to see if she could take another round, I'm sure that I can't.

She's still gasping and shivering when I right her chair. I reach behind her and undo the makeshift cuffs. Then I step back and give her room.

"Stand up and turn around," I order. It's the kind of order I'm not used to issuing, and yet it sounds good in my voice. It feels good in my bones.

Especially when she obeys, which she does almost immediately. I love how her legs are jelly as she moves to follow my command. She can barely stand on her own, so I tell her to brace her hands on the desk.

Well, and because I just like the look of her bent over like this, her skin glistening with sweat, her curvy ass displayed prominently.

I want to bite that ass. I want to spank it. I want to mark it as mine.

Almost absentmindedly, I fold the belt in half, and before I know what I'm doing, I'm swatting it down on her behind. The leather thwacks against her skin and she gasps, and instantly I decide there has never been a more erotic combination of sounds in all of history.

I have to hear it again.

I repeat the motion on her other cheek, and now there are two red belt marks along her skin. I rub my fingers lightly over her burning flesh.

Fuck. It's so hot. It's so kinky. I'm so hard. So...

Wait.

"Genny?" I ask tentatively, all of a sudden concerned I'm the only one into this.

"I'm good," she says through gritted teeth, apparently reading my mind. "It's good. Keep going."

That's all the permission I need. I smack the belt down again. And again. Who the fuck am I? I don't even know. Five more times until her ass is bright red and warm to the touch, and now I know I'm going to break my promise about keeping things in my pants, but I have a feeling she won't mind. So, in between lashes, I get a condom ready with my other hand—yeah, I'm better at it than I thought I'd be too. Then I drop the belt to the ground, undo my tuxedo pants, and slide on in.

She's so tight in this position, so warm, so wet— even through the condom I can feel how wet she is. It's fucking incredible.

"Oh, god, that's scrummy," she says with such a blissful sigh that I have to assume that she's enjoying herself. Enjoying *m*e.

"I'm taking scrummy as a compliment," I tell her as I pull out to my tip. "But whether it is or isn't, you're about to get bloody fucked."

She tries to laugh at my use of her slang, but it's cut short when I slam back in. I'm relentless now, driving into her over and over and over, pummeling her like she's the last woman I'll ever fuck, like she's the only woman I was made to fuck, like I've never wanted to fuck anyone in my life, and I know that's a bad sign. This is familiar territory—a place I specifically try to avoid.

I don't want to be here. I want to only be here.

When I come, I close my eyes, and all I see on the back of my lids is her, and as my seed spurts long and hot from my body, I can't decide if I'm falling apart or if, finally, I'm coming together.

• • •

Afterward, Genny slips away to the bathroom to clean up.

And I take my belt, wrap it around my neck, and try to strangle myself before falling face-first onto her bed.

What. The Fuck. Am I doing?

I whipped a girl. *Whipped* her. This isn't who I am. What the hell is she bringing out of me? Will I ever be able to go back to my usual loverboy ways?

Do I even want to?

Of course I want to. No questions asked. This is just good sex. Really good sex. That's my excuse for being here.

But I know better than this. There are so many rules I've broken, and now I'm paying the price because my insides feel like goo and all I want to do is take off all my clothes and stay the night in her arms.

Which would be a big fat mistake.

And what the fuck was I doing inviting her to a weekend in the Hamptons? And telling her that I'll help her with Hudson? Why would I stick my neck out for a girl I barely know?

Great. Now my chest aches.

Oh, god, am I…am I falling for this girl?

And fuck, if I am, is she taking advantage of me? That's always how it goes. I fall then I get hurt then—

Nope. It's not possible.

She can't be pulling the wool over my eyes because firstly, I'm the one who invited her to get all business-buddy with my brother, which is stupid and will probably piss Hudson off, but that's reason enough to follow through with my offer.

And secondly, I'm *not* falling for her. I broke my rules, but it doesn't mean anything. My mission statement is still clear in my head.

But, my chest...

Moaning, I roll over on my back, rubbing the spot at the center of my sternum. I'm too young for a heart attack, right? It's got to be heartburn. Or a pulled muscle. I did put a lot into that whipping. I probably strained something. It's definitely not emotions. I am not feeling things for her. I. Am. Not.

I've got to get going.

I bolt up and loop my belt around my waist, and then start frantically searching for my cell.

"Have you seen my phone?" I ask when she returns from the bathroom.

She peers up at me, surprised. "You're leaving already?"

I try not to meet her eyes, afraid if I do I won't remember all the reasons I shouldn't stay. Mainly, because it's not Chandler protocol. "Just as soon as I find my phone."

"Here it is." She holds her hand out, and sure enough, my phone is in her palm.

"Thanks." I swear I already looked on the dresser near where she's standing. "Where was it, anyway?"

"Oh, uh. You left it in the bathroom. I brought it out with me."

"Ah. Well." I pocket my phone quickly, eager to get out of there. "I better go."

"Yes. You said that you were leaving. See you Saturday, then." I'm not sure if I'm imagining the disappointment in her voice or not because I'm ignoring it.

I wait until I'm safely in the elevator before I let out a sigh of relief. It's so much easier to think when she's not standing in front of me, all soft curves, her plump lips ready to nibble, her long dark hair perfect for pulling.

She's sexy. That's all it is. Pure sex on legs.

And, man, those legs…

Focus, Chandler.

See? That's definitely what it is. Desire, pure and simple. I don't feel anything except unadulterated lust. I don't really care about getting her in with my brother. I just want more time between her luscious legs. Yeah, that's it.

I'm so good at reasoning that, by the time I make it to my car, I almost believe what I'm telling myself.

But it's not until I'm halfway home that I'm thinking clearly enough to remember that I never went in her hotel bathroom.

So why on earth did Genevieve have my phone?

CHAPTER TEN

I wait until after nine the next morning to give Hudson a recap about dinner. I don't expect him in his office, so I'm not surprised when I peek in and see it's empty. Plopping into his chair, I sit back and prop my feet up on his desk.

I mean, I'm already here.

But even though I dial his cell, it's his wife that answers.

"He's asleep," Laynie says, presumably picking up his phone for him. "The twins kept us up most of last night. Well, they keep us up most nights. We've been sleeping in shifts, and it's his turn now. I'd wake him, but we're driving up to Mabel Shores this afternoon and I want him rested."

"You guys are going up today?" It's only Thursday, and I hadn't expected them to go up to our Hamptons home so early, but I guess it's not *that* early.

"Yeah, we are. I want to make sure the kids are settled in before people start showing up. Should I have Hudson call you later?"

"Sure." I change my mind immediately after I answer.

"Actually, no. I'll catch him up on Saturday." I can use it as a lead-in to get him talking to Genevieve. Just because he's said he doesn't want to hire Edward Fasbender, doesn't mean I won't try to get him to hire her—for bonus points with the girl, of course.

"Perfect then. Thanks." She sounds exhausted, and I'm pretty sure I can hear the gurgling of a baby in the background.

I wonder if she's nursing.

Shit. Now I'm picturing Laynie's boobs. My brother's wife is hot, and yes, I've had the inappropriate thought now and then before he put a ring on it. But now she's practically my sister and gross.

Sure way to clear my mind is to think of Genny's boobs instead. Her perfect, perky, round tits…

"Oh, Laynie." I catch her before she's hung up. "I also wanted to mention that I'm bringing someone this weekend. I hope that's okay."

"Like a girl kind of someone? Do tell." As tired as she must be, she still manages enthusiasm, and it nearly makes me want to spill my guts.

Except I have nothing to spill. Because I don't feel anything for the person I'm bringing. "Her name is Genevieve," I say, coolly. "She's got some good ideas for the company, and I thought this weekend would be a great time to hear more."

Laynie seems dubious. "Yeah, that's why you're bringing her. You're probably not sharing a bedroom while you're up there either."

"Obviously I'm sharing a bed. Who do you take me

for?" Though it feels kind of irreverent to be talking about Genevieve like my only interest is sex.

Even though it *is* my only interest. Definitely my only interest. Not her smart-as-hell head. Not her chill-as-fuck personality. Not her cool-ass ambition.

"Hmm," Laynie says, curiously. "Do I sense you might… *like* her?"

"No. Of course not. Honestly, I don't even know a lot about her."

"That's why you go on dates," Laynie says. "Find out things about each other. See if you're compatible." With a burst of excitement she asks, "You know what you should do? The first time I went to Mabel Shores with H, I didn't know a lot about him. So we played a get-to-know-you game on the drive. It was really fun, and I learned a ton."

Um. Ew. "How…adorable of you."

Apparently I don't hide my disdain well enough because she lets out a frustrated sigh. "I was trying to help."

I feel bad. I swear. "I know. I'm sorry. It was very nice of you. I can see how that probably was a good trick to get inside the brain of my tight-lipped brother. I just don't see me playing any sort of game that doesn't involve taking off clothing. But thanks for the suggestion."

Then I listen to what I've just said, and an idea forms. A really great idea, if I say so myself.

• • •

"I have a thing to keep us occupied on the ride up," I tell Genny as I pull my Bugatti onto the Long Island Expressway. "Strip True Confessions: This or That style."

It's mid-morning and the party at Mabel Shores begins at one. I made sure we got a late start so that we wouldn't be the first ones there. It's best if there are people around when Genny meets my mother. I love my mom and all, but sometimes she isn't on her best behavior, even when there are other people present.

Genevieve raises a brow. "*Strip*? This sounds intriguing."

"It's a get-to-know-each-other game. But with a naughty element."

She folds her arms over her chest and points her chin up. "I told you this wasn't a date."

"And this isn't something I'd ever do on a date, thank you very much. But with someone I've banged a few times? It seemed like a fun way to pass the time."

"You do have a point about needing to pass the time. Go on."

She's so stubborn and determined to stand her ground. It's admirable, as frustrating as it is for me. Mostly, it just makes me want to know more about how she ticks, which is partly why I want to play this game. "I say two things to you about me, one true and one not. You pick which is the truth—this or that. If you pick right, then you get to take a turn. If you pick wrong, you have to remove an article of clothing first."

"I'm glad I decided to wear underwear today."

It's probably unfair that I'd already known about this game when I got dressed, but I'm actually wearing less than I plan to at the party, so it's fair. I brought a suit to change into at the house. Now I'm in a *Game of Thrones* T-shirt and long cargo shorts. Both easy to get out of while I'm driving.

Yes. I'm planning to get naked while driving. Is that a problem?

A beat later I register what she's said. "Wait. There was a moment where you'd considered *not* wearing underwear?" I glance over at her in her pleated floral skirt and plain white sleeveless top and picture nothing underneath.

Possibly that was a bad move. I casually shift in my seat.

Meanwhile, she shrugs all nonchalant-like. "I'm not fond of a thong on a long drive, and I didn't want panty-lines. Then I decided I'd feel uncomfortable meeting your mother without any knickers on and just decided to wear a different skirt."

"Good choice." Though I hope that she settles in quickly. My mother will be down the hall tonight, and I hope to get the chance to strip Genny completely.

…and now I've learned that Genny naked and my mother down the hall are not thoughts that should ever occur together again.

"Yes. I think it was a nice choice. As is this game. Bravo! Let's play! Will you go first, or should I?" Her enthusiasm does weird things to my stomach that are definitely not tied up in unexpressed emotions. Nope.

It doesn't mean I don't want to get her naked. Because I do. Always. Obviously.

"I'll go first," I say. "My birthday is in June. Or my middle name is Alexander."

She rolls her eyes dramatically, and I've never wanted to pull her hair and kiss her as much as I do right now. "Too easy," she says as though she's bored. "Hudson's is Alexander. Your middle name is Aaron. And your birthday *is* in June."

"You know my middle name?" It's ridiculous how happy this makes me.

"Of course. You think I wouldn't Google the man who's taking me away for the weekend? That's barmy. I'm not an idiot."

Damn. Why hadn't I thought about doing that for her? I'm not too bummed though because I'm too busy flying on the adrenaline of knowing she wanted to know more about me.

I mean, that's cool. She wants to know about me? Totally expected.

"My turn!" she exclaims, practically bouncing in her seat. "Hmm. Let's see. Oh, I have one. I've never been skiing. Or I've never been to the beach."

"Never been skiing," I answer quickly. "You've surely been to the beach."

"*Bzz.* Strike one. Take something off! Take something off!"

"You've never been to the beach? How is that possible?" That will be corrected today if I have anything to say about it.

"I'm pale, and I burn. And I'm not into sand in all my private places. The only interest I have in a beach is a stormy broody, northern England kind of landscape. The kind of scene you can admire from the window with a good book and a warm fire."

Huh. Maybe we won't be beaching today after all.

"Now take something off!"

She doesn't need to ask again. I start off big and take off my shirt, tossing it over my shoulder to the backseat. None of this take-off-something-little-like-my-watch-first bullshit. I like to raise the stakes from the very beginning. Makes it more likely for her to take off *her* shirt next.

Have I mentioned lately how good I am at gambling?

I glance at her ogling my bare chest, and I have to say, I like it.

"That's brilliant," she says, admirably. "I'm quite pleased with this game, I must say." She switches gears quickly, but I can still feel her eyes on me when she proclaims, "Your turn. Make it a good one. I'm warm sitting over here in all my clothes."

Seriously, god bless Alayna. This was the Best. Idea. Ever.

I tap my fingers on the steering wheel as I think. I really should have planned some of these beforehand, but what would be the fun in that? "I'm the only Pierce child who wasn't baptized. Or I was the president of our math club."

She considers briefly. "President of the math club. I think you're really brainy behind all that goofy exterior."

I whip my head in her direction. "Goofy?"

She laughs. "Let it slide. I'm here, aren't I? No need to get offended."

"That isn't comforting."

"Too bad. I'm very distracted by your lack of clothing, though. Is that better? You have a nice body." She reaches over to glide a hand over my pec. "Very, *very* nice."

Very, very nice indeed.

Obviously, I forgive her. "That *is* better. Now I get to be distracted by your lack of clothing because I wasn't the president of the math club. I was treasurer. But thank you for the compliment."

Her mouth turns down. "Only child not baptized? That's odd, isn't it? What's that about?" She reaches behind herself to unzip her skirt. See? Told you she'd follow suit in the high stakes clothing removal. It's also definitely distracting. "I, uh, think my mother was bored with god by the time I got around. I don't know. It's random."

The next time I look over, her long bare legs are draped on the seat next to me. "Speaking of god, holy shit you're hot."

I can't help myself—I reach over and run my hand over the creamy skin of her thigh. *So hot.*

"Actually, I'm feeling quite chilled," she says. "Mind if I turn down the air?"

At this point, a bucket of ice thrown over my lap will be the only thing that could calm me down so I tell her, "Whatever you need. Just take your turn." I might even lose on purpose to speed this along.

"I took piano lessons for years. Or I took cello lessons."

"I'm hoping it's cello. Because I'm dying over here thinking about you putting that big instrument between your legs." I'm glad we're on the highway, and I don't need to shift because I don't think I can stop touching her any time soon.

"You're right. It's cello, you wanker."

I grin. "That too. Wanking means jerk off, right? Because, yes."

"I meant you were a git. An idiot. But figures you're really a wanker too." She opens her legs slightly and runs two fingers across the flimsy crotch panel of her panties. "Sometime I'd like to watch," she says, and I have to think about my high school gym teacher Mr. Al so that I don't cream myself.

All of a sudden, she crosses her legs and folds her arms over her chest. "Or I'm just putting you on."

I groan. "I was enjoying the show. And it wasn't your turn. But you'd definitely like to watch. I can arrange that for you, you know." I move to work on my belt—not that I'm actually planning to give myself a handjob, but I would like her to notice how stiff I am at the moment.

"Not right now!" She half giggles, half screeches. "You're driving!"

"All right, all right." Reluctantly, I rest my hand back on the steering wheel—like she said, I *am* driving. "I'm really itching to get you naked though. So this one's going to be a really hard one. Let's see…" I trail off in thought. "I'm a big Marvel fan. Or I've never asked a woman to marry me before."

Whoa, Chandler. That's a little too much info for a girl you're just sexing.

Luckily she glosses over it. "*Marvel?* What's Marvel? I pick that one as the lie."

"Oh my god, you did not." I pretend she's shot me in the heart—which isn't far from the truth.

Her eyes widen as it clicks. "Oh, you mean those superhero movies? The ones with The Hulk and Superman?"

"Superman is not in the…" I shake my head. "I can't. I can't even believe I'm with a girl who doesn't know the difference between Marvel and DC Comics. You know what? You take something extra off just for that."

She's giggling again. Have I mentioned how much I love the sound? So much that I'd embarrass myself purposefully just to hear it. "Obviously I got the answer wrong," she says. "I'm not taking off two items. That's not how the rules go. But tell you what—I'll take off something good."

"Your panties?" I might sound eager. I'm not a proud man.

"I'll take off my shirt."

"That will do."

She looks around. There are other cars on the highway, and it's broad daylight. She's going to be seen by someone. I'm betting she's about to chicken out.

But she surprises me when she whips off her tank and tosses it behind her, leaving her in nothing but a matching white bra and panties.

The exclamations of gratitude that are running through my mind aren't even words. They're more like sounds. Grunts. Random syllables. I'm so turned on right now, it's not even funny.

"Don't get pulled over, okay?"

"Um, all right." I immediately ease my foot onto the brakes. "This game is going to get out of hand real soon." If it's not already. I adjust myself again, but it doesn't help. At all.

"Oh, I don't think so. I think I'm going to win! What do I get if I do?"

"A spanking." Which is also what she'll get if *I* win, but I don't tell her that.

"Hey, I didn't agree to touching."

"You already opened that door when you rubbed your hand all over my chest. Now take your turn."

"I did do that, didn't I? Hmm. Let's see." She strokes her hand up and down the strap of her seatbelt while she thinks. "I love live theater. But do I prefer musicals? Or plays?"

I answer without hesitation. "Plays."

"Take off the belt, buddy."

"Hang on." I hold up one finger to scold her. "First of all, you don't get to choose what comes off."

She pouts her full lips dramatically. "Come on. I should at least have a say. It's my reward, after all. Besides, the belt is easy when you're driving. I can even help you." She reaches over and why am I even arguing?

"Well. Okay." I let her work on my belt, let her brush my dick "accidentally"—spoiler: it's not an accident. We both know that she's fooling no one. "But, really? Musicals? I thought you'd be all into that serious boring shit. You know, Agatha Christie. Shakespeare. *Downton Abbey.*"

"*Downton Abbey* is a television show. Not a play."

I sit forward so she can pull the belt from its loops without snagging. "But it's BBC and boring. Isn't that what you Brits like? Boring things? Musicals seem so…*not* boring." I'm teasing her. Hard.

"You're a bit of an ignorant clod, aren't you? *Brits like boring things,*" she scoffs. "Who makes misinformed generalizations like that?"

"I think we already know the answer to that question. And now I've been schooled. Go on, tell me about your love of musicals."

Let me pause to say that I don't mind musicals. I've seen all of one in my entire life—*Wicked*, for Mirabelle's birthday a few years ago. It was fine. Entertaining. I could see more of the same for Genevieve's sake. You know, for the sake of a really good roll in the sheets after.

She wraps my belt around her shoulders, wearing it like a trophy scarf, her hands gripping both ends. "I will not. I'm afraid that you'll ruin one of my favorite things."

"I won't! I promise!"

She turns and narrows her eyes in my direction. "How about your next 'this or that' be *play* or *musical* and think carefully before you answer. I'm guessing you'll say musical."

I'm putty. Complete putty. "Musical. All the way. Musical."

She beams and it's like a fresh breeze cutting through downtown Manhattan. "Awesome. We should see *Hamilton* together some time. Tickets are sold out for the next year, but Hagan has a friend."

"Seeing *Hamilton* together? You mean, like a date?"

"No. I mean like two people who work together— hopefully—that go out with a bunch of friends. It will not be a date."

"Fine. Whatever you say." Not that I care if it's a date. But I am ready to take this game to the next level—speed round. "I love anchovies," I say. "Or I love olives."

"You must love anchovies, because I heard you ask if there were olives in your lasagna at dinner the other night, and people don't ask unless they don't want them."

"Yeah. That's right." I love how she knows things about me.

Or I hate how much she pays attention.

I refuse to answer that. But why *does* she pay so much attention?

I refuse to care about that answer as well.

Anyway, it's her turn. "I want children. Or I want to run the New York marathon."

"You want kids. Not now, but someday."

"Ding, ding, ding."

I want kids too. Now I'm imagining tiny people with my eyes and her cheekbones, and dammit, am I imagining having kids with *her?*

That realization punches me in the gut, but then it moves outward, shooting warmth through my entire body. It feels…right.

Our eyes meet, and it's like drinking champagne how sweet and light and bubbly I feel as I drown in the pools of her eyes.

And she doesn't even have a clue what's going on in my head.

Which is a good thing. Because nothing's going on. "I'm allergic to penicillin. Or I'm allergic to dogs," I say next, trying to get a grip. Trying not to feel like I'm drowning in quicksand.

"You seem to be the type who likes dogs, so I'm hoping for your sake it's penicillin." She doesn't look at me when she adds, "For the record, I love dogs."

"I love dogs too. And I'm not allergic." From the outside, it could look like we are subtly planning a life together. Kids—*check*. Dog—*check*.

"I detest mayonnaise. Or I want to have sex without a condom."

Good sex—*check*.

I can't tell you how fast my head twists toward her. "Please say it's the latter."

Her skin gets redder, and her eyes widen to the size of small saucers. "I don't know!" she gasps. "I really detest mayo, and I said the other off-the-cuff, but I am on the pill and when I think about it, think about going bare—it kind of makes me squirm in my seat, and I don't think it's just because I'm only sitting in my knickers."

I don't even bother adjusting anything down below—

there's no point. "I'd like to try that out," I say as calmly as I can manage. "Or I'm not into that."

"You'd definitely like to try it out."

I put on my signal, peeking at traffic over my shoulder, then head to park the car at the side of the road. "I'm pulling over because we need gas," I say. "Or I'm pulling over because I want to kiss you."

She's quick in her response. "Neither. You're pulling over because you want a blowjob." She's already undoing her seatbelt. Already bending over in my direction.

The game seems to have worked—she's practically naked, and I'd say she knows me pretty damn well.

Chapter Eleven

"I have hair on my arms and my legs," Mina says as she fills her coloring sheet with red scribbles. "But that doesn't make me a boy."

Genevieve bites her lip, stifling a giggle.

"That's right," I say, adding purple hair to the princess Mina's insisted I color. "Doesn't make you a boy."

When we'd arrived, the party was in full swing. I'd dropped our bags off in our room, changed into my suit, then instead of searching out my parents, I brought Genny to the designated children's area to meet the other most important girl in my life—my niece.

Not that it really mattered if they liked each other or not. If I were really interested in Genny, it would, though. Mina and I are tight. A girl wants to be in my world, she has to get that Mina and I are a package deal. I couldn't spend any real time with a woman who didn't understand that.

But Genny and I are only here for Hudson. So whatever.

Still, I'm quite happy when the two of them hit it off instantly. Really happy.

Which is why I'm hanging out in a tent in our garden at Mabel Shores, crammed onto a kid-sized folding chair, coloring from a *Frozen* activity book at a kid-sized round craft table while grinning ear to ear. Behind us, my other niece, Arin, is digging dirt out of the ground with a plastic spoon and singing to herself, as she frequently does. A handful of other children run between the tables, throwing grass at each other. And the most beautiful woman in the world is smiling at my side.

I'm telling you—this might be heaven.

Mina pauses her coloring and looks inquisitively at my date. "Do you have hair on your arms and legs too?"

"I do. Though I take it off of my legs."

"Why?"

Mina's three. *Why* is her favorite word in her vocabulary.

Genevieve frowns. "That's a good question. I guess I like the way it feels to have smooth skin." She absentmindedly runs her hand up and down her shin.

Mina notices. "Can I feel?" She doesn't wait for permission before reaching out her tiny hand to smooth it over Genny's skin. "Ooh. Soft."

It's only been an hour since our side-of-the-road sexcapade, but I can't pass up the opportunity to touch her. "Can I feel, too? Please?"

I'm met with a stern look, but how can she resist me?

"Go ahead," she says with chagrin.

I stroke up her calf, delighting at the path of goose bumps that arise at my touch. "You were right, Mina. Super soft."

She twirls a lock of dark hair around her finger and thinks for a minute. "Does it hurt to take your hair off?"

Genevieve shakes her head. "Not usually."

I study my niece as she tilts her head, her small features furrowed. "You've given her a lot to think about," I tell my date.

"I hope it's not anything that gets me in trouble with her parents."

Like me, I'm sure Genny's imagining Mina sneaking into her mother's bathroom and taking a razor to her own legs because a second later she says, "Taking your hair off your legs is only for grown-ups, though."

I lean toward Genny and whisper, "I'm pretty sure Laynie's had hers lasered off. No razor for the kids to get into."

"How did you know what I was thinking?"

I shrug, watching as Mina returns to her coloring. "I guessed based on my own experience. I borrowed my father's razor one morning when I was about six or seven. Wanted to be all manly like my dad."

"What on earth did you shave? Do I want to know?"

"One side of my head."

Genny lets out a boisterous laugh. "Oh, god. I bet you were adorable. And I bet you were also in a decent amount of trouble."

"My father didn't think it was a big deal, but my mother was furious. She didn't let me go to school until she could get me into a salon to get it all buzzed off."

"Then you got a holiday."

"I think she meant to take me in later, but she got a little hammered at lunch and we ended up going to the movies instead while she sobered up." I stretch my leg out under the table—a relief after having both my knees up to my chest—and turn my purple crayon in for a blue one.

Genevieve grabs the yellow and leans over to help me color. "Your mother likes to—" She mimes throwing back a drink.

I respect both how she's brave enough to inquire and how she isn't making a big deal about it. "She used to. Been clean for over five years now." We'd actually had an intervention for her, but it was my sister, Mirabelle, who'd been the driving force behind my mother's decision to go to rehab. Mirabelle had been pregnant with the first grandchild, and she'd declared that my mother wouldn't be allowed around her baby if she didn't sober up.

"Oh. That's fabulous."

"Well, except we'd all always assumed that my mother was mean because she was an alcoholic. Turns out she's just kind of mean normally."

"Who's mean, Uncle Chandler?"

Whoops. I somehow forgot there were small ears listening. Now I'm the one who's going to get in trouble with her parents, but it doesn't stop me from saying, "I was just saying some not very nice things about Grandma Sophia."

Mina's eyes widen in understanding. "Oh. Grandma Sophia *is* mean."

"See? Even Mina thinks so."

"You're terrible." Genny swats my thigh playfully, and I have to concentrate to keep my dick in line.

Arin, Mirabelle's daughter, picks up on our conversation and adds it to her song. "*She's so mean,*" she sings. "*So mean. So mean, mean, mean.*"

I chuckle to myself. Arin lives her life in a musical. It's freaking awesome.

Kira, another one of the kids, sets a child's teacup and saucer down in front of me. "Here's your tea, my good man," she says in a dialect that I suspect is supposed to be British. She sets another in front of Genny. "Here's your tea, my lady."

Genny grins in delight. "You're ever so thoughtful. Do we have biscuits to go with it?"

"It's pretend." The seven-year-old's tone says she doesn't think Genevieve is very smart. "There's not really tea in there. It's just imaginary."

Genny takes a pretend sip. "And it's very delicious. I'm imagining there are biscuits to dunk in mine." She mimes dipping something in her cup before bringing it to her mouth.

"Genevieve is from England, Kira," I explain. "That's a real compliment she just gave you. She has real tea and biscuits all the time, so she'd know delicious or not."

Kira beams. "Is that why you talk so funny?"

"It is. I live way across the ocean in an area of London called Brixton."

"I've never heard of it," Kira says, half curious, half skeptical that the place exists. "Do you miss it?"

"I do sometimes. But I'll probably go back there pretty soon."

"You will?" I try to sound nonchalant. It's just a question. I don't really care about the answer.

Though my pulse seems to slow when she says, "If the merger doesn't go through with Pierce Industries, yes. I will. I'd love to stay here, but I kind of need a job."

"Oh, right." Honestly, it hadn't occurred to me that her presence in the States might be temporary.

I look away so she doesn't notice it bothers me. Because it doesn't.

"And now you know why I have to run so much. All those biscuits with my tea make me fat." Genny pats her slim stomach, and I have to fight not to comment that there is not an ounce of fat on her—I know.

"*It makes you fa-at. Makes you big and fat,*" Arin sings behind us.

We both turn to watch her. Now she's moved on from digging to burying blades of grass.

"Yes, Arin's a strange one," I say. The five-year-old is also the happiest, sweetest child I've ever met.

Genevieve looks at her adoringly, the way I imagine I look at *her.* "She's precious."

Arin's volume sharpens as her refrain changes. "*She's dead in the trees. She's not alive anymore, she's dead.*"

"Well," Genny says, rethinking her last statement. "And morbid."

"*Precious Morbid.* That should be her band name."

She laughs and then glances around at the children who have gathered in the play area. "Are you related to all these little people, then?"

I scan their faces. "Not all of them. I don't think. I don't know a lot of them." I begin pointing out and identifying the ones I do know. "Mina is Hudson's oldest, of course. Arin is my sister's daughter."

"And she just has the one?"

"Uh-huh. She had a hard pregnancy, and she works a lot

at her boutique and her husband is a doctor. So I think they have their hands full."

"I'd say."

I nod next to the girl serving us tea. "Kira here is Norma's daughter. Norma is our head finance officer at Pierce Industries. She has an older son she adopted too, Tariq." I crane my neck to see if I can spot him. "I think he's over there in the pool."

Just then, a little boy in a miniature suit runs up to me, excitedly.

"And this is Jake. He's my man, aren't you, buddy?" We bump fists before he joins the other boys running circles around the tables.

I look up to see his mother waddling towards us in the distance carrying a toddler in a matching suit. "Be right back," I say to Genny then run to give Gwen a helping hand.

"I should have known you'd be hanging in the children's area," she says to me as I take Theo from her arms. "Thank you. That helps. Now I'm back to only carrying one of my offspring."

I chuckle as I survey her extremely large belly. "You look miserable."

"I *am* miserable. Thank you." She peers past me toward Genny, who's now concentrating heavily on her phone, her forehead creased. "Uh, hello. Who's that?"

"That's Genevieve, my *date*." I emphasize date because that's what she is, not because I like the way it sounds when I say it.

Gwen eyes me suspiciously. "That's interesting. You don't usually bring girls to these things."

"I don't usually know anyone I'd care to bring." I glance

over toward Genny and see her pointing her cell toward my niece. My pulse speeds up. "That's weird."

Gwen follows my gaze. "What? That she's snapping pics of Mina?"

"Yeah. Isn't that, you know, odd? Why would she be taking pictures of some other person's child?" The reasons I can think of make my stomach knot.

Gwen laughs and nudges me with her shoulder. "It means she likes you, you dolt. She likes your family and wants to make memories. She's maybe even imagining she's Mina's aunt."

The tension unwinds from my body. "Shut up," I say, rolling my eyes, but really? It makes me feel all gooey inside.

"Chandler and Genevieve sitting in a tree." Gwen taunts me with her chant. "K-I-S-S-I-N-G."

I shake my head then start walking toward the woman we're discussing. "Come on. I'll introduce you."

So maybe it's strange that I'm still such good friends with the person who broke my heart years ago. The truth is, it wasn't always like this. It took a good part of a year for me to come to terms with always seeing her, watching her life with JC grow and flourish. Really accepting that I wasn't the man she chose.

Eventually, I had to figure it out. Gwen's best friends with Laynie, and our lives intertwine a great deal. It's been a tough road—for me, anyway—but now our relationship is strong and warm. We're practically family.

Genny scrambles to put her phone back in her purse then stands so I can give the two a formal introduction. "Two boys? That must be a handful." She comes up beside me to take my hand, as though claiming me as hers. Which is not at all like her but really nice all the same.

"And another boy on the way." Gwen pats her belly, acknowledging our linked fingers with a raised brow.

It makes me feel confident and cocky. And a bit sassy. "You know, the sex of your baby is determined by the husband. Maybe you should have picked a different sperm donor."

I really don't love Gwen anymore—not like that—but I still like to give her shit about the guy who won her heart. "Where is your significant other, anyway?"

"He's finding me some watermelon. I need some, like, now."

Genevieve nods as though she understands. "My stepmother is four months along, and the cravings she has are insane. Good luck to you with them."

"Uncle Chandler," Mina says, tugging on my slacks. "What's a perm dona?"

I have to think through everything we've just said before I can figure out what term she's asking about.

Then I figure it out. "It's, uh, nothing, sweetie."

Arin belts out the next verse of her song. "*Sperm donor! Spe-ermm!*"

Yeah. Whoops. Again. "Maybe it's time for us to mingle with the grown-ups."

"Probably a good idea." Genny turns to my ex. "You have beautiful children, Gwen. So honored to have gotten to meet them and you."

"You too!"

I look down at where we're linked as we walk. "You're holding my hand. That's unusual, isn't it?"

"I was playing my part as a date. That's all." She pulls her hand from mine with annoyance. "She was an old girlfriend, wasn't she?"

"Wha-? How did you know?"

"It was a guess. The way you bantered. There was history in your subtext."

"I'm over her," I assure her. "*Way* over her. Have been for years."

She smirks. "Awfully defensive, aren't you?"

I stop walking, grab her hand and tug her into my arms. "I wasn't being defensive," I whisper, my mouth at her ear. "I just wanted to make it clear that there is only one woman on my mind these days, and it isn't her."

Where the fuck did that come from? They're words I should never have thought, let alone uttered out loud.

At least they seem to earn me points because Genny closes her eyes, as though she's taking in my words, soaking in the moment.

"You're good at this whole pretend date thing," she murmurs.

"Oh, I'm just getting started." And then I bend to kiss her. For show, of course. No other reason at all.

• • •

After a brief make-out session in the garden, we find my family where I expect them—on the patio off the house. Mirabelle is cuddling with one of the twins while my mother sits, sipping ginger ale and correcting everything my sister does with the baby. Hudson is standing nearby discussing something quietly with our father—business, I'd guess. I meant it when I said he's always working.

"There you are," Mom says, lifting her cheek for me to kiss. "I was beginning to think you were too caught up in chasing skirts to even say hello to your parents."

I ignore her jab, not wanting to draw more attention to my reputation in front of Genevieve. "Where's Laynie and Adam?" I had hoped everyone would be together when I introduced my date.

Mira barely looks up at me as she bounces the baby on her shoulder. "Adam got called into work this weekend. He'll join us later. And I think Laynie's nursing Brett inside."

"You'll have to meet them later," I say to my date. Then I address the small crowd. "Everyone, this is Genevieve Fasbender. She's from London and she's here for a month or so on business—hopefully longer, if all works out." Yes, I'm caught up on the minor detail of her possibly leaving. Much more than I've let on.

Even though this relationship isn't serious, I know my mother cares most about a woman's breeding, so I say, "We met at the Accelecom Charity Banquet last week." I'm careful to emphasize *Accelecom*. "Genny helped put the gala together, didn't you?"

"I did."

My mother stands, which is already more than I'd expected, her eyes narrowed as she scrutinizes the woman beside me.

"Genny, this is my mother, Sophia," I say.

Then I start to pray. I'm telling you—that's the only way to survive an introduction to my mother. That woman is unpredictable at best.

146

"So honored to meet you," Genevieve says with as much grace as a princess.

And with the authority of a queen, my mother says, "Charity functions of that scale are quite an undertaking. I oversee the Pierce Annual Autism Awareness Fashion Show as well as several smaller events. I know the work that goes into them. It's impressive."

I lean toward my date. "I think that's a compliment." The entire interaction has been a happy surprise.

Until my mother turns her attention to me. "She's too thin, Chandler. She'll never be able to carry a baby to term if you don't put some weight on her bones."

"Yep. She just said that. Out loud." *We were so close to a perfect start!* I let out a long breath, reminding myself it's not polite to punch your mom.

Unfazed, Genevieve responds with a smile. "Actually, Mrs. Pierce, my size is deceiving. I'm broad in the hips, as is my mother. She had particularly easy births with both my brother and me. I imagine I'll be just fine."

"Perhaps."

Somewhat harsh, but it went...well, better than it could have.

My mother sits back in her chair and throws a scowl at her husband. "Jack, stop ogling the poor girl."

"I'm not ogling, I'm being attentive." My father steps in to shake Genny's hand, and to his credit, is completely appropriate with the length of time he grips it as well as where he keeps his gaze. "Did I hear your name correctly? Your father is Edward Fasbender?" He exchanges a glance with Hudson. "He's quite a respectable businessman."

Maybe I was wrong about which parent would be more interested in my date's family ties.

"That he is." Genevieve gives her father more respect than I'd give a man who thought so little of me. "I'm honored to be able to work with him, though I'm pretty sure I got the job because of my name." She winks, and she's so enchanting when she does that I have to hide a shiver.

"Hell, that's how Chandler got his job too." My father slaps his hand on my back and laughs, as though he's just made a joke.

Now I briefly wonder if it's bad form to deck your dad but decide to let it slide.

"I didn't realize you were bringing anyone today," Hudson says, and I guess that's his form of a greeting, because he doesn't offer anything else besides a nod in Genny's direction.

I hope this isn't a prelude to how he'll react when we try to discuss Accelecom and Werner Media. Though that's business talk. Business talk always cheers him up.

I'm overly convivial in my response, making up for my brother's lack of cordiality. "I guess Laynie didn't tell you?"

"She didn't mention it. No."

I try not to be too pissed at his lack of manners. He isn't sleeping well, I remind myself, and he's not warm under the best circumstances. Maybe I misjudged when I'd assumed he wouldn't care if I brought a date. Or maybe he's irritated that I'm mixing business with pleasure. Still, doesn't please me when he acts like a doucheface.

"Hi, I'm Mira!" My sister pops up from her chair and, with the baby cradled in her arms, nods instead. "Sorry, my hands are full."

"No worries." Genny gazes at the newborn. "He's quite beautiful."

I surmise she's about to ask to hold him, but before she can, my mother seems to sense it as well and has to get in first. "Mirabelle, give me that baby. You've hogged him all afternoon."

"Because he's a boy! I don't know what boy babies are like. But fine." With a reluctant sigh, Mira hands the baby off.

My mother settles her grandson on her lap and stares affectionately. "He's so attentive. Look at how he watches everything around him. Just like you were, Hudson." She leans down to coo to the baby, "Yes, you are. Just like your daddy!"

Genny frowns in my direction. "Your mother doesn't seem that mean," she says so only I can hear.

Nope, today it's my brother who's being nasty.

I don't say that though, and I don't bother to keep my voice down when I say, "She's only nice until they're walking. I think she even liked *me* when I was still in diapers."

"Which was longer than she liked any of us, since you were still in them until you were four," Hudson adds without invitation.

Genny's eyes light up. "You weren't. That's hilarious."

"Isn't it?" Mirabelle asks. *Traitor.*

"Hey." I sweep my finger in the air, pointing at all of them. "There was enough of you willing to wipe up my shit—why wouldn't I let you? Hashtag: benefits of being the youngest."

"Hashtag: spoiled," Hudson retorts.

"You're one to speak, Mr. I Get Everything I Want."

"Because I work for it. Not because it's handed to me."

This is how my brother and I tease, but I'm aware as much as the next guy that there's always truth underscoring Hudson's words. He's very opinionated, and he doesn't mind if people know it.

Usually, I can handle him. Today, I prickle at his innuendos. "Are you done?" Because I'd like to get past the bullshit and start a meaningful conversation. Preferably one that lets Genevieve show off her beautiful brain.

"Actually," he says, "I wondered if we could talk for a few minutes."

"I've already told you, H." He hates it when I use his wife's nickname for him, so I use it a lot. "You have to choose to share to your selected friends list and not public if you don't want Mom commenting on your stuff on Facebook. The list she's not on. Remember? I helped you set it up."

"Chandler," my mother says, not looking up. "You're not funny. I know how to use Facebook."

"Yeah, but does Hudson?"

Genevieve at least thinks it's funny. She covers her mouth with her hand to hide her giggles.

Hudson, however, does not appreciate my humor. "Cute," he says dryly. "Let's talk."

"Fine. Shoot."

"Privately. Please."

"Uh…" I consider insisting we talk here, but his expression says he's not budging. And I can guess what he wants to talk about—he wants me to catch him up on the dinner the other night. It wouldn't be appropriate in front of Genny, but it might be my opportunity to talk her up.

I place a hand on her arm and am about to ask her if

she'll be okay with the wolves when my father interjects. "Not now, Hudson."

Hudson seems reluctant. "It will only take—"

"It can wait," Dad insists.

I'm willing to slip away and get the business taken care of, especially because I'm more interested in convincing my brother to consider what the Fasbenders can bring to Werner Media since Genny made her remark about returning home.

But before I can say so, Laynie shows up with a swaddled baby in her arms. "H, you aren't trying to work, are you?"

His smile is tight, and his eye twitches, and in the look that passes between him and my father, I'm suddenly very nervous about what it is that he has to say to me. Now I'm not sure I want to get it over with or postpone it as long as possible.

Hudson decides for me. "Of course not, precious." He puts his hand affectionately around his wife.

It's not long before I've forgotten all about business myself. Instead, I'm holding the littlest baby Pierce, staring into her blue-grey eyes, and trying not to imagine it's my own baby I'm snuggling.

Definitely trying not to imagine who I'd want her mother to be.

CHAPTER TWELVE

The sun is setting, and the party's winding down when I persuade Genevieve into slipping away with me. Wanting to show her the ocean, I lead her along the path that passes through the thick trees lining our estate.

"What's with the dense woods?" Genny asks, as we curve deeper into the trees. "Isn't the view the reason people buy beachfront property?"

"Huh." The landscape has essentially been the same my entire life, and until now, her point hasn't occurred to me. "I guess it is. But the problem with a view *out* means that there's also a view *in*. Too many people walk along the beach, even with the private property signs. Too many boats pass by. Too many passengers with binoculars. My mother prefers our life be kept confidential."

Genevieve flashes me a teasing grin. "Then she must adore your relationship with the paparazzi."

I wince at her reference to the frequent media buzz about my social life but ignore addressing it directly. "Let's get this straight right now," I say instead, "my mother adores nothing. Even if I were squeaky clean and as reserved as Hudson, I don't think I'd own any more of her affection than I do now."

Genny looks sideways at me, her eyes scrutinizing. "Does that bother you?"

"Maybe?" My brows knit as I consider. "I know she has emotions somewhere deep inside her. Just like this property, she hides behind a bristly-needled exterior. I think I'm used to it."

She scoffs. "I think you convince yourself you're used to it. I don't believe that anyone who lacks their mother's love doesn't feel its absence." She sounds like she may have experience with the subject herself, but she doesn't give me a chance to ask. "Maybe your mother isn't the only one hiding behind landscaping."

My steps slow as I take in what she's said. Am I more like my mom than I've realized? I'm not cold and guarded like she is, but that doesn't mean I don't wear my own form of armor—my charm. My business-plan approach to relationships. What emotions am I hiding behind those barriers?

Genny purses her lips as though she knows exactly what's going through my mind. "Shame, really, about all those trees. Because this view is absolutely breathtaking."

We've stepped out from the woods onto the cliffside, the ocean spread across the horizon below us, but she keeps her eyes pinned on me for long seconds before casting her gaze across the panorama.

I happen to think the view I have is breathtaking as well. And I'm not looking at the water. "I had a feeling you'd like it. Away from the sand and once the sun wasn't so high, that is."

She squints over at me. "Does this count as having been to the beach? Can I now cross that off my to-do list?"

"Eh," I shrug. "Real beach enthusiasts would probably say not until you've put your feet in the sand. The path continues over there if you'd like to try that out." I nod in the direction of the wooden staircase that winds down to the shore.

She wrinkles her nose. "I'm fine up here, thank you. I'm enjoying this part of the beach experience. We should quit while I'm still enchanted." Leisurely, she begins to stroll along the property.

I fall in step, hoping her sentiment applies only to the outdoor scenery. Not that she's enchanted with anything else at the moment. Not that I *want* her to be enchanted with anything else.

Yet, I'm so enchanted with her.

And I don't want to quit her. Not yet.

A cloud pushes in over my mood as I suddenly remember that my time with Genny is very possibly fleeting. That her job might soon take her from me.

I nudge the thought away, and a question that's been niggling at the back of my consciousness slips into its place. "Don't take this the wrong way, but there's something I have to ask."

Curiosity etches her expression. "Okay. Ask."

I ignore the connection trying to form between this thought and my last one and put it out there. "If your father is so against you working in this business, why does he let you work for Accelecom?"

"Ah. Good question." Her features relax. "It's because it's the only way I'll let him help me."

"What do you mean?" I sort of hate to admit it, but I'd assumed she was a trust fund baby, same as me.

"I had an account for college, but after school, I was determined to make my own way. And I do. I rely on public transport. I have my own apartment—a modest little place in a part of London that is not up to my father's standards, but I'm quite fond of it. He's tried over and over to convince me to let him pay for something in a nicer part of town— translation: a *snobby* part of town. I turned him down. He bought me a car for my birthday, which I refused. He kept sneaking me money. I kept returning it. Finally he offered me a job. A *dream* job. And I'm embarrassed to admit that I was weak. I accepted in an instant."

A breeze blows, and she hugs her arms around herself. "But I still have my silly little flat, even though he pays me an exorbitant salary."

"So what do you do with all your money?" I realize too late that it's probably an inappropriate question. I'm still trying to wrap my head around the fact that she doesn't own a car. Had she not mentioned the size of her paycheck, I would have assumed it was decent just based on what she does, and a car would have been the first item on my purchase list.

"I do like shopping. Shoes, in particular. But I'm saving most of it for when I don't have a dream job. I may need that money to make ends meet one day."

Her grey eyes widen suddenly. "Oh! A gazebo!" She skips up to the old forgotten rotunda on the edge of our property. "It's completely charming. I love it!" She spins around in the center of the structure then strolls to the opening and leans against the pillar.

I follow and pause at the bottom stair, my hands in my pockets, and cock my head up at her. "You don't like working at Accelecom?"

"I *love* working at Accelecom! It's exactly the kind of position I went to university for." She rubs the goose bumps off her arms. "But I don't love that it's my father's company. If he'd let me build more of it, that might be different, and I still hold out hope that he'll eventually change his mind. But if he doesn't, I'm prepared to go someplace where I can."

Realizing she's cold, I take off my jacket and walk over to give it to her. She's so interesting, I decide, as I wrap it around her shoulders. We're alike and so different. We've both been born into a dynasty of sorts, and she's turned down every handout while I've accepted—and *expected*—every privilege I've been given. Both of our families are leery about our careers but for very different reasons. She's worked her ass off to become something in her chosen field, proving that she deserves to be where she is even against her father's wishes.

And me? I've just coasted.

God, I'm kind of pathetic next to her. Scratch that—*really* pathetic.

"That's important to you, isn't it?" I ask as I pull the front of my jacket closed around her. "Making it on your own."

"It is. Extremely important." She tilts her head up to look at me. "Next you're going to ask why."

"I am now." I step back to lean against the post opposite her.

"I don't know. Probably a lot of it is that's just how I was made. But it's also probably my mother's fault."

I wait, sure she'll say more if I do.

And she does. "My parents got divorced when I was twelve," she explains as she kicks off one of her heels. "Before that, my mother was the best wife you could imagine. Devoted. Subservient. Put everyone else above herself." She points a foot out in front of her and circles it in the air, stretching as she talks. "My father so adored her. Doted on her like she was the queen.

"Then, one day, out of the blue, she up and left. Took off with another man and moved to Lisbon."

Huh. Hadn't been expecting that. "She left without warning?"

"No warning at all. We never saw it coming." She's quiet then, her brows furrowed.

I search for the right words to say—sympathetic and supportive—but just as I'm about to speak, she says, "Actually, that's not exactly true."

"Oh?" I sit down on the step and peer up at her, letting her know she has my full attention.

"There were subtle warnings, I think. Things I caught later." She kicks off her remaining shoe and looks down, as though studying her toes. "Like, once I'd overheard her tell my father that she didn't know who she was without him. Not in a romantic way but in a hopeless way. As though she didn't have any identity that wasn't tied to being his wife and our mother."

She tugs my jacket tighter around herself and meets my eyes. "I have no idea whether she was planning to leave him at that point or if the thought had yet to cross her mind. But even without knowing what was to come, I decided I didn't want to be like that. I didn't want to be a woman without a sense of self. I didn't want to rely on a man—or anyone, for that matter—to fill in the spaces of my existence. I didn't want to ever feel as lost as my mother sounded."

Her admission is so stark and bare and honest, and I understand. But what hits me is how vulnerable she is before me. Naked in a way I've never seen her.

It leaves me speechless. I *want* to be speechless. I don't want to break this spell, don't want to ruin this moment of intimacy.

After a moment, she looks away. I watch her throat as she swallows. Then she says, "My father was devastated when she left. I was pretty shook up too, of course. But a part of me also felt a smidgeon of happiness. For her. I really believed she was out to find herself."

She turns back toward me. "Then she went and got into the same boat. Married a guy who completely eclipses her. Had new babies that consume her entirely. Hagan and I only ever have contact with her at birthdays and Christmas now—at most."

So that was what she was hinting at when she'd talked about children missing the love of their mothers.

"My father, on the other hand, married a woman who isn't anything like his first wife. She's strong-headed, refined, independent. Runs her own business."

This surprises me. "Your stepmother?"

"Strange, right? Knowing my father." With her back against the pillar, she slides down so she's sitting on the step across from me. "But they're the happiest couple I know. Madly in love. Quite perfect together."

"Wow." I ignore the urge to wonder if she thinks *we* might be a happy couple together too and focus on what she's said. "And he's cool with her being self-reliant?"

She brushes a piece of hair behind her ear. "He is. He's extremely supportive of her work. Which is why I have to believe he'll one day come around about me. Honestly, I think he just wants us to be happy. He can see his wife is happy doing what she does. Hopefully one day he'll realize I am too."

I have a feeling she's trying to warm me up to her father, and because he's important to her, I want to make an effort. Just…

"I don't know if I can get used to the idea of your dad not being a bad guy," I admit.

Genny lets out a soft laugh. "That's fine. He can still be the bad guy in your story. He's just not the bad guy in hers."

"What about in your story?"

She frowns as if the answer is obvious. "In my story, he's my father."

My own relationship with my father is also that complex and that simple. Jack Pierce can bring on the charm with the ladies like I can, but he's so focused when he wants to be. So business-minded, like Hudson. Sometimes it's like I can't possibly share his DNA, we're that different.

But I still love him. I'd still care if he didn't love me.

My voice is gruff when I manage a response. "Enough said."

Her eyes slant with compassion, as if she knows what's going through my head. God, it makes me want things. Want to touch her. Want to hold her. Want to *keep* her.

I look away, stifling my emotions. With my eyes trained

over the horizon, I take a beat to process everything she's told me, letting the pieces click together in the puzzle that makes up who she is. I better understand now why she was worried to get involved with me—she didn't want to rely on anyone to help with the Accelecom/Werner Media merger.

But that begs a different question—why is she here if she doesn't want anyone's help?

I turn back to study her a moment. "You like me!"

"What? Where did that come from?"

"From you. You don't want anyone's help. You just said that. And yet you're here under the guise of me helping you. Why on earth would you accept help from me when you want to do everything on your own? Only one answer makes sense. You like me."

"Oh, for fuck's sake. I do not." But her skin turns scarlet.

"You're blushing. You totally do." I laugh, loving this new turn of events. "I can't believe it."

"Would you stop it? You're making a fool out of yourself." She purses her lips and shakes her head.

"There's no one here but you, and I don't care, anyway. It's worth it to hear the truth. You. Like. Me."

She shakes her head again, but this time she doesn't deny it outright. Instead, she meets my eyes, and I can see it clearly. She *does* like me.

And there it is again—that tightening in my chest. That feeling that I both want to ignore and hold onto for as long as possible. Words bubble in my throat, sentiments begging to be expressed.

With my gaze locked on hers, I scoot closer, needing to kiss her. Needing to occupy my mouth with something other than the things I shouldn't say.

Our mouths move slowly at first, tasting. Testing. Quickly, it grows deeper. I cradle her cheek with my hand and move my body in tighter, so she can feel the thick pressure of my erection on the inside of her leg. I know we're outside, that it's only dusk and we could be seen, but I'm desperate to have her.

I start to gently steer us to a prone position when she brusquely pushes me away.

I search her face, questioning—did I hurt her? Did I misread the mood? Is the outdoors a hard limit for her, and did I actually just think the term *hard limit*?

But that can't be it because she's given me all the cues. Her grey eyes are clouded with desire. Her breathing has become quick and shallow. Her tongue darts out to moisten her lower lip.

Then, in a husky voice, she says, "Make me."

I know exactly what she means. I know because it's what I want her to mean, and because we've become so connected in these ways that I can just tell. She wants to fuck as much as I do. But it's a game now. A game where I *make* her.

She gives me a beat to process. Her body visibly primes, her limbs prep to take off.

I'm ready when she lunges, though, and I catch her at her wrist. She pulls and twists, and I grin because all I have to do is grab her other arm, and I'll have her trapped.

Except I'm too slow, and she takes advantage of my hesitation. She stomps down hard on my foot, and before I can react, her free hand flies through the air. With a loud *smack*, her palm meets my face.

Automatically, I drop her wrist to rub my jaw. Our eyes lock and we freeze.

I can't believe she did that.

The look on her face says she can't believe she did it either.

And maybe it's messed up, and I should be pissed or confused but instead I'm turned on as fuck. My dick is throbbing, and I swear all my primal instincts have kicked in because I can smell her so clearly that my mouth waters. My want turns into need. Desperate, urgent need.

From the way her brow rises, I think she knows. And from the glint in her eye, I'm pretty sure she's feeling exactly the same. The edges of her mouth turn up into a wicked smile. Then, letting my jacket slip off her shoulders, she runs.

With her heels off, she's fast, sprinting back along the trees. But I'm right behind her, my adrenaline pushing me to chase, and even though she's an experienced runner, I'm on her in no time. I grab her by the elbow, and before she can pull away, I fold both arms around her in a tight embrace.

"You think you can run from me?" My voice is low and gruff at her ear. "You think I won't come after you?"

"Let go," she whimpers, and I know she doesn't mean it. She knows she can end this, knows all she has to do is say *stop*.

And as long as she's not saying that, every other word she utters means *go*.

"No way, little girl. You got me hot, and now you've got to pay for it."

But she's not giving in that easily. She fights back, pushing her elbows up into my sides. It surprises me enough to lose my grip. She stumbles forward, out of my arms and onto her knees.

Immediately, she tries to stand. This time, though, I'm

quick, and while she's still halfway down, I lunge my weight onto her, knocking her to the ground. She wrestles as I shift my body over her, pinning her down forcefully. All the while, she repeats the same words as she struggles, "Let me go, let me go!"

She's really into it, screaming, even. But we're far enough from the house for her not to be heard easily, and I'm into this too, so with one hand wrapped in her hair, I twist her head sharply to the side and push her cheek to the ground. "One way or another you're taking my cock, and if you don't shut the fuck up, it's going to be down your throat."

She gulps but she quiets. I nudge her legs apart with a knee, and with my free hand, I reach up under her dress as I continue to play the part she's asked me to play—a part I've taken on happily. "This is going to be so good," I promise her on a low rumble. "You know that, right? You want me inside you, you little dicktease."

"Please," she whimpers, and it makes my cock grow thicker because it feels like she's begging me to stop, when I know she's really begging me to go on. And somewhere in the back of my mind I recognize how perverted this is, how vile. I'm getting off on pretending to violate the girl I like. What kind of fucked-up fuckhead am I?

But she wants it. I *know* she wants it, and in case I don't know, she tells me with her body language, with the way she moves her legs farther apart, granting me better access. With the way her breath hitches with excitement. With the way her panties are soaked when my fingers find her crotch.

"See how much you want this? I knew you did." Suddenly, I remember something important. Thinking fast, I work the question I need to ask into the scene. "Are you still going to want it when I tell you I don't have a condom with me?"

"I don't want it," she squeaks, but at the same time, she nods.

It's the green light I need. "Oh, you want it, little girl. Don't lie to me."

It's not easy, but somehow I manage to pull her underwear down one-handed. Then I tackle my belt. Then my zipper. All the while, she writhes below me, hissing, protesting, never using the one word that will end this.

And then my cock is out, and I'm shoving inside of her, and Jesus, it's ecstasy how tight and warm she feels around me. She gasps as I fill her, her character breaking as she lets out a soft, "Yes."

"That's it," I tell her, driving into her again. "I knew you wanted it. Hard to fight me now, isn't it?"

She grunts in response, shifting beneath me, but this time instead of struggling, she's reaching her hand down to rub her clit, and goddamn it's so hot how she wants this as much as I do. How she wants it *the way* I do.

I find my pace quickly, and while it fits the scene, I'm not playing anymore, uttering dirty, vulgar honest truths as I rut into her. "I fuck you every day," I confess. "Did you know that? In my head, with my hand. I fuck you in so many ways. In your mouth. On your knees. By force. Willingly. So many ways I fuck you, but it never feels as good as when I'm inside you. Your pussy is so tight, Genny. So, so good."

I'm crazed with my lust. I'm barely restraining her now, but the illusion of the scenario has set fire into my veins, fire that won't be smothered until I've given her everything I have. Until I'm making her fall apart beneath me. Until I'm spilling my release inside of her.

She's the one to get there first. "Oh god, oh god, oh god," she says as she starts to clench around me. "Oh god, like that. Harder." Then, "I'm coming! I'm coming so hard."

I pick up speed, racing to my own finish. And when I cross that line, I explode like never before, ramming so far into her, I'm not sure where she begins and I end.

I'm not sure I want to know ever again.

She's breathless and panting when I roll off her and gather her into my arms. I study her closely. Her face is dirty and her dress is rumpled and she has a bruise forming on her upper arm, but she's smiling, and her expression appears happy and sated.

Still, I ask, "Are you okay? Was *this* okay?"

She nods. "I should be asking you the same thing." She rubs her hand gently over my slapped cheek.

"Very okay." I kiss her, wishing this would never end. Wishing I could find the way to make this thing between us last. Wishing she didn't live in another country and that the power to keep her here were in *my* hands and not my *brother's*.

As always, though, I hide those wishes behind a landscape of charm. "You can ask me to *make you* anytime you want," I tell her, and I mean it.

But all I'm really thinking is how much I wish she'd ask me to make her *stay*.

CHAPTER THIRTEEN

Later, it's my turn to be vulnerable.

We lie wrapped around each other naked in bed, and in the dark, I tell her about Gwen. Tell her how I fell in love. Tell her how I got my heart broken.

"So her ex had been gone for how long when you started seeing her?" Genny asks after I give her the basic gist of the story.

I rub a hand up and down her back while I talk. "About nine months maybe?" I don't remember the exact timeline really. JC had been in witness protection without any contact with Gwen. "But they hadn't totally broken up. He said he would come back."

"And yet she still got involved with you?" I can't see her face in the position we're in, but from the tone of her voice, I suspect Genevieve is frowning.

I get it. It was a situation that once made me frown too. A lot.

It makes me happy that she cares enough to have that reaction.

"I think she thought he'd be back by then," I tell her. "I was just supposed to be a distraction while she figured out what she did next."

Genny tilts her head up toward me, and this time I can *see* she's frowning. "That doesn't sound very nice of her. You're just her plaything while she decides if she's waiting for her real lover to return? That's a load of tosh."

"Well." Once upon a time I would have agreed. Now it doesn't bother me like it once did. "I actually didn't mind being a plaything." Gwen had been ten years older than me. The sex had been hot. The whole situation had been hot, whether she had feelings for me or not.

But back then, it had stung more. "I *did* mind not knowing her heart was already spoken for. Even when she'd always been clear it was just sex, it would have been nice to know."

Genny sits up and stares at me, her eyes aflame. "I can't believe you're so cavalier about it. '*It would have been nice*'? She should have told you. Plain and simple. That she didn't is just mean."

Jesus, I love it when she's feisty.

"And how could she expect you not to develop feelings for her? It's natural to fall for someone you're intimate with. Especially when it's repeated intimacy. No matter what our culture tries to make us believe, it stirs things. How could she not have fallen for you as well?"

Our eyes meet, and in unison, we both realize what she's said. How it could apply to our current situation. Genny's cheeks turn beet red, and she lowers her eyes, and all I can think is *Oh my god, is she really falling for me?*

I want to know so badly that I almost ask.

But in the end, I'm chickenshit, and instead I only make allusions. "That is the burning question, really," I tease, trying to lighten her embarrassment. "How can anyone not fall for me is an even more accurate question."

She gives me a lopsided grin and settles her head on my chest without remarking on my comment—maybe she's chickenshit too. "I've decided I don't like her," she says after a beat. "I'll be nice to her in person, of course. But she's heartless."

I chuckle, stroking my hand through her hair. "Gwen isn't heartless. We're friends now. Good friends."

Genny harrumphs, her finger drawing lazy circles over my chest. "Doesn't mean I have to like her."

I love how good her touch feels on my skin, and I almost miss her subtext. But then it hits me—"You're jealous!"

I love that she's jealous.

Her hand stops mid-circle. "Do I have a reason to be jealous?"

I shake my head then realize she can't see it. "I don't have any feelings for Gwen any more beyond friendship. I told you that earlier."

"Then I'm not jealous."

"Well. You are. But that's cool. I like it."

She sits up and scowls playfully at me, but she doesn't deny my accusation a second time. Is it fucked up how much I love her attitude toward my ex? Because I love it a lot.

When she lies down again, it's on her side, facing me. I move toward her until our noses are inches from touching and wrap my arm around her waist. She fits so perfectly against me. Like we were made to be this close.

With her eyes pinned to mine, she asks, "Have you ever been the way you are with me with anyone else?"

I squint, trying to understand exactly what she's asking. "Like what way that I am? Like where I hold you all night? I'm holding you all night, by the way."

"We'll see."

"I'm holding you," I say with an authoritative tone I know she won't refute.

Goose bumps sprout up on her skin. "Like that—like bossy and…I don't know."

"Dominating?"

"Yeah. And rough. And primal."

I bring my finger up to trace the line of her lips. It gives me an excuse to look somewhere other than her eyes when I answer. "I told you before that I haven't."

"I want to hear it again. You've never tied someone up?"

"Nope."

"Pushed them to the ground?"

I shake my head.

"What about spanked them?"

"Not like how I spanked you." Not with a belt. Not so hard it left marks. My gaze flickers up to hers, suddenly worried. "Can you tell?"

"No," she says softly. "And yes."

I stay silent, waiting for her to expand, and she does. "When we're like this, it feels like you're never anything else. Like this is who you are. Kind and gentle and kind of cocky but also goofy."

"There you are with the goofy again…"

She ignores my interjection. "It doesn't seem at all like you'd be the type of guy to strap a belt around a woman's wrists or shag her in a bathroom or pretend to force her in the backyard of your parents' summer home. But then, when you're doing that, it seems like there's no other way you'd ever fuck. You're natural at it. And the only reason I suspect that it's new to you is because of that first time. The awful time."

"Oh my god. It wasn't awful. Would you stop saying it was awful?" I pretend to strangle her, taking note for the future of how it makes her eyes cloud with desire. "It wasn't maybe as good as the times after, but I couldn't stop thinking about you afterward."

"Fine, it wasn't awful." Her lids lower and she gets abruptly bashful. "I actually enjoyed it more than I let on."

Yes! I knew it hadn't been terrible!

Containing my excitement, I use a single finger to lift her chin up. "Look at me, Genny." Her eyes flutter up to meet mine. "Why didn't you tell me that before?"

"Because I didn't want to like you."

My mouth gets dry. My pulse picks up. My chest tightens, as though my ribs are trying to close the gaps in my skeleton, desperately trying to protect anything from getting inside. She's told me this before, but this time it really sinks beneath my skin and into my blood. Into my bones.

"And you really do *like* me?" Somehow my words come out steady, despite how shaken I feel inside.

"What do you think?" She glances down at my lips, and I take the cue, moving in to kiss her. Her mouth molds easily to mine, even when I get brutal—which I do. I wrap one hand around her neck, my thumb lightly pressing against her windpipe—not enough to hurt her, but enough so she's aware.

It arouses her. I can tell by the nature of her kiss, how it gets hungrier. Wanton and wild, mirroring everything I'm giving her.

Soon I'm hard and eager to press into her, but at the same time, I'm not ready to move on from this kiss. From this moment. From this out-of-breath, on-the-edge-of-a-precipice, scared-out-of-my-mind feeling scratching inside of me.

I pull away to look at her.

"I like this." Her eyes are heavy and dark. "I like that I'm the only one you've been like this with."

"I like that you're the only one who brings it out in me." *I love it, actually.*

And that's when I know.

Goddammit all to hell.

I'm in love with her, aren't I? That feeling in my chest, that desire to help her out with her job, my fear of her leaving—this is the explanation. This is the emotion I'm hiding. I've tried so hard to ignore it, but I'm fucking head-over-heels in love with her.

I'm pretty sure I should have seen this coming.

Then why do I feel like I've been run over by someone else as they're stealing my Bugatti?

"Is this fast?" she whispers, and now I know she's feeling something too.

"Don't think about it," I whisper back, praying that the dark and the thinness of our voices can keep the words from holding weight. From anchoring in and changing everything.

"This is fast," she says again on the softest of breaths.

Neither of us moves, both of us completely encapsulated in this single moment, frightened and thrilled all at once. Like a roller coaster. Like speeding down an empty highway. "Fast things aren't bad things."

"But they're often over too quickly."

"Or they're not. The thing is sometimes you don't know how long a stretch of highway is going to be until you get to the end. All you can do is buckle up and enjoy the ride." Funny how I sound more confident than I feel.

"Pretty sure I've already been buckled up with you, and yes, I enjoyed the ride."

I grin, grateful that she's lightened the tension. "Pretty sure I'll be riding you again real soon."

She licks her lips and nods once, and I'm pretty sure she's talking about more than the next round when she says, bravely, "All right. I'm ready."

All right then, I'm ready too.

CHAPTER FOURTEEN

I wake up to a soft nudge and the whisper of my name.

"Hmm?" My arm is wrapped around Genny's waist, and even though I'm awake enough to take victory that I did indeed hold her all night, I'm not ready to open my eyes.

"Chandler." She reaches around to poke my shoulder.

"What is it?" I say on a yawn, but by then, my eyes are open, and I can see exactly the reason Genevieve had woken me up. "Uh, hi, Mina."

The three-year-old stands at the edge of the bed and bats her brown eyes at me.

"Guess I need to learn to lock the door," I mumble in Genny's ear, glad that the sheets are pulled up around our naked bodies. "Well, hello there, ninja-child."

Mina blinks. "What's a ninja?"

"Someone who's good at sneaking up on people. Like you." I'm already preparing for the lecture that Hudson is sure to give me later. But seriously? Kid needs to learn some rules about privacy.

Mina smiles, accepting my words as a compliment. "I didn't even try to sneak on you. I'm a reawy good ninja, aren't I?"

"Really good. Whatcha doing in here, anyway, kid?"

"Gramma Sophie said you were 'spending the day in bed'." *Not an unattractive idea.* "Are you sick, Uncle Chandler?"

Genny stifles a laugh as I glance at the clock on the wall. *Jesus, Mom, it's only nine-thirty.*

"Nope. Not sick. Just sleeping in." I sit up, careful not to reveal anything too, uh, traumatizing. For me. Not her, necessarily.

Apparently, I wasn't cautious enough because next thing I know, she's tilting her head and asking, "Uncle Chandler, are you naked?" She's an observant little ninja, my niece is. "My mommy says that people sleep together naked when they love each other."

"Um." Awkward. Because, yes, I do love Genny. But this isn't quite how I want to say it for the first time. And I certainly don't want her to feel pressured to say it back.

Then Genny floors me when she says, "That's right."

Two words and my heart is pounding in my chest like a bass drum. *Did she just…?*

Genny looks over her shoulder at me. "I wouldn't want to undermine anything her parents have taught her."

"Right," I say, my breath still caught in my lungs. That's what she meant by that. Still, I can't help but think there's a layer of honesty to her statement. We've hinted at feelings for each other now, and yet we keep dancing around actually saying it. But moments like this? I have to think the words aren't that far off.

My stomach twists at the thought, in a mostly pleasant

way. And a little bit not so pleasant. I mean, this is a big thing we're talking about—or *not* talking about, exactly—and while it's exciting, it's also fucking terrifying.

Also terrifying is what comes out of Mina's mouth next. "Are you going to have a baby now?"

I scrub a hand over my face. "Wait…what?"

"Mommy says that when two people—"

"Hey, Mina," I cut her off once I get the gist of where she's going with this. "Why don't you go downstairs and see if Millie saved me any of her famous pancakes? I'll be down in just a minute, okay?"

She pauses, not completely sold on the idea of leaving me, but then suddenly she says, "Okay," and darts out of the room.

"Damn. That was…" I trail off, not sure how best to finish the sentence.

Genny finishes it for me. "Precious. That's what it was."

"God only knows what she'll say to everyone else about this encounter. I better get down there." Reluctantly, I hop out of bed.

Genevieve stares after me with glassy eyes. "You're going to be a really good father, you know."

"Now that's *really* terrifying." I use the excuse of digging through my suitcase to hide my face from hers because, seriously, I'm imagining children waking us up in the future, children that don't belong to my brother.

I wonder if Genny's imagining the same.

Which reminds me of something else that we should probably address. "We haven't used a condom these last few times." I pull on a pair of jeans and turn to face her. "This isn't your way of saying you're not really on the pill, is it?"

She laughs. "No. I'm definitely on the pill."

"Not that it wouldn't be okay. I mean, we're too young. And just met. And we have other agendas right now. But it would be cool. If you were. You know, just in case." God, I sound like an idiot. No wonder she calls me goofy.

I meet her eyes, and yes, she's laughing at me, but there's something else too. Adoration, maybe? It's how I imagine I must be looking at her.

"I'm not worried about it," she says, completely in control of her speech, unlike me. "I'm not worried that I'll get pregnant," she clarifies. "But I'm also not worried about what would happen if I did. I know you'd be supportive."

Supportive? I'd be goddamn-father-of-the-year if I had the opportunity.

Whoa. This really is moving fast.

I take a deep breath as I throw on a T-shirt. We're just talking. That's all. The kind of conversation all responsible adults have when they start having sex without latex. It's all good.

When I turn back to her, she's on her side, propped up on her elbow watching me, and it takes every bit of strength I can muster not to crawl back into bed with her. A day in bed sounds so perfect, and not only because my dick is twitching in my jeans, but because I can't get enough of this woman. I want to talk to her and touch her and just *be* with her. All the time.

"If you keep looking at me like that, you're never going to get out of here, and there will be one sad little girl waiting downstairs."

"More likely she'll come looking for me up here again."

I sigh, resigned to the fact that I have to leave her. But not without a good morning kiss.

I crawl over the bed toward her.

"Chandler, no! I haven't brushed my teeth."

I shake my head. "I don't care." She didn't seem to care when we woke up in the middle of the night for yet another round of let's-see-how-deep-I-can-go. She doesn't fight me now either when I wrap my hand in her hair, tugging it sharply before ravishing her mouth.

I swear she tastes like fucking candy. I love it.

I love her.

"Are you going to come down too?" I ask when I bring myself to pull away, surprised I didn't spill the contents of my heart instead.

"Yes. I want to shower and then I'll join you." *Fuck, showering with her sounds even more delicious than my housekeeper's pancakes.* "Is that okay?"

Little girl. Waiting for me. Got to go.

I kiss Genny once more on her nose. "As long as you think of me while you're in there."

She agrees, and I'm not sure if it's that or the kiss that caused the hard-on I'm sporting. The sight of her naked body as I watch her slip into the bathroom definitely doesn't help.

Needing a few minutes to cool down before I go downstairs, I pace the room and recite the Pledge of Allegiance until something catches my eye—a folder sticking out of Genny's suitcase with the Pierce Industries logo at the top of it.

I'm curious.

Okay, I'm a goddamned snoop.

I pull the folder out and find dozens of pages of financial transcripts, all belonging to Pierce Industries.

Which is weird, right? I mean, she wants to do business with us, but her interest is in Werner Media. So why on earth does she have this? I'm not sure where she'd even get that information. Not sure if it's even public.

The water in the shower suddenly turns off. And not wanting to be caught with my hand in her bag, I shove the folder back in and rush out of the room. Outside the door, I take a moment to clear my head.

And realize I'm being a moron.

Genevieve is a businesswoman through and through. Of course she'd investigate all the parties she was looking at working with. That's all. I make a mental note to ask her about it later to be sure and then head downstairs.

• • •

I find my family eating breakfast on the patio, and except for Laynie, it looks like Genny and I are definitely the late risers.

"Wow, look who managed to put some clothes on," my mother says, her tone filled with its usual disdain.

I narrow my eyes at Mina. "Seems someone told on me." And really? I'm twenty-four. Am I supposed to pretend I'm celibate? God knows Hudson didn't.

"You have to be careful how you behave around little ones," Mirabelle chides, but I can tell from the twinkle in her eye that she's poking at me more than lecturing.

"Hey, I didn't realize that I needed to lock my door." I turn to Hudson, who is scowling quietly over his coffee. "She didn't see anything, H. I swear."

He glances over at his daughter, as if to be sure she isn't listening before he says quietly, "Oh, if I believed she had, you'd be missing your nuts by now."

"Ha ha." At least now I'm totally soft. No one kills a boner like my brother.

No one kills a breakfast like my brother, either. He's moody and tense, probably because he's not sleeping, but I can't help but feel like it's directed at me.

Sure enough, I'm only midway through my stack of cakes when he says, "Chandler, we need to talk."

"Not this again," my father grumbles, and all of a sudden I remember the strange foreboding I felt the day before when Hudson had wanted to pull me aside.

My eyes dart from Hudson's to Dad's and back to Hudson's. "Is there something I need to be worried about?"

"I'd rather discuss this privately." Although he obviously already told my father. How private is this really?

Hudson stands, expecting that I'll follow suit.

"Is Uncle Chandler in trouble?" Mina asks no one in particular, and I have to say, I'm wondering the same thing.

"Of course not, baby." Hudson's features relax as he addresses his child. "We just have some grown-up talk to get to." He bops her on the nose with his finger, his smile warm and full of love.

Then he turns to me and a cold front moves in over his expression. "Let's go."

"Yep." I follow Hudson into the house imagining all the possible things he might want to talk about. He can't be that upset about the way Mina came upon us this morning, can he? I finally decide he's just eager to get an update on what happened the other night at the Advances in the Media banquet.

At least, I hope that's all it is.

Hudson is quiet as we walk. Even when we reach the study, he doesn't speak until he's poured himself a scotch and offered one to me as well.

"Day drinking?" I accept the glass, hoping this isn't an indication that this conversation is going to be serious. Though everything is serious to Hudson, so what my concern is, I don't know.

"I'd offer a mimosa instead, but you know those have been nixed from the menu since Mother's been sober." He swirls the liquid in his tumbler before taking a swallow.

I walk to the window and take a sip myself, letting the liquor burn my throat. As I stare out, Genny joins my family on the patio, and at the sight of her, all my anxiety disappears. I can't hear them, but her inquisitive expression says she's asking about me. Mirabelle responds and then they're laughing and sitting down together. Warmth shoots along my spine, and I don't think it's from the scotch. Is it ridiculous that I love how perfectly Genny fits in? It's like she belongs here. Belongs with my family. Belongs with me.

"Rumor has it," Hudson says, interrupting my daydreaming, "that you took Genevieve to the awards banquet the other night. Is that true?"

So that's what this is about.

I turn from the window to find him leaning against the desk. It's such a stance of authority, like he's a principal reprimanding a student.

I'm pretty sure that's how he wants me to feel—like I've been sent to the principal's office.

It makes me want to do what I did every time I found myself there growing up—roll my eyes.

I take a long sip from my glass to rein in my irritation. "It's really not how it looks. You told me not to bring a plus one, and I didn't. I ran into her there, and she had a sort of mix-up and didn't have a ticket, so I said she could take my extra spot. And it was fine because guess who else was seated at our table?"

Hudson shrugs, sets his glass down and folds his arms across his chest, waiting for me to tell him.

"Edward Fasbender and his son Hagan. How the hell did you expect me to feel out Nathan Murphy with them at the same table?"

He's surprised by this information. "They were? Well, damn. What are the odds?"

"Whatever the odds, it happened. But I did my job and found out—subtly, don't worry—that Nathan is indeed interested in running Werner Media. You should give him a call for a meeting. I'd like to be there for it, please."

And now that I've given him what *he* wanted, it's time to ask for what *I* want. "While you're setting up meetings, set one up with Genevieve. I'd like to be at that one too."

"Genevieve?" His forehead wrinkles with confusion.

"Yes. She's young, I know, but she has some great ideas and you should really hear her out."

"You want me to talk to Genevieve Fasbender. About Werner Media."

It sounds like a statement instead of a question, but I confirm anyway. "Yes. I do. She's brilliant. She's a grand-scheme kind of thinker. More aware of the current market than her brother, that's for sure. Completely on top of her game."

"Jesus," my brother mutters, "you're gushing."

He's mocking me, but that's all the invitation I need. I hadn't realized how much I'd been dying to talk to someone about my feelings. Next thing I know, I'm sitting in the window seat, spilling my guts. "I'm in love with her, Hudson. I think she might be the one."

"Please," Hudson says dismissively. "You're not in love with her. You just met her."

"What does that matter? Aren't you the guy who moved his girlfriend-slash-future wife in after two weeks of knowing her?" He doesn't show it, but I have a feeling that down deep he's romantic. Why else would he let things happen so quickly?

But if he *is* romantic deep down, he's not letting me be privy to it. Instead, he's giving me brusque and snippy. "I'd known her longer than two weeks."

"Sorry, two and a half." Honestly, I don't know exactly when he'd met Alayna, but it was fast. He's definitely not one to talk.

But he does anyway. "Don't compare your relationship with this, this…girl to my relationship with my *wife*. It's not the same."

Okay, despite our differences, I was ready to open up and share everything, but now I'm pissed.

"Who the hell are you to decide that?" I stand and point a finger at him. "Maybe it's exactly the same. Maybe this is the beginning of exactly what you have with your wife. You don't know how deeply I feel about Genny. I'm in love with her, and just maybe I'm going to marry her."

Hudson picks up his drink and finishes the contents in one swallow. Then he slams the empty glass on the desk next to him. "You cannot marry that woman. I forbid it."

Like hell. "You can't forbid shit."

"I can tell you that if you put a ring on that finger, you and her family will be banned from coming anywhere near my family again."

I'm speechless. My brother has always been a bit aloof, and he's more often than not a pain in my ass, but he's never been downright shitty. I don't understand this, don't have any idea where it's coming from, and the only comeback I can manage is the most obvious one. "What is your fucking problem?"

"Her family!"

"I know that you're not fond of Edward Fasbender, but so what?" Even if he doesn't end up giving the man a job, it shouldn't have anything to do with what happens between Genny and me.

"It's not her father I have a problem with," Hudson snaps back, his hands wrapped around the edge of the desk behind him. "It's his wife."

I don't say it, but I give him the look that says, and *what's your deal with her?*

Hudson's eyes widen with realization. "You don't know, do you?"

"Know what?"

"That girl you're so fond of? Her stepmother is Celia Werner."

CHAPTER FIFTEEN

I know Hudson has beef with Celia Werner, but I'm perplexed and still trying to piece together all the reasons this affects my relationship with Genny when I hear Laynie at the door.

"Celia's back?" she says, holding one of the babies and looking paler than I've ever seen her.

Hudson winces, and I know he regrets that his wife overheard this bit of news. Seems Mina isn't the only one who needs to learn about privacy. Hudson did leave the door open. I feel less bad about forgetting the bedroom lock now.

He recovers quickly and rushes toward Alayna. "Millie?" he calls out into the hallway. "Could you take Holden for a bit, please?"

"Gladly!" Millie steps in and scoops the baby from Laynie's arms then quickly disappears, humming as she goes.

Hudson shuts the door after her. A little late for that, isn't it?

"Celia's back," Laynie repeats, drawing the attention back to the issue at hand.

Hudson puts his arms around his wife and looks her in the eye. "She's not back, precious. I will not let her be back; do you understand?"

"But she's that girl's stepmother? I thought Genevieve was someone you met from work," she directs to me. Then back to Hudson, "She got to us through Chandler?"

I frown, irritated at what my sister-in-law is inferring.

"She *hasn't* gotten to us," Hudson says. "And Celia is *not* back. That's the point. She's exactly where she's always been, and we've been fine. I won't let her get any closer to this family than she already is."

He throws a glare in my direction at that last part. Then he walks Laynie to the couch. He holds her as they sit down together, delivering reassurance. It's sweet. It's the kind of relationship I want with my wife one day, and I can't help that I see Genny in that position now more than ever.

So while I hate to interrupt this private moment, it seems *our* private moment was the one interrupted first. "Hold up, Hudson. You're talking about Celia. That has nothing to do with Genevieve."

"It has *everything* to do with Genevieve," he sneers. "Anyone who has any association with Celia should be considered a threat. That's how Celia works."

"Wait. Back up," Laynie says, putting a calming hand on Hudson's thigh. "How did Genevieve meet Chandler in the first place?"

"I met her at a charity thing last week that I went to in Hudson's place. Her father is Edward Fasbender, and your husband wanted me to do some schmoozing."

Laynie's eyes widen and she whips her head back toward my brother. "You sent Chandler to get close to Celia's husband?"

"No. That's not why I sent Chandler there. I wanted him to send a message. Prove to Celia that I still have eyes on her and her family, in case she was at the event."

"Would have been nice if someone had told me!" Now I understand why I needed the scotch. I throw back the rest of the drink then put the empty glass on the bar.

Alayna ignores me. "Well, your plan backfired, H, because now Celia's here. Practically in our own house!"

Much as I like to hear her scolding Hudson, I'm not at all about to stand by the allusion that my girlfriend—yes, I'm calling her that—is merely an extension of someone they think is not a good person. "You're overreacting," I say, trying not to overreact myself.

Hudson jumps to his feet and faces me. "Do I need to tell you the things she's done? Not just to other people, but what she's done to us? She blackmailed me. She's threatened us. She tried to get me to put Alayna in a mental hospital. This is not behavior I take lightly."

Um, damn. A lot more serious than I'd imagined.

"I'm not taking it lightly, either." And I'm not, now that I know about it, that is. "But if it was so terrible, why didn't you have her arrested?"

He looks back at his wife before answering. "It's complicated. Mostly because there wasn't enough evidence to charge her. But other reasons too." Other reasons that I sense might not shed too favorable of a light on my brother.

I know him well enough to know he's not going to give more explanation than that. So I don't pursue it.

Instead, I address the more important matter. "She's done nothing to you in years, though. Right? Because you…" *Because he took over control of Werner Media.* But now Warren is retiring and that leaves Hudson without any leverage. Which was a problem on its own, but now…if the Accelecom merger takes place, Hudson will essentially be handing the company back over to the Werners by giving it to Celia's husband.

Hudson studies me. "You're working it all out now, I see."

"That's why you aren't interested in giving the job to Edward Fasbender." Fuck. There goes Genny's chances for her dream job.

Yeah, I probably should have worked out that her chances were shot before this. It's not that I'm slow—it's that I'm hopeful. Or, I was.

The way the picture is being presented now, my hope has pretty much evaporated.

Hudson takes advantage of my epiphany and proceeds to back it up. "There is no telling how that woman might plan to destroy us. What she could do to our business. Our income. Our family. Through her husband. I do not want that man or his wife or anyone connected to her anywhere near my family. And if I had known you were bringing *her* this weekend— " he enunciates the word *her*, as though Genny is something awful or disgusting "—then I would have considered banning you from the premises."

I let out a laugh because he can't be serious. "Like hell you would. You're the oldest, Hudson, but this isn't even your property."

"You're right. I don't own Mabel Shores. But Mom and

Dad are on my side where Celia is concerned, so like hell we wouldn't."

It's a loaded statement, one that proves I've been the only one in the dark. Just like always, Hudson is the one in the know, the one adored and respected. The one who rules the roost.

My anger increases sharply. I bolt out of my seat. "That's not fair, you know. None of this. Genevieve had no hand in deciding whom her father married, and yet she gets to be punished for it? No. Not fair."

"Doesn't matter if you think it's fair." He shrugs like it's no big deal, and I swear I've never wanted to sock him as much as I want to right now. "If you continue to associate with her then consider yourself out with us."

I feel my fists tightening at my side, but I'm too struck by his latest remark, the implications hitting me in the gut. "What exactly are you saying?"

"I'm saying that we will keep our distance from Celia in every way we can."

"You mean distancing yourself from me. Because the girl I'm in love with is related *by marriage* to someone you dislike." I'm seconds from going full-out Hulk on him, but I know the weapon to use with my brother is control, so I rein it in.

"If it were just the matter that Genevieve was associated with someone I dislike, we wouldn't be having this conversation. It's much bigger than that."

That's it. I'm furious. So much for control.

"Well, fuck that," I shout. "And fuck you. If you're making me choose—"

"I'm not making you choose—I'm forbidding you to be involved with that girl."

What the actual fuck?

"Are you even listening to yourself? You can't forbid me to be involved with her. I'm a grown man, and you're not my parent, or even my boss. You're my business partner and my brother and neither of those positions gives you any authority over my love life."

"You are my family," Hudson says, pointing an authoritative finger in my direction, "and as I said, I will do what I have to do to protect *every member* of my family from falling into one of her games. That includes you. And I'm telling you that you need to seriously consider the motives of this girl's involvement with you."

I shake my head. I'm at a loss. Hudson is treating me like I'm a teenager who's frustrated that his car keys have been taken away for the weekend. Does he really believe that I'm not capable of looking after myself?

And his latest insinuation is the worst. "Are you suggesting that she's only with me to get to you?" Ironically, Genny half-admitted to going home with me that first night because of who I am and what a relationship with me would gain for her father.

But then she tried to distance herself from me for exactly the same reason.

So I hear him, but I'm not buying what he's saying. "She's not with me because of you, Hudson. She's with me *despite* you."

His eyes narrow. "Are you so sure about that? Is that what she's told you? Why *is* she with you?" He's calm in his questions. Reasonable. "It seems awfully convenient how the two of you continually cross paths, doesn't it? How you didn't know who her stepmother was. How she shows up at your office. At your dinner meetings. Awfully convenient."

In a matter of seconds, I replay our entire relationship. That night at the gala, had she been interested before I gave her my name? Then, it was her who'd shown up at the office. She'd shown up at the dinner. Are there reasons to suspect she'd been after me, despite the times she's made me chase her? "You think she's playing me. For Celia."

"I'd bet on it."

No. I won't believe it. I had to fight for her interest. And the chemistry between us is legit—I'm sure of it.

"You're a conceited asshole," I tell my brother. "You know that? I try to tell you about the girl I'm in love with and you immediately make it all about you."

"I'm not making this about anyone. I'm telling you that if you continue to spend time with that woman and her family, there will not be a place for you anywhere near us." He turns away from me to retrieve his tumbler and carries it to the bar, leaving it right side up to indicate it's been used. He's done with me. Done with this conversation.

"Asshole is too good of a word for you." I start for the door when Alayna speaks up behind me.

"You're right, Chandler."

I turn back to her, relieved someone's talking sense, and though I don't look at him, I feel Hudson's attention is equally directed at his wife.

"It's not fair," she continues. "This poor innocent girl is caught up in the middle of something bigger, and placing judgment on her for something completely out of her control is a pile of shit. I'm always the first one to give a person the benefit of the doubt. We're all slaves to our weaknesses, but we also have a great amount of strength and resilience. It's very possible that Celia is no longer interested in harassing us. It's also possible that Genevieve is simply a woman who sees the incredible man you are. Who wouldn't be with you? Why wouldn't any girl fall head over heels for you?"

Have I mentioned I've always liked Laynie? And not just because she's hot. Right now I could kiss her.

"Thank you," I tell her. "Now that's the most sensible thing I've heard since I was brought in here."

"You're welcome, but I'm not done. See, with Celia Werner," Laynie's eyes are sympathetic as she looks at me, "you can't take any chances. She'll take advantage of anyone and everyone. She'll play very deep, manipulative games, and her pawns rarely know they're playing into her hands. So I'm sorry, but Hudson's right too. It was bad enough when it was just H and me that she terrorized. Now we have the children to think about. If there's any reason to believe that Celia has influenced Genevieve—and I'm afraid there is—then I have to do what's best for my family."

Of everything that's been said in the last half an hour, these are the words with the most impact. "Laynie. You know I love those kids more than almost anyone. I'd do nothing to bring them pain, and I'm telling you, Genny is a good person."

She smiles, and I can see that, despite her exhaustion, she's got her head on straight. She knows what she's saying. "And Mina adores you to the moon and back. As for Genny, she might very well be the most decent person on this earth. I feel sorry for her. If she's involved in a Celia scheme at all,

I'm sure she's being manipulated or bullied into her actions. Which makes me sorry for you too."

"I don't need your pity," I say, harsher than I mean to.

"You don't need pity," Hudson agrees. "You need our wisdom. Alayna and I are telling you from experience that you need to run while you can."

I shake my head again, as though it will block out the words he's saying. The thing is—he's an asshole. I'm convinced of that in this moment. But on the other hand, he's never done anything like this to me before. Laynie's definitely never been against me like this. Until now, I've trusted them both with my life. Even when he's been irritating, I've never had a reason to believe Hudson was against me.

I just…I don't want it to be true.

"You're wrong. What's going on between Genny and me is real. She tried to push me away. I'm the one who pursued her. I'm the one…" But the doubts are creeping in like thick fog. Is this why she's letting me help her when she wants to do everything on her own?

Hudson steps toward me and puts a hand on my shoulder. "I've done everything I can to protect my family from falling victim to her schemes." His voice is low and gruff, his eyes locked on mine, and I know when he says *family* right now he means *me* too. "Don't make the same mistakes I have. Please."

It's the closest I've felt to Hudson in a long time—here in this moment as the life I'd envisioned for myself falls apart. Why does Genny really have Pierce Industries financial reports in her suitcase? Who is she planning to share them with? And why was she was messing with my phone that night at her hotel? Was she looking for something? Did she find it?

And what pictures would *I* find if I looked on *her* phone? Is it really possible that she's only here because she's acting as a spy for Celia?

"You're wrong," I say again, shrugging out of Hudson's grip.

Only problem is, I'm not a hundred percent sure I believe that.

Chapter Sixteen

Remember when I said I fall in love fast?

Well, I also act fast. Too fast sometimes. Often I start moving before my brain can fully process if it's a good idea.

Like now.

I'm pedal to the metal the way I storm out of the study and up the stairs to our bedroom. I don't know what I'm looking for. Standing in the doorway, I scan the room for something—anything—that will prove Hudson's suspicions are out of place. My eyes land on her phone by the bedside table.

I'm not proud to say I don't even hesitate. I don't second-guess. I snatch it up and pray there's no security code set on it.

There's not.

Would someone who was trying to fuck me over be so trusting?

There's only one way to know.

I search frantically through her email—mostly related to Accelecom business. And her photos—there are several of the kids from the day before and even a few of me I hadn't seen her snap. Then her texts.

And that's where I find it—a text sent this morning to a number with no contact name. The message includes nothing but a close-up picture of Mina.

Fuck.

My face heats as my blood turns hot. There goes Gwen's notion that Genny was collecting memories. There is no good reason my date can possibly give for sending pics of my three-year-old niece to some rando number.

Hudson's right.

He has to be.

That's the most obvious conclusion. If there are any others, I don't wait to consider them. With a burst of righteous determination, I toss her phone onto the bed and rush down to the patio. I'm full-on action, my head still trying to fit everything together, and even though I know I should pause to think this through, I can't stop myself from marching up to where Genevieve is sitting next to Mirabelle and asking point-blank, "Why are you with me?"

Everyone goes suddenly quiet around her, forks frozen in the air, mouths half-open.

I ignore them all, their figures blurring in my periphery as I focus only on Genny, whose brows are perked in astonishment. "What?"

"Why are you with me?" I ask again. My tone, my posture, everything about the way I'm speaking to her is aggressive. Mean. Hurtful.

But I'm hurting so fucking bad right now that everything that comes off of me is poison and sharp.

Her cheeks flush as she gives me a tight smile. "I'm not sure this is the best place to discuss this."

My mother, in typical Sophia Pierce fashion, pipes in. "Chandler, leave your lovers' spats to—"

I raise my voice over hers, still addressing no one but Genny. "Is it because of your stepmother? Is she the reason? Did Celia tell you to worm into my life, and in exchange, you'll get your dream job at Werner Media?"

"Celia?" my mother and Mira say in stereo.

Genny drops her napkin onto her plate and scoots her chair out. "Excuse me," she mumbles politely to my family before standing and walking away.

Yeah, maybe it is best to continue this elsewhere.

I follow her into the house, dead on her heels. "Did she tell you to play hard-to-get? Huh? Then I'd never suspect a thing. It would be *me* pursuing *you*. Brilliant thinking, actually." I feel the bite of my words as they shoot from my tongue. "Was that your idea or hers?"

She spins around suddenly to face me, and she looks so betrayed that it punches me in the gut. "I do not like the way you are speaking to me. It's embarrassing and mean, and I don't have to stand for it."

But even though I see her pain, it's not as vibrant as what I'm feeling. I pause only a beat before my next attack. "You can't even answer me, can you?"

"What?" She throws her hands up. "What do you want to hear? That Celia is my stepmother? Yes, she is. Is that a problem? All this talk about worming into your life and blaming her—I don't know what to even say to that. Where the fuck did it come from?"

I glance behind her to Hudson standing in the hall

outside the kitchen. He frowns sympathetically then turns to leave, giving us privacy.

Genny traces my gaze with her eyes, catching sight of Hudson as he walks away. When she looks back at me, her expression is pinched. "What did your brother say to you?"

I fold my arms over my chest. "He simply told me I needed to look harder at the situation, and I am. And you know what it looks like? Like you're sidling up to me for your own benefit."

Her hands tighten into balls at her sides as she fumes. If she were a cartoon, there'd be smoke coming out of her ears. She opens her mouth to say something. Closes it. Then opens it again. "Sod off," she says finally before twirling away from me.

I trod after her, stopping at the foot of the stairs when she turns to go up them. "Where are you going?"

She keeps climbing as she speaks. "I'm going to pack my bag, and then I'm calling a taxi. I'm not going to stay here and be belittled and interrogated when I've done nothing wrong." She curses under her breath. "I knew I should have stayed away from you. I *knew* it."

"That's good. Playing the part through to the end. Really good." I'm frustrated and mad. About everything, but right at this moment, I'm especially pissed that she's leaving in the middle of this fight.

At the top of the staircase, she swivels to face me. "I'm not playing at anything, you shithead. You're breaking my heart." Her voice cracks, and god, her expression… She's so crushed, so defeated, and suddenly it occurs to me that she's not just walking away from this fight—she's walking away period.

Somehow I didn't predict this outcome.

My lungs suddenly feel empty. I wish I could draw her into my arms and make that look go away. This isn't what I wanted. This isn't how I wanted this to go.

I put my foot on the bottom step, ready to come up after her, but she puts her hand up in the air to stop me. "I don't want to talk to you anymore. Don't follow me."

My stomach sinks. I'm frozen in place while I watch her disappear down the upper hallway.

Once she's out of sight, I bring my fist to my forehead and bang it a few times. My brain is going through thoughts at light speed, and I'm only sure of one thing—I did not handle that well.

Desperate for a redo, I start up the stairs despite her request not to follow her. Halfway up I decide I should probably think things through a little before I talk to her again, so I go back down. Anxious adrenaline runs through me, and I pace the front foyer, trying to figure where to begin sorting out the jumble of facts rattling in my brain. She didn't deny it. That's got to be telling.

On the other hand, her expression, the way her voice cracked…

I'm so wrapped up in my head, I don't notice Mira behind me, and I bump smack into her on one of my turns. "Chandler Aaron Pierce, what the hell was that?"

Yeah, I was just asking myself the same question.

I scrub my hand over my face. "I, uh, really don't know."

"Do you want to explain what you *do* know?"

Not really.

Maybe.

Actually, this is good. Mira can help me put things in perspective. Just…where to start?

I settle on the revelation behind today's turn of events. "So, Celia Werner is Genevieve's stepmother, and—"

Mira shakes her head. "That's not good."

…and I guess I don't have to explain the significance of that. Of course I don't. "I was literally the only person in the dark about her being the family's archnemesis, wasn't I?"

"Well…" She shrugs guiltily then quickly recovers her annoyance. "But that doesn't explain why you were a total douche to that poor girl. You were terrible to her. In front of everyone!"

I'm about to defend myself when I remember the look on her face when she was standing at the top of the stairs. *"You're breaking my heart."*

"God, I was. I know I was." I cup my hands over my mouth and blow into them like they're a paper bag. "I don't know what I'm doing anymore, Mira." I drop my arms to my sides. "I don't fucking have a clue."

"Oh, Chandler." She reaches up to rough my hair then sweeps her palm around to cradle my cheek. "Love does that to a person."

"How did you…?" The only person I've declared anything to was Hudson, and he hasn't had time to tell anyone.

Mira rolls her eyes. "It's freaking obvious. You're head over heels, aren't you?"

I nod. I am totally head over heels. I'm so head over heels that I'm pretty sure my brain's in my ass. No matter what Genny's done or what game she might be playing, my feelings are the same. And what kind of a fucktard would talk to the woman he loved like I talked to her?

"Yes," Mira says, guessing at my thoughts, "you were a total prick. Now go fix it."

I want to. I want to take everything back and beg Genny to forgive me for being an asshole, except there's still that one issue. "I can't. She's spying on the family for Celia."

Mira wrinkles her face in disbelief. "She is? No way. Are you sure?"

"I think so?" I don't know what I think, honestly.

But those pics on her phone and the word of my brother... "There are reasons to believe she might be. Hudson thinks so."

"Does Hudson *know* or just *suspect*?" She doesn't wait for my answer. "Did you actually ask her?"

"Uh..." I sort of asked her. It's what I meant when I asked why she was with me. But I didn't ask her directly about the pictures or the business files, which, now that Mira mentions it, sounds like probably a better move. "Not really."

With surprising force for her petite frame, she punches me in the shoulder. "You idiot! She at least deserves a chance to explain, don't you think? Instead of you just jumping to conclusions. Seriously, between you and Hudson..."

She trails off as Genny appears at the top of the steps with her overnight bag in hand.

"There she is," Mira whispers loudly. "Go fix it."

"But I—"

She pushes me toward the staircase. "Go!"

When I glance behind me, Mira's already darted out of the foyer.

Great. I still haven't had a chance to work out what to say. This is going to work out real well.

But I don't want things to end like this, so with a deep breath, I rush toward Genny as she descends the stairs. "Wait, Genevieve."

Without looking at me, she brushes past.

"Stop, please. Let's talk about this, okay?"

She ignores me, making a beeline for the front door.

"Stop!" I shout again. This time when she doesn't, I reach out, grab her elbow and turn her around to face me. Just like the night before.

And like she did the night before, she slaps me. Hard. Harder than last night. Hard enough that I'm not sure there won't be a mark.

Possibly, it's a warning.

Except, okay, I'm a dog. I'm easily trained. And maybe not the best move, but the way this scenario usually works out between us is I get forceful, and she's into it.

So I pull her to me and crush my mouth to hers. I'm eager and invasive, my hand pressed behind her neck to hold her in place. And she opens for me, meets my tongue, lets me in.

Then, suddenly, she shoves me away. "No. Stop." She locks eyes with mine, and it hurts worse than the slap when she says again, "I want you to stop."

My insides feel like I'm caught in a giant squeeze-press.

I step toward her. She steps back.

I reach my hand out. She shakes her head.

Studying her face now, I see that her eyes and nose are red, and since I highly doubt she was upstairs snorting coke, I can only guess she's been crying.

"Genevieve…" I don't recognize the smallness of my voice. "I'm sorry. I overreacted. Can we talk about this?"

She continues to shake her head. "What exactly do you want me to say?"

Right. That. "I don't know. You could start by explaining why you have business files for Pierce Industries."

For a second I think she won't respond, but then she says, "So I could be prepared when I talked to your brother, you jerk. Hudson gave them to my father."

Ah. Well. That is reasonable. But… "What about the pictures of my nieces on your phone? Who did you text those image files to?"

Her face goes white as her jaw drops in astonishment. "You went through my phone?"

"No. I…" Yes. The answer is *yes*. Totally the wrong thing, yet I try to defend myself. "You left it on the dresser."

"That doesn't give you the right to go snooping through it!"

"I wasn't trying to snoop. I was trying to find answers."

"You could have just *asked*." Funny, that's what Mira said.

"Fine. Are you spying on us for Celia?"

Immediately, I know it's another wrong thing. Genny's expression goes from mortified to indignant. Her mouth clamps tight, and she whirls away from me, headed toward the door.

I trip after her. "You told me to ask!"

"I didn't think you'd have to."

Her hand is on the knob when I run ahead and place my weight on the door, blocking her from leaving. "I'm sorry. You're right. I shouldn't have asked." Right now I'll do anything to get her to stay and talk to me.

She pulls on the knob, but I'm not ready to let her go. "What can I say to make this better?"

With a sigh, she drops her hand and hangs her head. "It doesn't even matter."

"It doesn't?" Because I'm an idiot, I perk up, hopeful.

"There's no reason to care anymore. It's pointless. If your brother told you this shit, there's no way he's going to strike a deal with Accelecom, and I'm not going to begin to try to figure out what bad blood there is between him and Celia because it's not my place, but I'm sensible enough to see where I'm not wanted."

I can't stand it. I don't care what proof there is against her or what the possibility might be that she's working against our family. My gut says she's innocent. My gut says she's really hurting, and I. Can't. Stand. It.

With a bang of my fist against the door, I say, "You know what? Fuck Hudson. I don't care what he wants."

Genevieve brings her eyes up to meet mine. "I wasn't talking about your brother."

Knife, meet heart. "Genny, no. I want you." I'm practically begging. "I want you so much. You have to believe me."

She raises a brow. "Like you believed me?"

And the knife twists.

I open my mouth, but what can I say? She's right. I didn't believe her.

"Yeah, that's what I thought."

This time when she tries the knob, I let her leave. There's nothing else to do. Her cab is already pulling into the drive, and I can't keep her when she doesn't want to be here. When I've given her no reason to stay.

I watch after her car until the taillights have disappeared down the drive, my emotions twisting and building into a hurricane of despair. Once she's out of sight, I take off in search of Hudson.

I find him alone in the study.

"This is your fault," I say, pointing an angry finger at him. "I was happy. You ruined everything."

His jaw twitches and his mouth tightens. "If you want to blame anyone, blame Celia."

Sure. That's easiest. Blame Celia.

But I know deep down the only person to blame for Genevieve leaving is me.

CHAPTER SEVENTEEN

The next day, I lie on the floor, my feet propped on the playroom wall, and with my hands over my heart, I let out a moan.

Mina looks up from the castle she's building with big block Legos and frowns. "Does your head hurt, Uncle Chandler?"

"No, no." I rub at my sternum with my knuckles. "My chest. My chest hurts."

Arin removes the clip she's placed in my hair and refastens it. She's sitting above my head so she's upside down when she peers over me. "Did you get hit with something sharp?"

"I did. Very sharp." That's a popular analogy about love, isn't it? That it's beautiful but thorny like a rose?

I still can't believe she left like she did.

For the millionth time, I replay the scene with Genevieve from the day before. She hurt me pretty damn good. But if I'm honest, I wasn't really very nice myself. "Actually,"

I correct, "I was the something sharp." Sharp tongue, sharp accusations.

After the way I talked to her, no wonder she's gone.

I moan again.

"I did everything wrong, guys. All wrong." I'd spent the previous day mad—mad at Genevieve for leaving, mad at her lack of answers, mad at what I was absolutely sure she'd done. *Fuck her* was my mantra by bedtime. Fuck her.

Today, the anger has worn off and the regret has seeped in.

Fuck her, but fuck me too.

With my fingers, I tick off my offenses. "I shouldn't have snooped. I should have asked her directly. Not in front of everyone. I reacted too quickly. And based on *her* reaction to *my* reaction, I think it's possible I was wrong about what I reacted to in the first place."

That's my emotions talking. I *want* to be wrong.

"Except, I'm not wrong. She texted those pictures. Why else would a person do that?"

"I like to take pictures," Arin says. Picking up a toy block, she puts it up to one eye and pretends to click. "Smile, Uncle Chandler!"

I pose for the fake camera, but my smile quickly fades. Everything feels wrong. Everything feels terrible. Everything feels pointless.

And nothing makes sense.

"Do you know I actually had to convince her to date me? That's the first time that's happened in, like, ever." I suggested she played aloof on purpose, but how could she really know that would work? "She didn't even want to come here. She was worried she'd be intruding on the family gathering, and I had to assure her it would be fine. I was wrong. Obviously."

I sit up to look at my younger niece. "I'm not blaming your father for this, Mina. I could. But he's not the bad guy in my story." I said I blamed him, but I can't. I know Hudson's just looking out for his wife and kids. Looking out for me.

I lay my head back down. "Frankly, though, neither is Celia. She's never done anything to me. I barely know the woman. Why would I be wrapped up in her Hudson drama?" Maybe she's the bad guy in his story, but in mine? In mine, I'm the bad guy.

At least, I feel like the bad guy.

Unless Genevieve is the bad guy. My head says it's a very likely possibility.

My heart feels quite differently.

My heart remembers how she felt in my arms. How she melted into me when we kissed. *This is fast*, she said, and it felt like she meant it.

"That's the worst thing," I say, working through the pit of despair out loud. "I think she might really love me too. The first woman who falls when I do, and I go and f—, uh, muck things up. I mean, she was perfect. We were perfect together. The way we bantered. Our career interests melded. We had similar family backgrounds. And the se—" I catch myself before finishing the s-word. "Well, anyway. You know what I mean. Or you *don't* know what I mean, but one day you will. The point is, she liked me and I liked her and things were good."

That's the part that hurts most. Whether she was working on behalf of someone else or not—I think she actually did fall.

LAURELIN PAIGE

"And then I accused her of doing something terrible. Of *being* something terrible." Which if she didn't do anything, well…then I'm a total ass.

I moan again.

I'm miserable.

I'm pathetic.

I'm *heartbroken*.

Mina crawls over to me and puts her hand on my cheek. "It's okay to make mistakes, Uncle Chandler. You just have to say you're sorry."

"I think it will take more than an apology to fix this."

And then there's Hudson.

Even if Genny is innocent, even if I could convince her to give me another chance, how could I convince him not to cut us off from his little family?

It doesn't matter anyway because she's *not* innocent. Probably.

The door to the playroom opens suddenly, startling me. I turn to see Laynie standing in the doorframe.

Mina runs to her. "Mommy!"

Laynie bends to pick up her daughter then narrows her gaze in my direction. "Are you really spilling your woes to the children?"

"Um…maybe?"

She nods toward the device on the shelf that looks like a walkie-talkie. "The monitor is on. I heard every word."

I resist the urge to let out another moan. "I'm sorry. Did I say anything inappropriate?"

"No." She sets Mina down to resume playing and perches on the arm of the child-size loveseat. "You just made me feel extremely guilty."

"Guilty?" I sit up, shifting my back to the wall so I can face her. "Why?"

My sister-in-law lets out a sigh. "Because I encouraged you to believe the worst about Genny. Or to believe the worst was a possibility, and I didn't think about the way you feel about her. I'm the one who should be saying I'm sorry."

I scoff. "You shouldn't be sorry. I should be sorry. For bringing her into your life."

Laynie shakes her head. "You couldn't have known."

"I should have known. I should have seen the signs. Because there *were* signs that something might be up. I didn't want to see them."

She tilts her head at me, her eyes searching. "But do you love her?"

"Yes. Yes, I do. I'm so in love with her." It hurts more every time I say it. "And I think she's in love with me. I don't know what part in our relationship Celia played, but I know how we feel is real. How *I* feel is, anyway. And now I've screwed it up too much to know for sure how she really feels or what she did. Not that it matters since Hudson's made it clear that I have to choose between you guys or her." I look at my nieces playing. "I could never choose to lose this."

"I know. I know." Her face is somber as she considers for a beat. "I think Hudson and I both forgot something important, though."

I perk up. "What's that?"

"That people can change. Especially when they're loved. H and I really should know that better than anyone."

I have a feeling she's talking about something personal, but all I care about is what she's saying about Genny and me.

I sit forward. "You mean…even if she did get close to me because of Celia—"

Laynie cuts me off. "I mean that whatever point she started at, she could have had a change of heart."

I'd thought the same, but Laynie saying it now gives me permission to dwell on it. What if she did start out as Celia's spy, fell in love, and then didn't want to go through with it? It would explain why she looked so hurt, and maybe why she left so hastily. She might have felt too guilty to discuss it.

I wish she would have, though. I probably would have forgiven her.

That thought hits me hard. I definitely would have forgiven her. Which means, I *do* forgive her. Because whether or not she loves me, I love her. And since I am the one thing I can control, all that matters is how I feel. What I do.

"So what do I do now?" I ask Laynie since I for shit don't know.

"I'm probably going to regret saying this, but," she takes a deep breath before continuing. "Forget about Hudson's ultimatum. Go after what you love. I'll, for one, support you. It might take time, but I can work on my husband."

I shake my head. "You can't do that for me. I don't want to cause tension in your marriage."

"Don't worry about us. We've overcome worse."

For half a second I'm hopeful. Like maybe this could actually work out, and I could win the girl back.

Then I remember there's more to the problem. "That's sweet of you, Laynie, but it's a no go. She'll be leaving the country now that the Accelecom merger has fallen through. The only way to keep her here would be…" I trail off as an idea starts to form. A long shot of an idea, but an idea nonetheless.

I stand up abruptly, almost knocking over a tower of blocks next to me. "I think I know what I need to do." Not just because I want a chance to win her back, but because it's the thing that should have been done all along.

"That's the spirit!" Laynie exclaims. "Where are you going?"

I'm already halfway out the door, but I peek back in to answer her. "I have to get to town. There's a lot of work to do before we're back in the office tomorrow." As an afterthought, I run in and give her a giant hug. "Thank you, Laynie. You're a great sister."

In no time, I'm packed and on the road back to the city, my head working overtime as I try to tackle the details of the plan that's emerging.

Just one problem I can see at the moment—if this works out the way I want it to, I'm going to have to have Hudson on board.

Yeah. I know.

• • •

Tuesday after the holiday weekend, I'm in Hudson's office first thing. I enter through his lobby this time—I know when to have tact—but the door is open, and his secretary isn't at her desk so I breeze on in.

"Good morning, Trish," I say when I see her standing over my brother's desk, giving him a rundown of his day. "You're looking fabulous. New dress?"

She beams. "It's a new hairstyle. I wasn't so sure about it."

"It's absolutely perfect," I assure her, stalling before I have to address my brother.

I'll admit it—I'm nervous. I spent all of the night before gathering the information I need to make the proposal I'd like to make, and I've got a solid game plan. One that deserves to be heard.

Still, it's Hudson.

"You know," he says, acknowledging me without looking up from his paper, "it's customary for people to schedule meetings with my secretary instead of bursting in unannounced."

"Trish, can you add me to the agenda?" I glance over her shoulder and see that, fortunately for me, Hudson's calendar is clear until nine-thirty. "Just pencil me in right now. And hold all his calls, please."

Trish likes me, but she knows who pays her salary. "Mr. Pierce?" She raises a brow in my brother's direction.

Hudson concedes. "It's fine, Patricia. You may go."

I sink into the chair in front of him. "I guess it's too much to expect coffee," I say, causing Trish to halt on her way out of the room.

"He doesn't need anything," Hudson says, shooing her away. "If you want coffee, go bother your own secretary."

"Huh. What an idea. I'll try that sometime." Usually, I stop and grab coffee from Trish on my way down to my office, but that's not something he needs to know. "Anyway, the reason I'm here—"

"You've had second thoughts about Genevieve," he says, cutting me off. "Alayna told me."

"Really?" Man, that woman's fast. "What exactly did she say?"

"That you want to give her another chance."

"And you'll support that?" My heart thumps in my chest. This can't be that easy, can it?

"No. My position stands, same as before."

I throw my head back. "Come on, H. How can you be so stubborn about this?" Ten seconds into my proposal, and I'm already off script. Well, I've always been better at improvising. Might as well go with it. "Don't you believe that a person can change?"

"It's possible, yes—"

I clap my hands together. "Exactly! Then why can't you believe that Genevieve could change?"

"You believe she's changed? Then she admitted she was working for Celia in the first place?"

"No, she didn't. But if she *had* been working for Celia, isn't it possible that she could change her mind?"

"Celia doesn't let people out of her schemes." He sounds like he's speaking from experience.

"Maybe she doesn't. I don't know about that. But I do know how I feel about Genny. And I'm pretty sure she feels the same, no matter who she might have been working for."

"*Pretty sure* is not *knowing*," he says, straightening a pile of papers that doesn't need straightening.

I sigh. "You're right. It's not. But I love her. And I don't believe you can truly love a person without trust. So I'm choosing to trust her."

Something I've said catches his attention, and Hudson looks up at me.

I sit forward, taking advantage of his focus. "Okay, I know that you have reason to be skeptical where Celia is concerned, but from what I understand, you were once caught up in the same games she's in and look at you now. You aren't very forthcoming with your past, but let me guess that who you are today has every bit to do with being loved by Laynie. And I know she trusts you, heart and soul."

"I'd be nothing without Alayna," he says somberly. "And that's why I can't risk her for a woman you still know almost nothing about."

"I know enough. I've done my research. And you haven't even heard me out. I'm not asking for you to bring Genevieve into the family. I'm asking—"

Trish's voice cuts over the intercom. "Mr. Pierce, I'm sorry to interrupt, but you have a visitor that insists on seeing you right away."

"Tell him to make an appointment," Hudson responds.

But Trish continues. "It's not a him. It's Celia Werner-Fasbender."

CHAPTER EIGHTEEN

I stand up to block Hudson on his way to open the office door.

"I'm staying for this." Like hell am I missing a showdown between Celia and Hudson, and not just because of the entertainment value.

"This doesn't concern you."

He tries to take a step around me, but I put my hand on his shoulder. "It concerns me very much, thank you. You owe me this."

Hudson maintains eye contact for three full seconds before he shrugs me off. "We'll see," he mutters, and before I can talk to him any more about it, he's opening the door and stepping out into the lobby.

I hang back but stay close enough to see the perfectly coifed, blonde, blue-eyed woman waiting for him. She must be in her thirties now and is visibly pregnant, but she's as stunning and beautiful as I remember. Anyone with looks like hers is dangerous, no matter what her agenda is.

"Celia Werner." Hudson keeps his hands to himself, not offering any form of touch as a greeting. "I didn't expect I'd ever see you step foot in my offices again." It sounds like a threat and I'm pretty sure that's the way he means it.

Celia's lip curls up slightly. "Don't get your panties all twisted. This visit is harmless. And it's Werner-Fasbender now, which I'm sure you already know."

"Yes, I'd heard."

Silently, the two study each other. The animosity surrounding them is thick and noxious like pesticide, and I briefly consider ducking out of this reunion.

But only briefly. My curiosity wins out, and I stay.

It's Celia who breaks the standoff. "Are you going to keep me in your lobby all morning, or are you going to invite me in? I'll say what I have to say wherever. I just think you might prefer the privacy."

Hudson's eye twitches. "Very well. Come on in." He spins to lead her in then spots me. "Celia, I'm sure you remember my brother, Chandler."

"Of course I remember Chandler. My," she scans the length of my body, "you sure grew up."

In general, I enjoy being looked at like man candy. It's flattering. Even when the onlooker is more than ten years my senior and was once basically engaged to my older brother.

But I've learned too much about this particular onlooker and what she's done to Hudson, and maybe I'm more protective about my family than I realize, because instead of flattered, I feel hostile, and what I really want to do is tell her to fuck off.

Don't worry—I don't do it.

"It's good to see you again," I say icily, taking Hudson's lead and keeping my hands to myself. "It's been a while."

"Yes. I've kept my distance. Haven't I, Hudson?" She's trying to goad him, which only makes me more antagonistic.

Hudson is cooler. He responds with a tight smile and doesn't acknowledge whatever Celia's referring to. I have a feeling that's how most of this encounter is going to go.

It's about now that I expect to be dismissed. I can understand why Hudson doesn't want me around while she drags up their rocky past. But I was serious when I said I'm staying. I'm tired of being left in the dark, especially where my own business is concerned, and Hudson does owe me the chance to be part of it.

More importantly, though, I don't want to leave him alone with her. Not that he can't handle things by himself, I just don't want him to have to. I have a soft spot for the guy. Don't tell anyone.

So I'm sure to give him my *I'm not going anywhere* look when he glances over at me, a look that has never worked where my brother is concerned.

Which is why I'm surprised when he turns back to his guest and says, "Whatever you have to say, Celia, I hope you're comfortable stating it in front of Chandler because I'd like him to stay."

Sometimes, man. Sometimes that guy really comes through for me.

The grin I give is quite cocky. "You won't even know I'm around."

"Afraid to be alone with me, Huds? I suppose that's fair." Her cold smirk sends a chill running through me.

It's not something Hudson will put up with. Not on his

turf. With a no-nonsense attitude, he ignores her dig and asks point-blank, "Why are you here, Celia?"

"So we're jumping right in then. I suppose it was too much to expect we'd catch up first." I have a feeling that Hudson has kept close tabs on her. He doesn't need to catch up. "You've changed the décor," she adds, scanning the room in a way that feels possessive. "Not what I would have done, but I like it. It suits you."

I promised to be quiet, but I'm about ready to step in and tell her, *You don't know fuck about what suits my brother, lady.* Except even in my head it sounds lame.

Hudson's got a better instinct of how to handle the situation. "Why are you here?" he asks again in the authoritative tone he saves for the boardroom.

She lets out a melodramatic sigh. "Can we at least sit?"

Hudson rubs a hand over his chin. "Fine. Sit." He gestures toward the sofa then waits until she's sat before taking a seat in his armchair.

I perch on the arm of the loveseat, too anxious to really get comfortable. Somehow I manage to keep my foot from tapping a million beats a minute, but I'm not so sure I can say the same for my pulse.

Hudson remains stoic, and I wonder if he's as calm inside as he appears. "Out with it, Celia. We don't have all day."

With her back straight and her hands resting on her protruding belly, she finally answers. "I have a favor to ask."

Hudson literally laughs. "That's ballsy of you."

"Perhaps. Or perhaps I just know what to say to get your attention."

"You have my attention. But it's waning quickly." His

tone says he's seconds from throwing her out. The awesome thing about my brother is that he'd really do it.

Celia seems to know that as well as I do. "I know you aren't going to go through with the Accelecom merger."

"Did your stepdaughter tell you that?"

The hair stands up on my arms at the reference to Genny.

"Genevieve?" Celia asks, surprised. Surprised as in she hasn't heard shit from Genevieve.

It's possible Celia's just a remarkable actress, but I'm taking this as a good sign. Such a good sign that I can't keep my thoughts to myself any longer. "You aren't the reason she's gotten close to me, then? That wasn't your idea?"

Hudson frowns at my interruption, but he looks with me toward Celia for her answer.

Her brow furrows. "I didn't even realize you knew each other. Genevieve and I aren't particularly close. We definitely don't talk business. If you've already told her the merger was a no-go, she didn't pass it on to me or Edward."

It stings a bit that Genny hasn't talked about me, but it's also in line with what she's told me. She said she didn't want her father to know she was with me. It's possible this is all part of their story, and they've both talked at length.

I really don't think so, though. I don't want to think so.

"If Genevieve didn't tell you, then how did you know?" Hudson asks, resuming control of the conversation.

"I know there's no way you'd hand over the company to my husband. It would contradict the reasons that you bought it in the first place."

At least the lady isn't dumb.

Hudson raises an amused brow. "Let me guess—you're going to try to convince me to give him the job anyway."

"You really do have a bad taste in your mouth where I'm concerned, don't you? I hope you understand when I tell you I feel the same."

"That's fair."

If I hadn't realized it before, I do now—there is history between these two that I'm not privy to, and in some ways I understand better why Hudson was so concerned about Genevieve's presence in our lives. Understand why he'd immediately assume the worst.

I, however, am more convinced than ever that Genny is innocent. There's no way that she's mixed up in what Celia is dishing out. I feel it in my bones.

"In answer to your question," Celia says now, "no. I'm not here to convince you to give him the job. Frankly, I'm happy with our lives the way they are. I'm not interested in moving back to the States, and I'm especially not interested in that kind of move with a baby on the way."

"Then the favor you want is for me *not* to give the job to Edward." It's not stated as a question. More like a clarification.

"I didn't say that. Let's be clear—I'd love for Werner Media to be back in the hands of my family. I simply know that isn't an option on the table."

I'll say it again—the lady isn't dumb.

"Then what is it that you're asking?" Hudson's taken the words right out of my mouth.

"My father. This company is his pride and joy. His legacy. He wants Edward to take his place because he thinks it will make me happy, yes, but mostly because he thinks it will be good for Werner Media. He hasn't even considered giving the job to anyone else. You and I both know that you will give the job to someone else. I'm willing to help convince him that's best."

"If…what?"

I sit forward, on pins and needles waiting for her response.

"If you let him believe it's his idea."

…and I was not expecting that.

Neither was Hudson, it seems. "I'm not sure I understand." Yeah, neither am I.

"I'm saying go ahead and pick who you want to pick for the job—I know you have other names in mind. I'm confident that you'll select the best person to head Werner Media in the future—you'd never let a good business fail, no matter how you feel about me. It's not in you. I just want my father to believe the decision is still up to him. Let him leave his company in a dignified fashion. Let him think it's his creative vision he's implementing, not just yours."

And this is when I have to bite my tongue. Hard. Because this…I know how to do this.

"What a noble endeavor," Hudson says. "Unfortunately, I don't know how I would begin to convince your father of anything."

I shoot up to my feet. "I'll do it. I can do it." The tongue biting obviously didn't last long. "Get me a meeting with him, and I got this."

Hudson eyes me with half irritation, half intrigue. "Chandler?"

"The proposal I was telling you about." I hadn't actually gotten to any of it before Celia arrived, but I silently say a prayer he goes along with me on this. "I'm confident Warren will be interested in it. I just need to be able to present it to him. Thirty minutes. That's all." I'm eager, and it shows, but this is exactly what I needed to make this plan work.

Celia has also perked up from my enthusiasm. "I can arrange that. If Hudson agrees."

He studies her with an intentness that makes me feel like he can see right through her, can see every thought and motivation that might be behind her request.

But after several long beats, he seems unsatisfied with what he's gleaned. "I can't figure out what game you're playing," he says steadily.

"Maybe I'm not playing any game."

"Wouldn't that be the most conniving scheme of all?"

"Wouldn't it?"

They stare each other down yet again, and this time, something's shifted in the energy surrounding them. It's less pervasive. Less aggressive.

"Random acts of compassion aren't like you. Thinking of anyone else's feelings isn't either." Hudson's eyes widen slightly, as though he's just figured something out. "You fell in love."

For the first time since she's arrived, Celia appears thrown. Her mask slips for a split second, and underneath she appears to glow.

But she recovers quickly. "Do you want the meeting or not?"

"We'll take the meeting."

I practically sigh in relief. My head starts spinning with all the steps of what to do next. Not the least of which, win Genevieve over to this plan.

Hey, I didn't say this idea was easy, I just said it was good.

"Thank you, Hudson." And it actually sounds like it might be sincere.

Without further ado, she stands. "I'll make arrangements with your secretary. No need for us to have any further contact, as far as I'm concerned."

"I appreciate that."

She's almost halfway to the door when Hudson calls after her. "Celia," he says, waiting until she turns back to him to go on. "Congratulations on your pregnancy. I once thought you'd make a good mother."

She nods to the most recent family picture he's added to his bookshelf. "Congratulations on your own little family. I once thought you'd make a good dad."

"She's changed," Hudson says the minute the door shuts behind her.

"You mean you no longer believe that she sent Genevieve to spy on us?" I'm practically giddy with how this day is turning out. "See? People can change. It's all good now, right?"

"No, I still don't fucking trust her," Hudson says, heading to his desk.

My elation is quickly deflated. "Then why did—"

"I trust *you*."

Here's where my jaw drops. Figuratively. I wouldn't really let Hudson see my shock. That would be giving too much away.

He smiles as though he can read me anyway. "You said you could make this work, Chandler. I believe you can. Go do it, brother." He sits down and addresses his computer screen, dismissing me.

I kind of want to hug him right now, but since he isn't really the touchy-feely type, I settle on running over and giving him a noogie.

Yep. That definitely feels more appropriate.

CHAPTER NINETEEN

I spend the rest of the day finalizing my proposal for Warren Werner. There are financial reports to gather and contracts to look over. Then, after a late meeting with Nathan Murphy, I head over to Genevieve's hotel.

My stomach knots when she doesn't answer my knock, and I wonder jealously where she's at and who she's with. What if she's already checked out? What if she's headed back to London right now while I rap insistently on her door?

This room is the only connection I have to her, though, so I sit my ass down on the floor and wait.

It's nearly three hours later when I spot her coming down the hall with her father and Celia. She sees me instantly, and for a half a second, she appears to light up.

Just as quickly, her smile fades.

She leaves the others at a door a couple of rooms down and heads down to her own. Down to where I'm waiting.

"What are you doing here?" she asks when she's only an arm's length away, her tone even and unreadable.

God, I wish I had the courage to pull her into me. Wish I had the strength to never let her go again. "We need to talk."

"There's nothing to say."

"Yes, there is." I'm conscious of her father standing within earshot as he works the key to his room, but his presence doesn't stop me from saying what I need to say. "Like, I'm sorry."

She takes a breath in, but her gaze remains steady and aloof. "You said that already. I told you it didn't matter."

"That's a lie, and we both know it."

"Do you need me, princess?" Edward's still in the doorway to his room, Celia having disappeared inside.

For one bleak moment, I fear she'll say yes. That he'll have security called, and I'll be fighting two guards as they attempt to escort me out of the building.

Because I will fight. I'll fight tooth and nail.

But eventually she says, "No, Daddy. I can handle myself. Goodnight."

I'm relieved but still daunted. This is only the first step. There's two feet between where she stands and where I stand, and yet it feels like a giant chasm that I'll never be able to cross. The smell of her drifts across the distance. It's punishing how much it makes me miss her. Need her. And I know in this moment that the way I feel about her is different than how I've felt about anyone else before because, though I want her, I want her to be happy more.

So even though I'm desperate to beg for her love, I hold back. "Look, if you'd rather ignore everything personal between us, then I understand. I'm not here for that anyway."

"Then why are you here?" She flinches as she recognizes

the words I said to her when I attacked her at Mabel Shores. "Guess it's my turn to ask."

I came to tell you I love you.

Except I didn't. This isn't about me—it's about her. What she wants. What she needs. "I came to talk to you about business."

She rolls her eyes and turns to her door, pulling out her keycard. "The Accelecom/Werner Media merger is dead in the water."

"I know. I have another idea. A better idea." I have her attention. She hesitates, tapping her key against the metal frame instead of sliding it in the card reader. "Give me fifteen minutes." I'll take five if that's all she'll give. I'll take one and it will be the best minute of my life. "Please."

A few more taps, and she closes her palm around the card. "I'm not letting you in." She's referring to her room, but I can't help but think she's referring to more.

It makes my chest twist and ache. I knew a second chance with her was unlikely, but it hurts to be faced with the truth.

Still, it doesn't change that I love her, and even if I never say it, I want to give her this one thing. "We can go anywhere you want. You name the place."

Slowly, she turns back to face me. She bites her lip as she deliberates. After what seems like an eternity, she nods toward the room at the end of the hall. "This way. The Executive Lounge should be quiet at this time of day."

As she's predicted, the lounge is practically empty. A couple talks quietly in the corner. In the center of the room, a man in a suit works on his laptop, his headphones leaking strains of something heavy and metal.

She chooses a seat near the doors. "In case I need to escape," she says, and I'm glad she's able to joke until I look at her expression and realize she's not joking at all.

"You're perfectly safe. I promise." I won't touch her because that's not what she wants, but even as I pull out my reports from my briefcase, I remember the touch of her skin against mine. Can you blame me for brushing my hand against hers as I pass her a copy?

She shivers at the contact. Then she pulls her phone from her purse and swipes at the screen. "I'm setting an alarm. You've got fifteen. Better get started."

Twenty minutes later I've laid out the entire plan and still haven't been kicked to the curb. When her alarm went off, she stopped it without any excuses or commentary and slid her phone back in her purse, letting me finish. Now that I'm done, she sits back in her chair and puts the report that she's now studied scrupulously on the table between us.

"It's a good proposal," she says, unceremoniously. "If Warren doesn't go for it, he's a fool."

But does it make you happy? "It's not the scenario you'd hoped for."

"The scenario I'd hoped for was unrealistic, and to be honest, my father doesn't have the vision that Nathan Murphy has, according to what you've told me. This is a much better move." She studies her finger as she traces the edge of the papers in front of her. "It's my best shot at being involved with Werner Media, and I'm grateful."

I let out a breath, slowly, relieved that she's on board, but not wanting to let on *how* relieved. "It's the least I can do," I start to say.

But at the same time, she says, "Why are you doing

this?" Her brow is wrinkled, and her eyes scald me with their burning curiosity.

The heat behind her gaze is too hot, and I have to look away. "Lots of reasons, actually. It's the best move for Werner Media." I busy myself with putting my reports back in my briefcase. "It's the best move for Accelecom, in my opinion. It's a good move for Pierce Industries, an even better move for me. It's about time I take more of an active interest in the business."

"It is a very strategic move for your career."

"I think so."

She crosses her arms over her chest. "Why else are you doing this? Why are you doing this *for me*?" From the look on her face, I can tell I'm going to have to give her a lot more than this. I'm going to have to be a lot more vulnerable.

It's hard, but I force myself to meet her gaze. "Because no matter what I think I am or what I want to be, I'm still a nice guy at heart. And I haven't been very nice to you. I want to apologize for that, and this is the best way I know to do that."

Her features relax ever so slightly. "Then you don't think I'm a spy anymore?"

"No, I don't."

"What made you change your mind? Did you realize your brother really did give those financial reports to my father?" There's no malice in her questions. She simply wants to know.

I shake my head. "I didn't even ask. I decided I didn't need to. I decided I trusted you." She chuckles to herself, which was definitely not the reaction I was hoping for. "What's so funny?"

She shrugs, sobering. "I guess, nothing. Just. I didn't even defend myself. I ran. I'm exactly like my mother. How on earth can you trust someone who runs?"

There's an ache in her voice, and I want nothing but to erase it. Want to take the blame. I lean forward, reaching for her hand before I remember myself and rest mine between us. "Why wouldn't you run? I bullied you."

"You only asked me a question."

"I asked it in front of everyone." I cringe as I remember how shitty I was when I interrogated her. "It wasn't fair. And I was aggressive. I didn't provide a safe space to talk it through."

She lays her hands on the table. "I was afraid I'd answer, and you still wouldn't believe me."

"Then you didn't trust me either." Like her, I'm not being spiteful—I'm working it out.

"I wanted to. But everything was moving so fast. It felt like I was waiting for the other shoe to drop. When you said what you did, I thought, *well, that's about right.*"

"Maybe I felt a bit like that too." Or more than a bit. Wasn't that why I refused to acknowledge I was falling for her? Wasn't that why I was so eager to latch onto Hudson's accusations? It feels so good to admit it. It feels so good to admit all of it.

"I'm sorry I ran," she says.

"I'm sorry I accused."

"I didn't spy on you for my stepmother."

"I shouldn't have let you leave." I should never let her leave again.

Her hand is so close, and when I stretch my fingers out to brush against hers, she brushes back. Warmth shoots up my arm, spreading through me like lightning. Though I'm trying to stay focused on her needs, I'd hoped—of course, I'd hoped—that part of what she needed was me. Touching her like this, the yearning grows. I want her so fucking much. And she feels so within my grasp.

Then she says the words that kill everything. "Chandler, even if this plan of yours works out, I'm still headed back to the UK. It's hard enough to have a relationship when we work like we do. Long-distance would be near impossible."

I close my eyes for the briefest second. "I know." I'm not keen on long-distance either. There is a way that she doesn't have to leave, but if she doesn't see it, then I have to think she doesn't want to. I test the ground one more time, to be sure. "At least you'll have what you really want—the job."

"Right. The job." She pulls her hand back, and that answers everything. She might have developed feelings for me, but the most important thing to her is still her career. It's what I should have expected.

Then why does it hurt so goddamn bad?

She clears her throat. "Thank you. This means a lot that you would do this. You can expect my help in any way you need."

For that, I'm glad. Not only because I want to spend as much time with her as possible, but also because I need her brain and her smart ideas. "Don't thank me yet. We have a lot to iron out, and we still have to win over Warren."

"You'll win Warren. I guarantee it. You sell him the way you sold me, and it's a hole-in-one."

I'm breaking inside, holding on to any scrap she'll give me like a starving dog. "You really think so?"

"I know so. You're really turning into the guy I've only seen in private. You should be proud." My cock stiffens at the reference to our sexual exploration. A vision of her naked and bent across the table flashes in my mind. It's possible she'd still be up for more of that, isn't it? She may be leaving, but we could spend the time before that having fun.

Except, holy shit—I'm not interested. I mean, I'm interested, but the idea of being with her now when I know it isn't going to last...

Well, that just sounds like torture.

Remembering Genny's earlier words about not letting me in, I think she's probably on the same page.

"We still have two days until the meeting." I stand, fiddling nervously with the handle of my briefcase. "Should I get your number so we can talk tomorrow?" It's funny, after everything we've been through, I've still never gotten this from her.

But she surprises me with her response. "Already done."

I glance toward the table, wondering if she's written something down for me when I wasn't paying attention. There's nothing. "What do you mean?"

With a mischievous smile, she gestures to my pocket. "Look at your phone."

I set my case down and pull out my cell. I flip through the contact screens looking first under Fasbender and finding nothing. Then I look under G, and there it is—*Genny*—followed by her complete number including country code.

I'm confused for a beat. *When*—?

Then I know. "You programmed this in that night in your hotel room." The night she'd said I'd left it in the bathroom.

"I can't believe you didn't notice," she says somewhat shyly.

"Obviously, I'm an idiot." I was an idiot the whole time.

"I won't argue."

I walk her to her room, and though I long to kiss her good night, I don't. When I walk away, part of me is proud of myself for showing restraint.

The other part of me thinks I need a kick in the ass, and I can't help but feel like I'm still the biggest idiot of all time.

Chapter Twenty

Friday morning, I'm downstairs early, despite staying up late to put the finishing touches on my proposal. Scratch that— *our* proposal. By now, it's as much Genevieve's idea as it is mine. We've both occupied the last two days in my office, buried in data and financial forecasts. Every second with her has been a torturous gift. I've never spent so much time with one person, from dusk until dawn, and then left yearning for more. Never spent so many nights completely blue-balled.

"Do you have the copies of the slideshow?" I ask when she walks into the boardroom holding her purse and two to-go cups. I flip through the handouts I already have. "I've got the projections for the next five years, the first and second quarter reports, the balance sheets. I can't find the slideshow."

I must sound anxious because Genny says, "I think I maybe shouldn't have brought you coffee. And yes, I have the reports in my bag."

"That's for me?" I take the cup without the lipstick

mark, wishing for a moment I could taste her one last time before reminding myself I need to focus. I chug half of the cup down. "Thank you. I needed that."

She laughs. "I'm not sure you needed that at all. Now your brother's going to blame me when you have a massive stroke in the middle of your presentation." She sets down her cup and looks me over. "Here, let me fix you."

"What?" I glance down at myself, but she's already in front of me, straightening my tie.

"There. Much better." Her hand lingers on my chest, and surprisingly, it calms me down. I suppose it would be inappropriate to ask her to keep her palm there throughout this meeting, but the idea crosses my mind.

"I'm going to make a fool of myself," I tell her, needing to be honest. "Warren's going to laugh at my idea, and Hudson..." I can't even think about how disappointed Hudson will be if this falls through.

"Shh." Genny yanks once more on my tie. "You've got this. Hudson won't be anything but proud."

She's wrong. I don't have anything because I don't have her.

But with her confidence, I do feel like I might be able to manage this meeting. I'm about to tell her how much I've appreciated her—and by tell her, I mean try my hardest not to stare at her lips—when Hudson arrives.

Genny immediately jumps away from me and starts busying herself with passing out reports to each of the chairs around the table.

"I'm sorry if I'm interrupting anything." Hudson's tone is chiding, as though he's telling me my head better be in the game.

I ignore the way that makes me bristle. He's trusted me, but I still have to prove myself. "Nope. We're just finishing the setup. How many people do we expect here?"

"The three of us, Nathan Murphy, Warren, plus he's bringing along three of his advisors. I've also asked Norma to sit in. Then there's Edward Fasbender and whoever he's bringing."

"Just Hagan," Genevieve pipes in. "My brother."

I mentally total the attendants. Ten people, not counting myself. I can do this. I can do this.

"I'll go back to my office and escort our guests down here when they arrive," Hudson says. "Patricia will be bringing up coffee and refreshments any minute now. The doughnuts are not for you."

Great, now I want a doughnut. "I don't like to eat before a presentation anyway," I lie.

"Do you need anything?"

I stumble on an answer. I'm pretty sure he's really asking for some words to assure him I'm capable of pulling this whole thing off. What am I supposed to say when I don't know myself?

Genny comes to my rescue. "We're good, Hudson." And, again, because she believes it, so do I.

Hudson leaves as Trish arrives with the refreshment cart. A few minutes after that, Norma shows up with her part-time assistant/husband, Boyd.

There will be eleven people now. *I can do this.*

"I checked those numbers one more time this morning," Norma says. "They're solid. Feel free to call on me if you want any further explanation."

"I'm sure she never has to tell Hudson to call on her," I mutter to Genny.

"And Hudson's run a million meetings. I bet the first time he gave a big presentation, Norma, or someone, was there saying the same to him."

"Hey, this isn't my first rodeo." I've run a boardroom several times before. Five times, at least. Okay, twice. Once for my graduate project and once when Hudson was on paternity leave.

"Well, it's *my* first rodeo. Which is why you're doing most of the talking." We'd agreed beforehand that I'd run the show since it was my company hosting.

A bustle is heard down the hallway. Boyd peeks out around the doorframe. "They're on their way." He claps a hand on my shoulder and whispers, "If you're nervous, picture them naked. Just don't picture Norma naked or I'll kick your ass."

"Got it." It's the perfect thing for him to say because it makes me laugh, and I'm still smiling when Warren and the other guests walk in shortly after.

The next few minutes are spent on introductions and getting settled. "Thank you for taking this meeting, Mr. Werner," I say when it's my turn to greet him. "Especially on short notice." Warren and his wife used to be good friends with my mother. It's strange to see him now in a formal setting when I remember him best in a Santa costume at our family Christmas party.

"I've known you your whole life, Chandler," he says, shaking my hand. "It's time you started calling me Warren."

"Thank you, sir. Warren, sir." Doesn't feel any less odd.

"My daughter was quite enthusiastic about your

proposal. Celia is very invested in the continued success of Werner Media, so when she came to me about meeting with you, I have to say, I was intrigued."

Hudson comes up behind me. "I hope we can keep your interest, Warren. Let's get started, shall we?"

The room quiets. My hands are sweaty, my throat is dry. All eyes are on me.

Showtime.

From the back of the room, Genny gives me a thumbs-up and a smile.

Then I'm ready. "Warren, let me begin by saying kudos. You have built a solid corporation with a business model that many of your competitors long to replicate. The whole of the media industry has their eyes on you as you pick a successor to take the helm."

The room nods in silent agreement. There's no one here who will disagree that Warren has done his job fantastically well.

"Naturally, you'd look to Accelecom, a giant in its own right."

Edward smiles at the praise, and Hagan sits up straighter in his seat.

I continue. "A merger between the two companies would strengthen your presence on two continents. The family connection has also got to be appealing.

"I'd strongly caution a merger, however. The time and resources that would be expended during the process would weaken both companies. Instead, I'd like you to consider a three-point alliance."

I go on to explain in detail an alliance between Accelecom and Werner Media, with Nathan Murphy taking over the board upon Warren's retirement. "With both companies performing at the top of their game, the overall benefit to each entity is illustrated in these projection reports I've handed out."

I'm careful not to look directly at Edward or Hagan for fear of finding disapproval in their gazes. I'd suggested bringing Edward in on our ideas earlier, but Genny had worried his opposition would be detrimental. So, instead, he's hearing for the first time that his daughter and I don't think he'd be the right person to take over for Warren Werner.

So I'm wary when he interrupts to ask, "You mentioned a three-point alliance? Where's the third company?"

And here's the pièce de résistance. The component that gives this idea any credence. Hudson will either flip his shit or want to give me an executive bonus.

He's the one I look to when I answer. "Pierce Industries."

Everyone buzzes. Pierce Industries has been primarily focused on finance, real estate, and computer technology. We haven't ever even hinted about moving into media, so this news is a surprise and everyone has a reaction.

Hudson, alone, is unreadable.

I wait for the room to settle before going on. "Accelecom has the technology to bring about a cable network that would compete with Google Fiber, but neither they nor Werner Media have the money to fund such an endeavor. That's where Pierce Industries would enter the picture. I've already begun the groundwork for opening a new division, one devoted completely to the expansion of hardware across the country. With our resources, Accelecom's technology, and Werner Media's programming, we're looking at the potential of creating an empire that dominates the industry."

The presentation goes on for another hour. Nathan Murphy delivers his ideas for Werner Media, Genny speaks to how an alliance will benefit Accelecom, and I dive deeper into what I see as Pierce Industries' role.

By the time we've finished, a lot of information has been presented, and I expect Warren will need time to think it over. "Why don't we schedule a follow-up meeting to—"

Warren interrupts me, turning to his son-in-law. "Edward, this is a pretty appealing scenario."

"It is. One I'm happy to support if you're on board."

A layer of tension drops away with one potential opponent out of the way.

Warren looks next to my brother. "Hudson, I've got to say, Pierce Industries as media players—quite a bold move. I like it."

"We try to be innovative whenever we can," Hudson says, and I'd like to believe that means he's not going to kill me later in private, but he's still not giving anything away, so it's hard to know for sure.

Warren stands. "I'd like to study these numbers more closely, boys. But if everything checks out, I think we have ourselves a solid strategy."

Oh my god.

Nothing's been set in stone, but I feel like I've won the lottery. I presented a major idea to major players, and not only did I not get laughed at, but I also seem to have closed the deal.

I've never felt so on trend. So on top of my game. So kickass.

Is this what it feels like every day to be Hudson?

With the promise of being in touch soon, Warren and his

advisors make their exits. The next several minutes are spent cleaning up and going over details with Hagan and Norma.

Edward approaches his daughter, and I'm a douche because I totally eavesdrop.

"Genevieve. You had a hand in this proposal?"

I hate how guilty she looks. Wish I could step in and take the blame.

She, however, handles the encounter with dignity. "I'm sorry, Daddy. I'm sure this feels like a betrayal. I know you wanted to run Werner Media yourself."

Surprisingly, Edward seems not all that pissed. "I did want to run Werner Media. Until this morning when Celia broke into tears and told me she really wishes we could stay in London. I wasn't looking forward to telling her father that I wasn't going to take his position. This solves that dilemma."

Manipulative on his wife's part? Possibly. But it sure works out for us. She did say she'd do what she could to influence the decision.

Genny's eyes widen with hope. "Then you're not mad?"

"I'm not mad." He takes a beat to seemingly evaluate his feelings. "I'm surprised. I'm also quite impressed. A lot of work went into this. Lots of those ideas I recognize as yours. It's first-rate."

"You think so, even though you don't want me working in the business?"

"The only reason I haven't wanted you working in this business was because I truly thought you'd be happier elsewhere. You've had ambitious goals for Accelecom, and I feared you'd never be able to achieve what you wanted if you stayed with us, but it seems you've found a way to make them possible. I'm proud of you, princess."

My breathing slows. I know how badly Genny wanted her father's approval, and I feel it now for her as deeply as if he were praising me.

I turn away as he pulls her into his embrace, wanting to give them their privacy. As I do, I bump into Hudson.

Oh, right—Hudson.

He's the one whose praise I'm most desperate to receive.

"Are these numbers good?" he asks, holding up the projections Genny and I have laid out. They're the most attractive part of our presentation, so it's understandable he'd want to make sure the facts check out.

Still, I'm nervous when I answer. "I ran them through financials and had Norma triple check them."

I sort of expect him to whip out a calculator and do the math himself. But he doesn't. "That's excellent news." He pats me on the back. "Good work."

I cough in surprise. "You approve?"

"It's a sound strategic move. One that looks to make us a lot of money. Why wouldn't I approve?"

I'm shocked. Literally shocked. I nod for five full seconds, speechless. Then, on impulse, I pull him in for a hug. Bro style, of course. Nothing too mushy 'cause I'm cool and he's, well, he's Hudson.

We talk for a few minutes more while everyone else disperses, and I agree to a more in-depth meeting with him later in the day. It will be grueling, but at least I know he's on my side.

Finally, he leaves.

And then it's just Genny and me left in the room.

Our eyes lock. Then she's running to me, giving me a giant celebratory hug. Every overtone says this embrace comes from exuberance and there's no reason to believe it's more, but I cling to her a little too long, sniffing at her hair, breathing in her very essence.

We break away in unison, and even with the excitement of the day, I note that I've never felt so empty as when she leaves my arms.

"We did it!" I'm awkward, like I don't know what to do with my hands. I stuff them into my pockets and that seems to help.

She corrects me. "*You* did it."

"Nah. I couldn't have put this together without you."

"Okay, that's true." She giggles. Is she apprehensive as well? "Thank you. I appreciate the credit."

"You're welcome."

Our gazes dance around each other, and I wish I had something else to say. Something magic. Something that would transform this situation between us into one that's bearable, because this—this standing so close to what I want and not being able to have it? It's the worst thing I could've ever imagined.

"Oh! I almost forgot," she says suddenly, rummaging in her purse. She pulls out something in a black wooden frame and hands it to me. "I, uh, got you a present."

I look down at the picture. A smile erupts on my face as I'm met with Mina's big brown eyes, her soft brunette curls. It's the image that I'd seen on Genny's phone. The one she'd taken in the Hamptons and then sent to a random number.

"It was a text-to-print service," she explains now. "You send them the image you want printed and then they mail it to you. I've used it a few times since I've been in the States.

Much easier than having to deal with finding a color printer in the hotel."

A text-to-print service. And I'd immediately assumed she was spying. I'm a dumbass. "Why didn't you tell me?"

Her smile is shy. "I wanted it to be a surprise."

"I love," *you*, "it." I really do. So much.

Her grin grows more confident. "I'm so glad. She looked so pretty in her party dress, and you clearly adore her. I didn't see any pictures of her in your apartment. So."

She swallows, and I notice her skin is red and splotchy at her neck like it always gets when she's nervous or turned on. "Also, I need to tell you something." With her eyes cast down, she barrels on. "I need to tell you that you were right to be suspicious of me. I *was* scamming you."

My shoulders tense. I can't have heard her right. "Go on."

Her breathing is shaky as she exhales. "I, um. I led you to believe I was after the Accelecom merger. That it was the reason I sought you out. But it was never the job I wanted most."

"Then what was it?"

"You." The word is soft but sure, and I want it to mean what I think it means, but I'm not certain.

"I don't know if I understand."

"You, Chandler. I just wanted you." There's no mistaking her now, and every coil of tension inside me unravels into euphoria. To hell with staying away. I tug her into me, my lips eagerly finding hers. She tastes like coffee and butter mints and relief.

I understand—I'm relieved to have her in my arms too.

I kiss her deeply. Possessively. Like I'll never stop kissing her. I never should have stopped in the first place.

Before we get too carried away, though, she pushes out of my grip. Leave it to her to remember we're in the conference room of my office building and that not all the obstacles between us have been removed.

Obstacles like the fact that she lives on another continent.

"Chandler." She brushes her lips with her fingers, as if cherishing the way it had felt to have my mouth on hers, before dropping her hand stoically at her side. "I don't want this to be harder when I leave."

"I know." I run my hands up and down her arms, searching her eyes. "But there's a way you could stay. Don't you see it?" I want her to see it so badly, want it to be a feasible option and not just some fantasy I've concocted.

Her brow wrinkles, and it takes her a beat before her eyes light with understanding. "Pierce Industries."

Yes. Pierce Industries. My company. "I need someone to head up the new department. It would be a high executive position, working right alongside me. You'd have a whole team. It wouldn't be the same as running Accelecom, but you'd still get to put your ideas into action."

"You'd give that job to me?" she asks tentatively.

"*Give* it to you? I *created* it for you. The job description matches your resume. The salary is negotiable, but—"

She cuts me off, jumping into my arms. "I love you!"

I blink, startled as much by her proclamation as her sudden movement. It only takes me a second to pull myself together. Wrapping my arms around her waist, I hold her tighter. "Is that a yes?"

"It's a *hell, yes*. It's also *I love you*."

She loves me. She loves me! Every cell in my body sings with that one simple phrase.

I draw back so I can study her, looking for any indication that she's jerking my chain. I find nothing but sincerity. "You really do love me, don't you?"

She nods. Then she repeats it because she gets that I need to hear it over and over before it sinks in.

And when it does, there's only one thing left for me to say. "I fucking love you, too."

EPILOGUE

"We should get a dog." It's the third time Genny's brought it up in the last few days. I'm starting to think she might be serious.

I stick my head out from the bathroom and pull the toothbrush from my mouth. "We can't get a dog," I say, but it comes out a garbled mess since I'm talking around toothpaste.

"What?"

I put up a finger signaling to give me a minute, then disappear to spit and rinse before returning to stand in the doorframe. "We can't get a dog."

She looks up from the Pierce Industries Employee Handbook she's been perusing all morning while I get ready for work. "Why not?"

There are a thousand reasons, but they're not so easy to remember when I'm in the same room with her. Especially when all she's wearing is one of the sleeveless shirts I use to work out in. We've been together four months now, and she still makes my pulse race every time I look at her.

"Why not?" she asks again.

"You live in an apartment building." We both live here, but she reminds me daily that it's her name on the lease. Stubborn as she is about being independent, she refused my invitation to move in with me at the loft and got her own place in Hell's Kitchen. Yeah, not my first choice, either, but it's roomy and within walking distance to the office.

It only took a week to realize that we might as well have gotten a place together. We agreed to wait until after the New Year for me to officially move in, mostly to make her father happy, but before that I only spent a handful of nights at the loft.

Now I'm here full-time, and spoiler: she's not getting rid of me.

"Thousands of people live in apartment buildings and still have dogs," she says now. We've been over this already. Nothing she's saying is new.

Nothing I'm saying is new either. "We work all day."

"We'll hire a dog walker."

"A cat would be easier." I'm not even a fan of cats. Just…are we ready for a dog?

"A cat is not the same as a dog. You said you were a dog person." She narrows her eyes in my direction. "I feel like I might have been duped."

"I *am* a dog person. I love dogs. I also love kids. It doesn't mean I want one of either *now*."

She tosses the handbook on the nightstand and stretches out on the bed. "Yes, you do. I know you do. Imagine it. A furry buddy sleeping at your feet. You could train it to bring you your slippers when you get home."

In her new position, the light blue edge of her panties peeks out from under her shirt. "You're too adorable." So adorable that my boxers are about to tent. I rub my semi through my underwear. "Lift up your shirt—I want to see your tits."

"Will that get me a dog?"

"Possibly." Probably. After all, my new mission statement is Make Genny Happy. Best job I've ever had.

She sits up, lifting the tank slowly to expose her firm, round breasts. Her nipples are pink and peaked and my mouth waters from the sight of them. After a bit of teasing, she pulls the shirt off all the way and throws it to the ground.

I let out a sigh. My life is pretty goddamn awesome; I'm not going to deny it.

"You're so fucking hot." I stroke myself, hardening completely. "Move your panties to the side. I need to see your pussy now."

She leans back against the headboard and, with two fingers, pulls aside the crotch of her panties to reveal the lips of her pussy. Jesus, she looks just like a *Playboy* pinup.

Guess what. It gets better. Because next she takes her panties off altogether. "If losing my shirt gets me a dog, what will losing my panties get me?"

It will get her finger-fucked, that's what it will get her. She already looks wet, and I can't help myself—I have to feel. I head over to the bed and stick two fingers inside her. Damn, she's soaked. I rub in and out of her a couple of times before pulling away.

"Done with me already?"

"I have to get ready for work," I say, licking my fingers. "And you're such a naughty distraction."

With her eyes locked on mine, she puts her own fingers inside herself. "You mean, I have to take care of myself?"

She's so fucking coy I want to either spank her or eat her. Maybe both.

I glance at my watch. I guess I have a few minutes to spare. And I do have that new mission statement to live up to.

With my boxers pulled down just far enough to release my erection, I sit on the bed next to her and bring out what she calls my bossy tone. "Climb up on my cock. I'm going to make you come."

I should mention that she loves my bossy tone.

She's scrambling over me in a matter of seconds, positioning my cock at her entrance before sliding down.

And oh my god, I practically forget my name. Forget everything but how tight and wet and luscious she is. She feels so good I have to take a few deep breaths to stop from coming right away.

I love it when that happens—when I have to struggle a little to get control. It's like racing my car around a series of tight curves. The challenge is what makes the ride so fun.

When I have myself in check, that's when I push on the gas. "Faster, baby." I spank the outside of her upper thigh.

She speeds up, her muscles tensing and her tits bouncing as she works herself up and down on my cock. "Just like that, Genny."

It's better than the goddamned Indie 500.

I run my hands along her hips, itching to take the wheel, but just as eager to see where she'll take us on her own.

Or, rather, with my guidance.

"Touch yourself," I command now. Like a good girl, she brings her index finger to her mouth and licks it before bringing it down to massage her clit.

"Like this?"

"Just like that, baby. Feel how hard that makes me?"

"Yes," she pants. "Yes. You're so hard. Fuck. I'm going to come."

"Do it." I shift so I can take over, lifting my hips to meet hers, picking up the pace and pounding into her like she likes. Reaching behind her, I grab a handful of her hair and tug it hard so her back arches.

She gasps and her body starts to shake as she nears climax.

"Do it, Genny. Come all over my cock. I want to feel you squeeze me so hard." I coach her to her orgasm, praising her and pushing her until she's reached the crest.

And then, with a groan that borders on a scream, she's falling apart on top of me. Her pussy clenches my cock, pulsing as her climax shoots through her in waves.

"There you go. Just like that, baby." We've discovered we both like it when I pressure her to come. Like it when we're both working toward her release. Both of us focused on the same thing. It's even better than when we come together.

Okay, I'm more than a bit whipped. Sue me.

While she's still in the throes of ecstasy, I flip her to her back and kiss her. I slide out of her and down her body, kissing her belly before laying a final kiss on the folds of her pussy.

I pull up my boxers as I stand, then stare down at my sleepy-eyed girl. Something in my chest pinches, and I swear, I wouldn't be surprised if I cracked a rib with how big my

250

heart is over her. Maybe we've moved fast, but the road goes on and on, and I know without a doubt that it's never going to end. I love her. Deeply. Completely. Eternally.

She smiles up at me, her breath still ragged. "What about you?" Her eyes dart to the steel pole in my boxers.

A steel pole I have to ignore.

I turn to the dresser and search for a pair of socks. "Unlike you," I say over my shoulder, "I have a job I have to get to." Genny's official start day isn't until next Monday. Though I put the development of the new department into action as soon as Warren signed off on it, it took a while to get everything ready to launch. Genny's worked on it with me as much as she could around moving across the Atlantic, getting a visa, and settling into a new apartment. There were also holidays to account for, as well as my own move. "It feels like it's taken forever to arrive, but your first day is finally around the corner."

"About that…" She reaches for the handbook and holds it up. "I've discovered one little snag in our relationship. This says you can't date someone who is your superior."

Ah, that. The good old Pierce Industries Anti-Fraternization Policy. It's not like I haven't thought about it. A lot. "There are ways around it."

"Such as?"

With a pair of socks in hand, I sit on the chair next to the dresser. "We could break up." I'm teasing, of course.

She pretends to mull it over. "Well, I'm not going to stop dating you now. I've just gotten used to seeing your hair products on my bathroom counter."

I pull on one sock as I talk. "Then we could ignore it. Hudson can't fire me, and I'm not going to fire you."

"I suppose we could do that. People will talk, though. There might be backlash."

I wait until I have the other sock on before bringing up the last option. "There's another loophole in the policy," I say then hold my breath. It's a loophole that's only existed for the past few years, one that allows fraternization if the couple is married. Hudson claims he made it so that he could work with his wife if he ever wanted to, but I'm pretty sure he added it so that Norma could marry her assistant, Boyd.

"I read about that," Genny says slowly. "One that involves a ring."

"Yes. That one." My heart is pounding in my ears. I wasn't planning on having this conversation for at least another week.

But I'm ready. And if she's ready too, then, what the hell are we waiting for?

I stand and step closer to the bed. "I would have brought it up earlier but didn't want to make assumptions."

"After what I let you do to me last night, I think you're allowed to make assumptions."

Hmm. Last night. When she let me tie her to the kitchen counter and whip her with a dishtowel...

Shit, I'm so hard.

She sits up and bats her lashes, but her expression is solemn. "In other words, make assumptions."

I move closer. "Maybe I should mention that I opened a line of credit at Tiffany's a few days ago."

She shifts so she's kneeling on the bed, facing me. "Maybe I should mention I prefer princess cut solitaire."

Bending so my lips are hovering over hers, I say, "Maybe you should be happy with whatever you get."

"Maybe as long as what I get is you."

"You win." Though, really it's me who wins. "Now, no more talking." Roughly, I take her lips, kissing her back into a prone position.

"I thought you had to be to work," she says, breathless, when I finally let her up for air.

Work. Yes, that. I have a meeting with Hudson this morning, and another with HR this afternoon, along with a pile of papers on my desk to go through and a long list of people I need to call. I'll be working overtime as it is, staying at the office long after my secretary has gone home, like I have most days the past few months. I've taken on a lot with this new department. With the job, moving to an apartment not owned by my family, a serious girlfriend, and a dog on the way, I just might be becoming a full-fledged responsible adult.

So I really should pull away and finish getting dressed.

But Genny is so soft and delicious beneath me…

"Fuck it. I'll be late."

About that responsible adult thing—I'll start tomorrow.

Let's stay in touch!

Join my fan group, The Sky Launch, at
www.facebook.com/groups/HudsonPierce,
like my author page at **www.facebook.com/LaurelinPaige**
and visit my website to sign up for my newsletter.

More books in the Fixed Universe:

Fixed on You (Fixed #1)
Found in You (Fixed #2)
Forever with You (Fixed #3)
Fixed Trilogy Bundle (all three Fixed books in one bundle)
Hudson (a companion novel)
Free Me (a spinoff novel – Found duet #1)
Find Me (Found duet #2)
Chandler (a spinoff novel)
Falling Under You (a spinoff novella)

Also by Laurelin Paige:

First and Last

First Touch (enjoy an excerpt at the back of this book)
Last Kiss

Lights, Camera...

Take Two
Star Struck

Written with Kayti McGee under the name Laurelin McGee

Hot Alphas
Miss Match
Love Struck
Screwmates (coming soon!)

Written with Sierra Simone

Porn Star
Hot Cop (coming soon!)

ACKNOWLEDGMENTS

To my husband and daughters—you brighten my life. You're the Chandler to my Hudson, and I'm so grateful for you. Love is love is love is love is love is love is love.

To my team Rebecca Friedman, Kimberly Brower, Flavia Viotti, Meire Dias, Mary Cummings and the staff at Diversion, Jenn Watson and the gals at Social Butterfly PR, Ashley Lindemann, Sheri Gustafson, and Melissa Gaston—you make me look cooler than I am. It's quite a task, I know. Also to the ladies who run The Sky Launch, Stephanie Raylyn, Annette Popa, Serena McDonald, and Lauren Luman—thank you for all you do and just for being who you are. Love you all.

To my squad, Sierra Simone (aka, #1 editor), Kayti McGee, and Melanie Harlow—you're the best snakes—er, I mean snatches around (yeah, I went there).

To the ladies who keep me in the know, Christine Reiss, Lauren Blakely, and Kristy Bromberg—I'm lost without you! There aren't words for how much I appreciate you. #FabFourForever

To my earliest readers Roxie Madar, Liz Berry, Serena McDonald, Stephanie Raylyn, Annette Popa, Holly Baker, Laura Foster Franks, and Ang Oh—your feedback helped shape this book. I'm so humbled by the time and friendship you give me.

To the bloggers and readers—I'm in awe everyday of your support and enthusiasm. To steal Chandler's words: Best. Job. Ever.

To my God—thank you for all the gifts you've given but especially for your patience.

FIRST TOUCH

PRAISE FOR FIRST TOUCH:

"Paige is unflinching in her depiction of a complicated relationship, and the results are explosive." Kirkus Reviews

"Edgy sex and pulsating mystery make this fast paced and sensual story impossible to put down." Jay Crownover, *New York Times* bestselling author of *The Marked Men* series

"Laurelin creates a romance that comes in many touches...Each chapter leads you deeper into mystery, twisting what you knew, making you love who you're meant to hate. A fascinating read!" Pepper Winters, *New York Times* bestselling author

"Dark, intense, and incredibly sexy, *First Touch* kept me on the edge of my seat from page one up to the very last word." Shameless Book Club Blog

"Gritty, edgy, dark and compelling, *First Touch* pulls no punches and just might leave you reeling." Megan Hart, *NYT* and *USA Today Bestselling* author of *Tear You Apart*

"*First Touch* is her best work to date ... it smolders, captivates, & rips you to pieces... we're obsessed!" Rock Stars of Romance Blog

"This spellbinding story will have you glued to the pages from the first page to the last. Paige's best work yet. Thrilling, captivating, sexy, and shocking. I am in love with this story." Claire Contreras, *New York Times* bestselling author of *Kaleidoscope Hearts*

"*First Touch* is shocking, stunning, and intense with a heat level that can only be measured on the Kelvin scale." CD Reiss, *USA Today* bestselling author of *ShutterGirl*

"*First Touch* ... will leave you on pins and needles, breathless and begging for more. Laurelin Paige has delivered her finest work yet." Jen McCoy, Literary Gossip Book Blog

"A beautifully executed maze of suspense, seduction, and ridiculously hot sex." Alessandra Torres, *New York Times* Bestselling Author

"A dazzling mystery to unravel ... wicked and yet sensual. Decadent in her ability to weave a captivating story from beginning to end, Laurelin Paige has another hit on her hands." Kendall Ryan, *New York Times* Bestselling Author

"*First Touch* is a heart chilling page-turner from a master storyteller – and the hottest thing I've read this year, hands down." M. Pierce, bestselling author of the *Night Owl Trilogy*

"Laurelin Paige writes an addictive mix of emotion and sexy that draws the reader in and doesn't let go until long after the last page is read." K. Bromberg, *New York Times* bestselling author of the *Driven* Series

"*First Touch* is a deliciously dark and sinfully sexy story that had me up way past bedtime. Laurel in Paige knows exactly what a woman craves, and I'm craving more Reeve." Geneva Lee, *New York Times* bestselling author

Enjoy an excerpt of *First Touch*

Prologue

When I heard the message she left, it had been more than six years since I'd spoken to Amber. Hearing her voice on my mother's old answering machine shocked me. It wasn't that we'd parted on *bad* terms, necessarily, but they were *final* terms. We were on different sides for the first time in our friendship. The only way past it was to separate.

The last words she'd spoken to me in person played in my mind so frequently it was as though they'd been scratched into the audio portion of my brain with professional recording equipment. They reverberated clear and crisp: *"I'm sure someday's gotta happen for us all one day. But it doesn't mean mine's happening at the same time as yours."*

So I left her to live my *someday* while she took off for Mexico on the yacht of the latest sugar daddy to buy her a designer bikini stuffed with hundreds that she'd later let him stuff with his pathetic excuse of a cock.

In our time apart, I'd grown up completely, reinvented myself, put the past behind me, yet her voice on the machine sounded as bright and young as it had when we were twenty-three. It instantly triggered a longing and regret that I hadn't let myself feel since we'd said goodbye.

"Emily." Her bubbly tone spilled into my ear. "It's been ages, I know. But I've been thinking about you. God, I'm not even sure if this is still your number." She paused for only half a second, the space of a sigh or maybe taking a moment to reconsider. "Anyway, I wanted to ask—do you still have that blue raincoat? Miss you. Bye."

She'd said nothing really. Her voice hadn't cracked or stumbled or betrayed emotion of any kind. But I knew one thing with clear-cut certainty: Amber was in trouble and she needed my help.

CHAPTER ONE

Even with my head below the surface of the water, I felt his arrival. My arms continued moving in fluid strokes, my legs kicking out behind me, but as drops of water trickled down my exposed skin, it itched with the awareness of no longer being alone.

I kept swimming—kept heading toward the end of the pool. The words I used to push me on in high school swimming competitions automatically repeated in my head: *This arm then that arm then this arm then that arm.* Now though, in the spaces between each beat, I thought her name—*This arm, Amber, then that arm, Amber, then this arm, Amber, then that arm, Amber.*

When I'd reached the concrete wall, I flipped and did another lap. I wouldn't let on that I knew he was there. I needed to control this situation, and for some reason, denying his presence made me feel like I'd gained another measure or so. Focusing on Amber, remembering she was the reason for what I was doing, made concentrating easier.

At first, anyway. Until I began to tire and the awareness of his nearness began to win the tug-of-war with my attention.

I forced myself to complete three more laps, the anticipation of finally being near him, talking to him, bubbling up inside me like a butterfly waiting to escape its cocoon. I had my reasons for not acknowledging him—but what were his reasons for ignoring me? What if it wasn't even him, but one of his security men? No, anyone else would have kicked me out already for sure. Then why had he let me continue my swim?

Soon the wings of curiosity fluttered and scratched with such distraction that I could no longer resist the urge to poke my head out.

At least I managed to complete my lap.

Then, after wiping the water from my eyes, I started to look around.

I'd expected him to be sitting to my side at the head of the pool so I was truly surprised when I spotted him in the lounge chair directly in front of me. His face was chiseled and serious underneath near-black hair. Metallic sunglasses paired with a layer of scruff made him appear both more laid back and more dangerous than the pictures I'd seen on the Internet. Even dressed in a standard hotel variety plain white robe, he was intimidating. His feet were bare and crossed at the ankles. His elbow was propped on the chair arm, and his thumb and index finger framed the side of his face as he without a doubt bore right into me with his gaze behind designer eyewear.

My heart flipped. He was infamous, famous, and if the rumors were to be believed, dangerous—a multibillionaire luxury resort owner and legendary bad boy. But my reaction wasn't fear; it was excitement. Not because he was ten times sexier in person—though he was—but because he was *here*.

Reeve Sallis.

Sitting mere yards from me. After all the work I'd done to make it happen, here he was. Step one. Success.

"Oh!" I weaved the thrill I felt into my lines hoping it passed as simple alarm. "I didn't realize I wasn't alone." An innocent smile curled my lip with a few flirty blinks. It was a look that had bought me quite a few drinks along with a fur coat and a nice piece of jewelry or two. But that was years ago. I was rusty, and I prayed under my breath that he didn't notice.

His stare had a texture I could feel on my skin. "And I *did* realize I wasn't alone when I very much should be. I imagine it's a similar feeling of astonishment."

I swallowed. "Yes, probably so."

"I'll help you out." He stood, swiftly. In two steps he was at the side of the pool, leaning down to offer his hand.

My gut told me that the smart thing to do would be to get out of the pool. I was trespassing on the property of a very powerful man.

But my heart told me I couldn't give up so easily. So I ignored the tightening in my stomach and stood my ground—or, rather, tread my water—and said, "No, thank you. I still have a few more laps to do."

His lip curled up into a half-smile. "You don't. You're done." Again he reached his hand toward me.

Ignoring his offer, I broadened my smile and turned up the charm. "Ah, you're one of *those* kinds of men."

He let his hand fall and tilted his head questioningly. "Which kind is that?"

Behind his lenses, I felt the command of his stare and even in his crouched position, he held himself with utter confidence. My eyes chased the broad muscles in his neck that disappeared under his robe. They, along with his entire demeanor, demanded my respect or, more likely, my capitulation.

Yeah, I knew his type. "The kind who gets what he wants when he wants it."

"Well. Yes." He chuckled as he, yet again, extended his hand out for me.

I was tempted to swim another lap. But I didn't have enough sense about him yet to know if that would piss him off or intrigue him. So I said, "I got it," and refused his hand, pulling myself up over the side on my own. I did know it was too early for physical contact. My exit of the pool was on his terms but our first touch would be on mine.

"Oh, you're one of *those* kinds of women." He stood with me and handed me a towel with sallis embroidered along the edge in gold.

I took it. I was dripping all over his bare feet, after all. And while I'd felt covered in the clear water, I now felt nearly naked in my salmon-colored bikini. Which was the point, but still. "Okay," I said, as I wrapped the terrycloth around the ends of my hair. "I'll bite. What kind of woman is that?"

"The kind who won't take help from a man."

There had been a time when nothing could be further from the truth. I'd been very dependent on men, relying on one or another of them to put a roof over my head, keep me fed and clothed and entertained.

But that was years ago. Now I only counted on myself.

That was perhaps the hardest part of the role I had to play—giving up the control I'd gained. Submitting.

If that was what it took to get the answers I needed, I'd do that and more.

I tilted my head to squeeze the moisture from my hair on the ground next to me. "That's not so. I took your towel."

His eyes were still hidden, but I knew he was checking me out. I could feel his gaze skidding across my skin, sending goose bumps up my arms. "That's nothing." His attention landed on my breasts. "There are hundreds of towels stacked around here."

My cheeks heated, sure that his choice of the word *stacked* was purposeful. Because there was no denying that's what I was—stacked. My breasts had come in early and grew rapidly, swelling until I filled a double D cup. They'd embarrassed me as a teen. No one else flopped and jiggled like I did in gym class. So I hid them behind baggy shirts and sports bras. It wasn't until I'd met Amber that I realized the power I'd been given through genetics. She taught me how to embrace my body, how to use it for my benefit.

With those lessons in mind—with *Amber* in mind—I pushed away my discomfort and bent over to run the towel up and down my limbs, exposing my cleavage. "That's proof that you're wrong. I could have easily gotten my own. I accepted it from you."

"You have a point there."

I had two points, actually. My nipples were standing tall and proud. It was the morning chill, of course, more pronounced after the heated pool, and I wanted to fold my arms over myself when I stood back up. But I forced myself to follow their example and rose up as tall and proud as they were.

When I did, I was met with my shoes. Reeve must have gotten them while I was swimming. He held them out to me now.

With a sigh, I took them from him. "You really want me gone, don't you?"

"What can I say? I like my routine. Swimming alone is part of my routine."

"Huh. I didn't take you for a man who was rigid." The media made Reeve Sallis out as impulsive and erratic. I was familiar enough with the difference between public perception and reality, but knowing Amber as I did, it made more sense that Reeve was that guy than the one he was playing at now.

He clicked his tongue at me like he was chiding a naughty child. "Now look who's making premature judgments."

"Touché." I sat on a deck chair to buckle my sandals. Leaning over to do it would have just been gratuitous at this point.

"But while I've got you here…"

I tensed as he undid the belt of his robe. *I can do this, I can do this,* I chanted to myself. This was what I'd come here for—to do what was necessary, no matter how much I didn't want to. Back then, I would have done far more for far less. And, I noted as Reeve discarded the item of clothing on the chair behind him, with far less attractive men.

Goddamn, Reeve Sallis was hot.

Like sizzling hot. He wore nothing but trunks—thank the lord it wasn't a speedo—revealing a perfect swimmer's body. His arms and torso were long and sculpted, his shoulders broad, and his waist trim. The six-pack he sported was nearly an eight-pack, and the muscles around his abdomen were so defined, so hard that I barely resisted the urge to lay my hand across them. My mind couldn't process how solid they would feel beneath my palm and wouldn't it be amazing to just find out?

While I was ogling—and probably drooling and definitely not breathing—he sat on the chair and faced me. "I hope you don't mind. I was getting a little warm."

It *was* getting a little warm. More than a little. And it wasn't the modern fire pit running nearly the entire length of the pool behind our deck chairs that made my skin scorch on the inside.

"Uh, of course I don't mind." Though, it sort of sounded like I did mind. Really, I was just disappointed that was the reason he'd undressed.

Jesus, Em, what the fuck? You're bummed that he didn't want you to blow him? Really, I was disgusted with myself. I mean, it was great that he wasn't unattractive considering what I'd probably have to do with him eventually, but what kind of bitch would I be if I looked forward to it?

Maybe old habits died harder than I had thought. I couldn't decide if I wanted that to be the case or not.

Reeve was apparently unaware of the battle going on in my head. "Good," he said. "Then we should probably talk."

"Interrogation time? I suppose that's to be expected." With his newly exposed body, I wasn't sure I'd be able to concentrate. And he had yet to take off those glasses, which was unnerving. Perhaps that was exactly why he kept them on.

"I'm glad you see it my way. If you didn't, this would be a whole lot less fun."

I finished fastening my shoe and sat up. "Is it fun now?"

His forehead wrinkled as he tapped a long finger against his lips. "I haven't entirely decided yet." His declaration came out low and raw, and it seemed, more honest than he'd intended.

Immediately, he changed gears, moving his hands to grip the arms of the chair. "But back to the interrogation. Why exactly are you here?"

It wasn't what I thought he'd ask first. I'd been expecting "who are you," but that he'd chosen the other question spoke volumes about my progress with him. He didn't care who I was. He only cared that my actions interfered with his own plans.

Dammit.

If my plan was going to work, Reeve had to want to get to know me. At least he hadn't dismissed me yet. I still had a chance to reel him in. "I'm here because I wanted a morning swim."

A hint of a brow peaked up over the frame of his glasses. "I assume you're a guest at this resort."

I bit my lip and nodded slowly. Even after our banter, there was a chance he could have me kicked out. A very good chance. Maybe the lip bite could make me seem virtuous.

Who was I kidding? He'd seen the girls. Once my chest was displayed, I'd lost all shot at claiming innocent, even if I truly was. And I wasn't.

The interrogation continued. "There are six other pools open to the public. This is the only one reserved in the morning for my personal use. Why did you choose mine?"

"I wanted the privacy."

"Wrong." He said the word as though he were buzzing a player out on a game show. "This wasn't about privacy. It couldn't have been easy for you to get in here. You went to a lot of trouble."

My shoulder hitched up in a nonchalant shrug. "It really wasn't that much trouble." That was actually the truth. I'd discovered pretty easily that any manager had the power to program my resort key card to let me in to the pool during Reeve's reserved time. A few days of prowling and I'd found a night manager who seemed he would be vulnerable to my seduction techniques. He was twice my age, balding with a ridiculous hairpiece. I'd been prepared to give him a hand job. Turned out he could be bought with a hundred. That had surprised me. I'd grown up with my body as my only asset, and I'd learned to use it. I was still getting used to having money as an alternative.

He frowned. "That doesn't speak well for my staff."

"Or it speaks well for me."

"Ah. You don't want to get anyone in trouble." It wasn't a question.

Teasingly, I tapped my own lips and threw his words back at him. "I haven't entirely decided yet."

He laughed. It was a good sign.

"You see," I said, lacing my hands and stretching them above my head, "I'm not loyal to the person who helped me. But on the other hand, I'm not loyal to you either."

He leaned forward, a smile dancing on his lips. "You'll tell me if I ask you."

"Maybe. Are you asking?" I'd totally throw the manager under the bus. But not yet. It was information that he wanted that I had—it kept him engaging with me. I'd likely keep the secret until the next time we met, no matter how much he asked.

That was the idea, anyway. Then Reeve surprised me. "I'm not asking. I don't really care about my staff at the moment. I'm more interested in you."

My pulse kicked up like I'd downed a shot of espresso. Because it was a victory. Because it was a moment of triumph. There was no other reason I cared. No other reason his interest keyed me up.

Reeve steepled his hands together then pointed them toward me. "Why this pool?"

I mirrored his leaning, lacing my fingers together and resting my chin on top. "I wanted to meet you." *Needed* to meet him. I had a long list of questions and as far as I was concerned Reeve Sallis had the answers.

"The truth comes out. Why would you want to meet me?" He seemed honestly perplexed.

"Are you joking?" There were certainly thousands of women who wanted to be his bimbo of the month. Word was he treated his sex toys well. He had enough money to lavish on them without even noticing a dent in his wallet. Then there were those who likely wanted to meet him just to claim the brush with fame. Plus he was, well, hotter than a man had a right to be.

But if it was flattery he needed... "You're a very interesting human being, Reeve Sallis. Not to mention, you're easy on the eyes. More than easy on the eyes, actually. Who wouldn't want to meet you?"

"I can name quite a few people, and I'm sure there are many more that I can't name. You could have met me in other ways." Though he'd verbally ignored my comment about his appearance, his mouth twitched ever so slightly letting me know it had pleased him.

Why did that make my belly flutter?

It didn't. It was nerves. It had to be. I transferred the emotion to my words, letting my voice get breathy and unsteady. "I wanted to meet you alone. Without your goons and your public."

"A lot of people would be scared to be with me alone."

"Who said I wasn't scared?" I should have been scared. He had a reputation that, as far as I could gather, was either completely fabricated or totally underplayed. The former was more likely, but what if it was the latter? What if I was truly unsafe in his presence?

It was also possible that I *was* scared. In all honesty, it was probably the core of his allure. But I couldn't let fear or captivation take over. I had no other choice but to see my plan through. For Amber.

Reeve tilted his head. "That's an interesting combination of traits—a stalker who's scared."

"Only scared enough to make it fun." Strange that I once lived for that kind of scared. "And not a stalker, Mr. Sallis. I merely have a curiosity that gets away from me."

"I like your curiosity. And your philosophy on fear." He shifted gears again. "I think I may have started off with the wrong line of questioning. I don't even know who you are."

He removed his sunglasses, and I couldn't help but gasp. His eyes…. At the surface, they didn't seem special on their own. A common blue and gray that could be easy to overlook. His brows were the prominent feature, what most people likely noticed. They were thick and arched. They darkened his expression and distracted from what lay in the icy pools below them.

But his eyes caught me. There was something I recognized in them—a sorrow or a longing that was both gripping and haunting.

I saw myself in those eyes.

Reeve noticed. As soon as he did, he looked away, scanning the horizon. I didn't blame him. Small as it was, it had been a revealing moment. Far too intimate for strangers.

When he turned toward me again, he'd hidden whatever it was that I'd seen. "There's something familiar about you, though. We haven't slept together, have we?"

I laughed. "No, we haven't."

"Good." He clarified before I could feign indignation. "I mean, I'd hate myself if I'd forgotten you."

"You haven't. And you won't. Forget me, I mean." I meant to allude that we'd sleep together eventually. It was as close to offering myself as I'd get. Anything more would be slutty and set me up as one-night-stand material. I needed to be more like flavor of the month.

More important at the moment was the delivery of my name. I had to be honest—I was too recognizable not to be. There was no reason to be deceitful about it anyway. If Amber had mentioned me ever, she would have used my real last name, not the one I'd taken on when I'd reinvented myself. There was a chance, of course, that she'd figured out my new identity. A possibility she'd mentioned it in passing—*Oh, that girl? You know, the voice on that sitcom? I used to know her....*

It was a risk I had to take. I extended my hand. "It's Emily. Emily Wayborn."

Reeve hesitated—was he as determined to be in control of our first contact as I was?

Whatever his reluctance, he quickly overcame it, taking my palm in his. His grip was strong and sure and aggressive. Almost too tight, but just barely not. He held it without saying anything for several seconds, and, I don't know how—somehow, though—I knew he was making his own allusion. His own promise. He wanted me to know what he'd be like.

In bed.

With me.

He'd be powerful and controlling and forceful, even. Almost too forceful, but just barely not.

Was that how he'd been with *her*? Did *almost* become *too much*?

I couldn't let myself go there. So instead of entertaining the thought further, I entertained a new one—Reeve Sallis had good hands. Really good hands.

After what seemed like ages and yet not nearly long enough, he let my hand go. "A qualified pleasure, Emily Wayborn. Qualified because you did interrupt my swim time."

"Qualified pleasure is the only kind I seem to give." That had come out dirtier than I'd intended. Or maybe exactly as dirty as I'd intended. God, my confidence in flirting was nil. "Anyway, I get the familiar thing a lot."

"It wasn't a line."

"I know." Though for half a second I worried he found me familiar for other reasons. Because I was like Amber. We'd been inseparable and so much alike at one time, everyone thought we were sisters. But that was years ago. I'd changed so much, even if she'd stayed exactly the same.

No, it was the other reason he found me familiar. "It's because I'm famous." I sounded embarrassed because I was. "My voice is famous. I'm the computer on *NextGen*."

"You're joking."

"Nope." I took a deep breath and then repeated my famous catch phrase in the lilting tone I saved for the show. "User error."

He laughed. Heartily. Like, full belly laugh.

Really, it *was* funny. All the years I'd worked to keep my figure, going to audition after audition trying to land my big break, and when I finally did it was in a role that only utilized my vocal cords. The hit show of the past two seasons, *NextGen* was the story of a family living in the not-too-distant future. Pitched as the movie *Her* meets the old cartoon *The Jetsons,* I played the part of the household mainframe—the computer that controlled each and every aspect of their lives. Practically overnight I was recognized by thousands, but only when I spoke.

Funny thing was I had a knockout body. A knockout body that no one ever saw. I got the humor in it. Really, I did.

When he'd stopped laughing enough to speak, he apologized. "I'm sorry to say I've never seen it. But I've heard about you. The show, I mean. It's quite a hit."

"It's…" There was nothing to say except, "Well, it pays the bills."

He smiled again, and this time I noticed the hint of a dimple. "At least I can be assured you aren't after me for my money."

It was my turn to laugh. "I don't make that kind of dough. And who said I'm after you?"

"Aren't you? Well, if you're not, that's a shame."

My belly flipped again. I had him intrigued. It was time to make my exit. Next time I'd bump into him more casually, more seemingly accidental, and then, if I was good, he'd ask me out. "I'm sorry for intruding on your morning, Mr. Sallis."

"Reeve," he corrected.

"Reeve." His name slid off my tongue a little too easily. "I'll let you get to your swim now."

I stood, and he followed. "After all the trouble you went to, you're not going to stay and watch? I'm disappointed."

It was tempting. I scanned his amazing body once more. He probably looked like a god in the water.

But I had to leave with the upper hand. Leave him wanting more. "Is it a lofty goal to want you to learn you can't have everything you want?"

"It is lofty. And not true." His voice grew deep and certain. "I want you to join me for dinner. And you will. Won't you." It was a statement—plain and clear.

And, damn, I hadn't predicted that. "When you put it that way, I suppose I will."

"Tonight. Seven-thirty. In the Cherry Lounge."

"I thought the Cherry Lounge was closed." I'd been at the resort for more than a week and the room had been off limits the entire time.

"It's closed when I'm in town. It's where I dine. It's where *we'll* dine."

Though he hadn't moved, it felt suddenly like he was closer to me than he'd been only a second before. As though his presence had extended out from his body, invading my own space. It flustered me, but I managed, "Formal or casual?"

"You can't come as you are?" He grinned a grin so wicked that I knew he meant the double entendre, and, though I shot him a disapproving glance, I also smiled. And I shivered. Because while I had ulterior motives for getting close to him, Reeve Sallis got to *me*. I'd read about his natural charm and sex appeal, but nothing had prepared me for the fullness of it in person. It was indescribable. Any adjective I tried to pin on him felt contrived and unoriginal. He was magnetic and provocative and commanding.

And he did scare me. There was a possibility he'd done terrible things to people—things that would frighten anyone with half a brain. Still, were it not for Amber, I might be able to overlook the rumors. Might be tempted by his charisma. That might have been the scariest thing of all where Reeve Sallis was concerned.

He shook his head. "Don't answer that. It was inappropriate, and anyway, there's no way you'll respond the way that I want you to."

He was wrong. I'd respond however he wanted me to if it got me what I wanted. What I needed.

But not yet. I couldn't go that far *yet*. "That sounded like an apology until you tacked on another thing you probably should be apologizing for. So how about I ignore everything you've said in the last ten seconds and we try this again. What should I wear to dinner this evening, Reeve?"

"Nothing too fancy. A dress, though, please. It would be a shame to hide those lovely legs of yours." But he said that with his eyes on my rack.

It was where I wanted his eyes. Another moment of triumph. A minor one. Partly because it meant he was attracted to me, but mostly because if they were elsewhere, if they met mine instead, I wasn't certain I could keep the advantage.

Thankfully, it was hard for anyone to look elsewhere. I had a nice rack.

I pushed my chest up and out just enough to let him know the attention was welcomed. "I know exactly what I'll wear. Until tonight."

His gaze rose to meet mine and lingered just long enough to threaten my control. Just long enough for me to glimpse the burden of his own restraint. Then, without a goodbye, he turned and dove into the pool, his form so tight and perfect that he barely splashed.

Despite my intentions to leave, I stayed long enough to see him swim the length and back. He was mesmerizing. His body was strong and lithe all at once, his arms gorgeous as they flexed and stretched, cutting through the water with powerful strokes. His tight ass could hold my attention for hours.

Though he never looked up, I'm sure he felt my presence, just as I'd felt his. There was an attraction between us. An electric pull that made the air crackle and twist around me even at that distance. It was something that I couldn't have faked, and I was grateful for it. It would make it easier to take the steps I needed to take next.

At least, I hoped that was the reason I was grateful for our connection. I didn't want to believe the alternative.

FIRST TOUCH

LAURELIN PAIGE is the *NY Times, Wall Street Journal,* and *USA Today* Bestselling Author of the Fixed Trilogy. She's a sucker for a good romance and gets giddy any time there's kissing, much to the embarrassment of her three daughters. Her husband doesn't seem to complain, however. When she isn't reading or writing sexy stories, she's probably singing, watching *Game of Thrones* and *The Walking Dead,* or dreaming of Michael Fassbender. She's also a proud member of Mensa International, though she doesn't do anything with the organization except use it as material for her bio.